dedicated to L—*for revealing the boundless capacity of my heart to love, even when it feels full, and for teaching me that strength forged in adversity, paired with your unwavering presence, is all one truly needs!*

a note from the author

Dear Readers,

What a delight to reconnect as we venture deeper into the At Night series with *Pursued at Night*! Weaving this series has been an exhilarating journey, melding the sweeping passion of historical romance with the bold, unapologetic edge of modern dark romance. *Pursued at Night* dials up the intensity from *Awaken at Night's* slow burn, drawing you into a richer, shadowed world. So, brace yourself, it's a thrilling chase!

I still love the term "dark*ish*" for this series. It's not an official label, but it captures the vibe: not feather-light, yet not pitch-black. And I hope, with your help, to make it a label someday! Releasing *Awaken at Night* was a masterclass in craft, showing me the adage about writing being learned through doing is so true. But I would also add it is learned through relentless, red-pen-wielding edits and immersing myself daily in the works of today's stellar authors. I half-joke to myself, "I want to be just like them when I grow up!" I had better pick up the pace, though...time's flying!

Thank you for diving into the shadowed world of *Pursued at Night*! This dark*ish* historical romance delves deeper into the intensity of the *At Night* series, blending passion with raw, mature themes. Your trust is everything to me. I'm dedicated to offering clear content guidance for *Pursued at Night* and the entire *At Night* series, ensuring you can descend into the story with ease and excitement. This book contains explicit content and may include distressing elements, so please prioritize your well-being and proceed with care if sensitive to any of these themes.

a dark*ish* historical romance

pursued

at night

HARLOW BRÍGH

ISBN 979-8-9919917-4-2 (Paperback)

ISBN 979-8-9919917-3-5 (eBook)

ISBN 979-8-9919917-5-9 (Audiobook)

Any reference to historical events, real people, and real places, are used fictitiously. Other names, characters, and places are products of the author's imagination.

Cover design by Muhammad Waqas

First print edition 2025

HA! Harvick Anderson Publishing

ha-publishing.com

To that end, please be aware of the following:

Stalking and obsessive behavior

Bondage and domination (consensual power dynamics)

Impact play

Group sexual activities (orgies and public settings)

References to consensual same-sex intimacy

Attempted sexual assault (graphic non-consensual advances)

Sadism (desire to inflict pain in non-consensual contexts)

Kidnapping and forced confinement

Graphic violence (fights, beatings, blood, and detailed injuries)

Murder and attempted murder (on-page and referenced)

Physical abuse (including torture and restraints)

Emotional manipulation (gaslighting and psychological distress)

Grief and trauma (past deaths and emotional betrayal)

Underground sex clubs (depictions of vice and debauchery)

Explicit consensual sex (BDSM, rough play, and power exchange)

Jealousy and possessiveness (evolving relationship dynamics)

References to alcohol abuse and neglectful parenting (in backstory)

Misogynistic language (historical context, challenged in narrative)

Hopefully I have piqued your curiosity. But if any of these themes feel overwhelming, please take care of yourself!

Love, Harlow

I pursued her with all the ardor of my heart, each step a testament to a longing that burned through the night. She, knowing she was pursued, felt her pulse quicken, a secret thrill in the chase that bound us.

—André Aciman, *Call Me by Your Name*

watching her... again

Well, well, well.
Well, well, well.
This has turned into a very interesting day. At first, I thought it was going to be a complete disappointment, but I suppose you never really know.
Do you?
Especially after I put so much effort into getting Lady Haven by herself. I was so damned close this time, waiting behind a copse of weeping birch trees, when I saw her. I first watched her get off her horse and walk alone by the Serpentine, as the sun shone on her beautiful face and a soft breeze twisted her skirts around her legs. She had the barest frown on her face as she waited, pacing impatiently like she knew I was there for her.
She was waiting for me!
Then, she was talking with Marien, but the stupid trollop was supposed to bring my darling girl deeper into the wood, right to me. Instead, they stopped so far away that I could not simply grab her and get her into my carriage. It was a perfect plan, but Marien could not even get that right. I was just working

my way closer when that cumbering lout came and blew my whole plan to complete shit.

Fucking Warwicke!

He ordered my *Lady Haven to leave the park. Like he has any right at all to tell her to do anything! He was lucky I did not have a weapon on me, or I would have shot him in his big dumb face for daring to talk to* my *woman like that. I then had to follow Marien and him, though I figured out easily where he was taking her.*

Nox House!

So, I was sitting here in my carriage, wondering if I ought to bother with breaking the stupid bitch out or if her usefulness is over. But I figured she was at least slightly helpful in reaching Lady Haven this season. Getting my girl alone has been damned near impossible, despite my best efforts.

I have only been close to grabbing her once before. One night, while I was watching Nox House, waiting for Marien to come out after I had sent her in to gather some information, I saw both de Clare brothers and that same stupid Scot pull up. I assumed I had lost Marien to them and was just about to leave, thinking the whole evening was a complete failure, when Lady Haven shocked the hell out of me by riding up in a hired hack and going inside. If not for my amazement, I would have simply snatched her from the front porch and been done with it. She had taken her time going up to the door, as though she were not sure of herself or where she was going.

It would have been the perfect time!

But if wishes were thrushes and all those bollocks! Instead, I watched for several hours after she went inside. Even after the younger de Clare and Warwicke took Marien away. I immediately dismissed any thought of following them and pretty much assumed Marien was a goner. Either way, I would not have left without finding out why Lady Haven was there.

Not for anything in the world!

Then I finally saw her being rushed out quite roughly by the damned Duke of Windemere himself, covered from head to toe in a hooded cloak. Like I was stupid enough to fail to recognize my beloved.

I would know her anywhere!

Now tonight, Marien is inside again, and up comes the duke with his brother and Warwicke. Again, those three. I want to smash all their bloody faces! Until any woman who sees them screams in horror instead of swooning in love. Especially since their arrival slammed the door on any chance I might have had to get Marien out of there myself. I was about to leave, when who came driving up in the second de Clare carriage?

Not just my Lady Haven this time. No, not just my lovely girl. The duke's amazon sister and that pretty blond chit, Miss Atwood, were with her. They strolled up to Nox House, like it was no big deal. Like it was not the back entrance into one of the most notorious and unsuitable places for young ladies in all of London. Like it would not ruin all of them if anyone were to let it whisper to the ton where they were seen.

Of course, I would never be one to tell tales. Emerson Haven's character must be unimpeachable. She is to be my bride, after all. Which means, by extension, Lady de Clare and Miss Atwood need to be protected as well.

At least for now!

Interestingly, soon after their arrival, Lady de Clare and Miss Atwood were basically dragged from the house by Lennox de Clare and Warwicke. Miss Atwood even dug in her heels, forcing de Clare to a stop on the walkway, about five feet from the carriage. He shrugged, picked up the blonde, and threw her over his shoulder. *She began scratching at his back like a hellcat, before he dumped her into the carriage and jumped in after her. They drove off immediately, not waiting for Lady Haven. I must assume she is still inside. With the damned duke.*

Again!

Instead of having her back at my house all day, holding her in my arms, whispering about our lives, I waited here. Outside of Nox House. For her, I watched, and I waited all night, with terrible thoughts of what might be happening inside, feeling myself getting angrier as every minute passed. I got so pissed I considered going home for my pistols and going in after Lady Haven myself. Then the de Clare carriage returned and the black door of Nox House opened once again.

Lady Haven just walked out with only that old Muscovite whore waiting by the door as she got into the carriage. My sweet girl is obviously upset, with tears running down her ivory cheeks. Even from here I can see them. I cannot help but wonder what that bastard de Clare did to her. He better not have touched her. She better not have let him. I would be furious. I might be driven to hurt her, which would be a pity.

After all, she is meant to be mine. I knew it nearly three years ago, when I first saw her. She was walking on Bond Street, and she smiled at me. It was one moment, but it changed my world completely. It brought me the one reason I have to exist. Since then, I have either been nearby or had someone watching her.

Every day, I watch!

It was not easy or inexpensive. Though, admittedly, it was much simpler to slip a few bob to a servant at her school than it is now. These bloody people working for the duke are remarkably close mouthed. I have only found one scullery maid who will

4

tell me anything at all. And even then, it is only about upcoming balls and events. Stupid things I could find out any number of ways. This season has been particularly difficult for me, though.

Watching her dancing with all those men.

Watching all the men going into de Clare House to see her day after day.

Watching her smile at them all, letting some of them touch her.

Someday, everyone will know she is mine, and I will destroy anyone who dares touch her.

"Hey, follow that carriage." *I ask my own driver through the open window as soon as her carriage pulls away.*

I am pretty sure she is going back to de Clare House now, but I will follow her anyway. I would not be the right man for her if I do not make sure she gets home safely. Plus, I might be able to speak with her. Hearing her voice is always the highlight of my day. Or perhaps I might even be able to grab her, if I am very lucky.

Yes, it was an interesting day indeed.

chapter one

Peter Jenkins leapt down from the footboard with practiced ease, swiftly opened the carriage door, and offered Lady Emerson Haven his hand. Like all de Clare family employees, he was excellent at his job, and he subtly turned his face to respectfully avoid seeing her tears. Ignoring her soft sobs proved far more challenging. His heart stirred with a quiet sympathy he dared not voice.

As he shut the door, Peter winced, hunching his shoulders as her cries became desperate, drifting from inside. He was well paid to overlook such displays, however. Returning to the rear of the carriage, he climbed back onto his perch just as the driver flicked the reins, urging the horses into the night. The rhythmic clatter of hooves and wheels on cobbles did little to drown out the sound of her grief.

Even from there, he could hear her anguished sobs and wished there was something he could do. Instead, he wrapped his hands tighter around the rail and gazed at the night sky, letting the cool evening air cleanse him. The stars above offered no answers, only a silent reminder of his place in the world.

Emerson could not stop herself. She was unraveling. Something had cracked open deep inside her and was spilling out. Just an hour ago, she was glowing with hope for her future. Now, she sat huddled and shaking, her thoughts a tangle of loss and confusion.

Indeed, so much has happened today.

That morning, she received a mysterious note from someone claiming to have information about her dead brother, Kit. When Emerson arrived at Hyde Park, at the designated meeting spot, she encountered Marien, a mysterious woman claiming to be her brother's fiancée. The meeting triggered a chain of events that resolved many lingering questions about her brother's death eight years ago.

Unfortunately, Marien could not tell her everything at the park because they were interrupted by Lord Warwicke, her brother's old friend. Yet Marien's words, sharp and insistent, raised more questions than answers. She heavily implied that His Grace, Lathen de Clare, Duke of Windemere, was responsible for Kit's death.

'It is because of him your brother is dead!'

This revelation devastated her for many reasons. Not least because Kit and Lathen were the closest of friends. Worse, Lathen was now her guardian and, in the last few months, had become her secret lover, though she had not surrendered her virginity to him. Yet, their illicit kisses and daring caresses in shadowed rooms and private carriages had deepened her trust.

She had begun to desire a lasting connection with him. That very morning, before Marien's note, she believed they were well matched, dreaming of marriage and the happiness she always lacked. To say this news destroyed her was like saying it rained occasionally in England. It was simply not strong enough to describe her heartbreak.

Confronting Lathen when she returned from the park, she met his usual stone faced silence, devoid of denials or affirmations. He merely asked if she truly believed he could harm Kit, as if that was answer enough to all her questions.

After she left him, Emerson realized she did not believe it. Not at all. She knew Lathen would never intentionally harm Kit or her, yet her mind wrestled with the truths he withheld. His continued secrecy was killing her.

Her first instinct was to flee. To leave London. To leave Lathen. To leave all the secrets behind. As she packed in haste, her friend Hazel found her and intervened. Soon after, Leighton, Lathen's younger sister, arrived with news of Marien's whereabouts.

The three of them, united in their resolve and friendship, decided to immediately go to Nox House. Emerson knew Nox House was forbidden from past experience. Yet, her determination outweighed any caution, and her only concern was finishing her conversation with Marien. She had long sought the truth about Kit, and nothing, nor any person, would stop her. The risk of deliberately defying Lathen's wrath was worth it.

Upon their arrival, a tense confrontation erupted with Lathen, his brother Lennox, and Lord Warwicke. Emerson's two friends were immediately taken away by Lennox and Warwicke, but Lathen had relented, granting her what she was asking for. He led her upstairs to finally confront Marien together.

The conversation with Marien was excruciating, each word a dagger to her broken heart, yet it revealed the truths Emerson had long sought. She learned how and why her brother had died all those years ago. Marien had been her brother's mistress, not his fiancée. When he ended their affair, her rage drove her to push him down a staircase, killing him.

In some ways, knowing the truth brought Emerson comfort. Yet its senselessness, coupled with Lathen's concealment of Marien's crime, also left Emerson bitter and angry.

Her heart burned for Marien's punishment. Some kind of fate to mirror her brother's. She wished to see her sent to prison or watch her hang at the gallows. An eye for an eye had never been clearer.

After all, she tore my beloved brother from me! The only person who ever loved me as a child. Certainly, such a heinous act cries out for retribution!

In the end, she conceded Lathen was right. From the very beginning, he shielded her, doing what Kit would have wanted. Her brother would have never wished for her to be tainted by his mistakes. London society could be vicious and cruel, and the *ton* would have devoured the scandal of a young lord being killed by his mistress in a seedy pub.

And they never truly forget the juiciest bits of gossip.

Even more than seven years later, it would have haunted her debut season. At the Queen's Birthday Ball, titillating whispers would have rippled through the room, the resulting stain branding her as unmarriageable. Moreover, she risked losing the title she inherited from her father.

Emerson never understood how her father secured a special remainder for her title of Earl of Haven. She doubted King George would have granted it if it was known how her brother died.

She finally realized that she had to accept the truth and trust that Lathen would handle Marien in the right way. Letting go proved surprisingly easy, as the release of anger opened her heart to Lathen. As though the truth about her brother was the only reason she was holding back.

In truth, she had desired Lathen for over two years. It was only his restraint holding them back. The night's painful revelations only fueled her determination.

She wanted him. And she finally had enough knowledge about making love that she was able to pull him in and overcome all his proper sensibilities.

Their passion was more than she had ever imagined it could be. It was incredible. She had felt her body explode into a million pieces and then come back again for more. Despite her sorrow and regrets, she still wanted him. As if he alone could make her whole.

What is wrong with me? He is not what I believed. It is not just that he is a duke who is used to throwing around his authority. He is not just a stoic. He is perverse! Her thoughts screamed as her trembling fingertips grazed her kiss swollen lips.

It was only after they made love in the Blue Room at Nox House that she began to realize the enormity of her mistake. She had woken alone and went in search of Lathen with hope and joy in her heart. When she finally found him, her heart leapt, believing the revealed truths would unite them.

Finally, we could get married. He had once vowed never to marry, but surely their shared passion had changed his mind. Now that all their secrets were revealed, there was nothing to keep them apart.

But Lathen still had another secret. One that was even darker and quite literally deeper. He led her through a secret door in Nox House's library, down a dark passageway, down steps, and further still to a heavy ancient door. He knocked once, spoke secret words, and the door opened.

It revealed another world.

Noir.

Night. Darkness. Shadow. An underground cathedral of debauchery and licentiousness. Men and women, entwined in naked, carnal embraces, the scent of bergamot and honey swirling with desire.

And the sounds! The moans of passion echoed in her mind, undimmed by distance or her desperate attempts to block them by pressing her hands to her ears.

Lathen let her glimpse the main hall's debauchery briefly before leading her past. His goal was the room he called the Cantilever Chamber. Inside was a strange apparatus, hanging from a huge beam. Her stomach churned when Lathen explained it was designed to keep her helplessly suspended. Leather straps, chains, and ropes would bind her immovably in place.

So, he could hurt me! He wants to cause me pain because he needs that to feel complete!

Emerson was not sure what was worse. That he wanted to hurt her or that he tried to convince her that she would crave it. He insisted she would come to love it, claiming it would heighten her passion.

It struck her as utterly mad. That was why she was crying so hard. It felt like a profound loss, akin to another death. To think she had turned a corner and could be with Lathen, to give him her innocence, only to find him on a path so dark and twisted she could not follow him.

It is tragic, really. I am not certain that my heart can take this pain.

Emerson's sobs deepened until she realized she must compose herself. She was already returning to de Clare House after dark. Alone. It would not do for the neighbors to see her face covered in tears or to hear her crying. Shuddering, she dabbed her eyes with a handkerchief, blowing her nose between slowing, hitched tears. She noted absently it was embroidered with little daisies and had her initials. Hazel had made it for her on her last birthday.

Oh, Hazel, my darling friend. How am I going to explain all of this to you? What will you think of me after I have freely given Lathen my innocence and have nothing to show for it? And Leighton. I can hardly tell her all that has happened tonight.

As the carriage rounded a corner, St. James Square came into view through the window. She wiped her eyes gently one more time and took another deep, shuddering breath. They halted, and the same footman opened the door for her. His fleeting look of relief betrayed his gratitude for her composure.

The poor man has no idea I am breaking still, but I suppose I must hold this heartache inside. It would not do for anyone in that house, besides perhaps Hazel, to know that I am anything other than perfectly happy. At least until I can get away.

Emerson took the footman's gloved hand and stepped onto the sidewalk, shoulders back, head held high. Only a slightly reddened nose and shining, overbright eyes hinted anything untoward ever occurred.

As she released the footman's hand, a cheerful voice called from across the square, startling her.

"Lady Haven!"

chapter two

After Lathen bid a stoic farewell to Emerson, the mechanical door clicked shut, its lock engaging with a sound that seemed to reverberate like a slam. The echo resonated in the hollow of his chest, a pang so sharp it nearly drove him to turn back, to rush to her, pull her close, and whisper assurances that they could find a way forward.

Together.

Instead, he pressed himself against the cold door, forcing himself to remain still. His body trembled violently, sweat beaded on his brow, and tight knots of tension coiled in his shoulders and thighs from the effort of restraint.

Lathen always knew revealing his true self to Emerson, showing her what he needed to exist, might make her bolt.

And it did.

The truth was a heavy burden for a young woman to bear, too heavy, as it turned out. Yet it was a risk he had been willing to take to keep Emerson.

Unfortunately, she asked to leave. He had promised she could, so he let her go. Now, hurt and anger churned within him, tightening painfully. He craved release, the kind that came from inflicting pain on another, a need that pulsed with urgency. The dark passageway before him offered countless options for such relief.

Ruby is still there, of course, and she can handle everything I need to unleash.

Somehow, that seemed wrong. Earlier, when he and Emerson had encountered Ruby, Emerson's discomfort at the idea of him with another woman had been palpable. Her jealousy, oddly endearing, mirrored the depth of his own feelings for her. To seek out Ruby now would feel like a betrayal, a violation of the bond they had shared.

Who then? Cora, with her long blond hair and huge breasts? That woman has an appetite for sex and loves being tied and hanged from the ceiling. She likes when I use a flogger to flick across every inch of her skin, turning it bright red as blood rushes to the surface.

He shook himself. Cora would expect him to bring her to completion. That, too, felt wrong. Lathen brought Emerson to the Cantilever Chamber to show her a world of possibilities, to share moments of raw connection as she swung toward him, their bodies colliding in passion. To do that with Cora would betray not just Emerson, but himself. Emerson's taste still lingered on his lips. Her touch was still warm on his skin. No other woman could replace that.

No, he did not want intimacy. He needed to hurt someone, to purge the pain within him.

Then it must be Marta. She is the only one, really. Her Prussian sensibilities are exactly what I need.

Marta was a twisted soul who liked to be beaten. Hard. She thrived on being pushed to extremes, her desires for pain matching the intensity he needed to expel. Lathen rarely sought her out as her tastes often crossed lines that even he found unsettling. Tonight, however, she was the answer.

He pushed off from the heavy door and slowly began the long descent to *Noir*. His steps echoed off the damp stone walls, and he could hear his heart beating loudly with every footfall. A sad musical salvo only he could hear.

When he got to the empty vestibule, he stood before the huge wooden door and paused. It was where every person who came to *Noir* passed through. For him, it was many years of going down this same dark path. He recalled when he first learned of the existence of the club, when he was just twenty-one years old.

It seemed like a lifetime ago. His father had just died two weeks before, making him the new Duke of Windemere. He came to London, from the country, to take over the estate. One after the other, from morning until evening, various employees came for meetings. The only reason he was able to do everything without feeling overwhelmed was the training his grandfather had given him since birth.

'Never show weakness. Always stand strong and tall so others must look up to you. You ARE to be the duke and will be the only authority that matters!'

Those sentiments might as well have been my first words after hearing them so often. His mouth twisted wryly at the memory.

Then one night, after an exhausting day of meetings, Madam Irina summoned him, asking him to come to Nox House to discuss a property his father had owned. The missive was vague. Just an address and a question: *What did he, the new Duke of Windemere, wish to do with Nox House now?*

Puzzled, as he had seen no record of another house in the city within the family ledgers, Lathen went. What Madam Irina showed him had shocked him.

At first.

Not the acts within, but that his father had built Noir, an underground haven for the *ton's* darkest desires. It explained his father's frequent absences, his lack of a mistress or new wife after their mother's death, and perhaps why he had sent Lathen to India after his grandfather's passing. There, Lathen had learned to channel his cravings, perhaps guided by a father who understood those needs, shaped by the same iron-willed grandfather.

Nevertheless, Lathen's first inclination was to close the whole place down. If the *ton* learned of its existence, his family would be ruined. Neither he nor his siblings would ever have been able to show their heads in proper society. His sister would never be able to marry well if she were to be tainted by such a thing. That was the way of things in their world.

Then, after thinking about it, he realized the *ton* did know. They were there, in that cavernous space, night after night. There were members of the peerage, including royalty, dukes, marquesses, earls, viscounts, barons. They were all there. Gentlemen, and even some ladies. Yes, the rest of the *ton* would be shocked if their nightly activities were exposed. But, for their own sake, they kept the secret.

To protect them, and himself, he kept their confidence as well. On a trial basis, he agreed to learn more about the club. Madam Irina taught him the club's rules, its safeguards, and how to maintain its secrecy. Over time, Lathen transformed *Noir* into a sanctuary where, for a price, the elite could explore their deepest desires without fear of judgment or exposure. He became its Master.

Of course, there were whispers among the rest of the *ton* about *Noir*. It was impossible to truly keep a secret in the upper echelon of London society. Yet it never became more than whispers. Even the Regent was rumored to visit on occasion, though there was no proof of that beyond what knowledge Lathen and Madam Irina had. Everyone who entered the door had to wear a disguise, and no one ever used their true names or titles.

Most came through a small, gated carriage house behind Leicester Square. They would get dropped off at the old iron gate and use their member key to open it. Then it was a short walk to a nondescript door that led to a set of stairs, down to a maze of old tunnels. The tunnels were always lit with beeswax candles, and members knew the way to the entry room, where Lathen now stood before the large door.

He, of course, did not come that way. Only his closest confidants knew of the tunnel he used. His father had purchased Nox House for the simple reason that it was one of three properties with tunnels that all led to this door. His father had bought them all, but it was Nox House that he kept to himself, and Lathen did his best to keep that secret as well.

He never learned how his father found *Noir*, or the tunnels that led there. Even Madam Irina did not have that answer for him. It was a vast cavernous space that was obviously built hundreds of years ago. Carvings on the stones suggested it was part of an ancient Templar complex, but other evidence hinted it was used in the time of the Tudors. Either way, it managed to be kept hidden through the centuries. Right under the noses, and under the homes, of some of the wealthiest families of London.

Lathen took another deep breath and rolled his tight shoulders. Thinking about how *Noir* came to be, and why he was standing there, was not helping his anger and hurt. If anything, the regret made his locked heart skip a beat.

Yes, Marta. It must be her tonight. Resolved, he nodded to himself.

Lathen pulled his mask out of the pocket of his greatcoat. He slipped it over his eyes, a well-practiced motion, and knocked on the door. A small opening near the top slid open to reveal the masked face of the doorman for the evening.

"Yes?"

"*Nox omnia secreta tenet,*" Lathen spoke the words quickly. He had told them many times. Not always the same ones, of course, as they changed often to ensure no one who was not supposed to be there got inside. Tonight, it was the second time he said them, and somehow, they sounded flat in his ears.

The heavy door was opened quickly, and the young man bowed to him again.

"Master," it was whispered reverently.

"Is Marta here?" Lathen did not feel like going through the formalities.

"Oh, yes, I believe she is. Shall I send her somewhere for you?"

"Yes, I want her in the Cantilever Chamber. Now." Lathen said brusquely over his shoulder as he walked away. Then he stopped suddenly and turned back.

"Have her bring a flogger and clamps with her."

"Yes, Master. Right away."

Lathen nodded quickly, then turned back toward the main hall. It led to the high opening of the cathedral like chamber, where bergamot and honey assailed his senses. He barely looked toward the activities that were still going on in the huge space and in the alcoves that were carved out on every wall. It was enough he could hear them as he walked through. The moans and screams echoed off the arches and vaults, coming at him from every direction. He winced as he thought of Emerson's delicate gasps and sensual, uninhibited cries she made when he touched her. He lengthened his stride, rushing to get to the other side, where a long hallway led him toward the chamber. There were many other doors on each side, but none of them had what he wanted right then.

Lathen reached the Cantilever Chamber, and he pushed open the old door. Inside, the faint remnant of orange blossoms surrounded him. It was the delicate scent that Emerson wore, and he could still picture her standing before him, not half an hour before, staring with her huge lavender eyes at the device hanging from the wooden post. It was his hope to have her in it. To show her how magnificent it could all be. The eroticism of giving in to him, for him to take responsibility for giving her pleasure.

Instead, she left me! His mind screamed.

He rubbed at his chest again, but it did not give him any relief. Instead, it magnified the hollow. He wished Emerson had stayed. He had known she was going to be shocked and frightened. That was unavoidable. Yet a part of him truly believed she was strong enough to handle it. To take what he wanted to show her. To enjoy it. She always seemed to enjoy what little he had shown her thus far. In fact, the first time he ever punished her, she had gotten so excited and wet that he barely touched her, and she came tightly around his fingers.

Instead, what was going to happen in this room was going to be different. It was going to be rougher. Darker. Far more than what he would have shown Emerson tonight. He wanted to strike out and hear the flogger hitting flesh. Over and over, until the sounds of Marta's screams drowned out the memories of Emerson's soft sighs. Until her sweat and tears overwhelmed the scent of orange blossoms. They had to. Or he was going to give in and rush home to her.

There was a succinct knock on the door.

"Enter!" he bellowed.

Marta came in quietly. She did not attempt to pretend she did not know what he wanted. After all, she was carrying a flogger in one hand and, though he had not asked for one, a cane in the other. Around her neck, held by a thin rope, was a pair of simple clamps. They were each made from two pieces of carved wood, fitted around a small dowel in the center acting as a pivot.

Marta slowly bent down to her knees on the hard stone floor, carefully placed the objects on the ground in front of her, and bowed down. All the way, going prone over her lap with her arms splayed to the sides, until her forehead touched the floor.

"Master," she murmured worshipfully with a heavy Germanic accent, "I am here to do your bidding."

chapter three

In the lamplight of the late spring evening, Mr. Brown was crossing the street from the park toward Emerson, his arm raised high in greeting.

She was not really in the mood to talk with him, or anyone else, but it would be impolite not to wait. She plastered a smile on her face, lifted her hand in a slight return wave, and watched as he reached her side, removed his top hat, and bowed.

"Mr. Brown. How lovely to see you this evening. Do you live near here? I was not aware."

She realized it was true. She did not know much about Mr. Brown. She never sought him out for conversation. Not when he called each day at de Clare House and not when they met at parties or balls. She only ever danced with him when his name was written on her card and would exchange pleasantries with him because she had to. He was nice enough, but she found him a bit boring. Luckily, when calling on them, he spent all his time sitting near Hazel instead of her.

"N-no, n-not me. I actually do n-not have a home in L-london. N-not yet. I have rooms just down on P-Piccadilly at the Albany for when I come to t-town for the season."

Oh, poor Mr. Brown. I wish he was not so nervous all the time, she thought sadly.

Mr. Brown had a stutter that always seemed to get worse whenever he was around them. Especially when he spoke to Hazel. At least from what Emerson had seen. It appeared to be getting better as the season went on, however. The first time they had all met, the gentleman could barely get a word out until she had taken over the conversation, chatting until he calmed himself. Emerson sincerely wished that he would find a woman whom he felt comfortable around, even though she really hoped for more for her friend. Not that there was anything wrong with Mr. Brown, per se. He just was not exciting enough in her opinion.

Hazel needs someone who can keep up with her brilliant mind. Someone to challenge her. Otherwise, she will get wearied and lose her shine. That will not do. Plus, she will always be in my life, and I cannot seem to picture Mr. Brown always being around as well.

"Then what brings you to St. James's this evening?" she asked as she turned halfway toward de Clare House, trying to work out a way to leave him.

"I had a d-dinner with a friend just across the square on the P-Pall Mall, and I thought I might w-walk it off back to my apartments. It is s-such a n-nice n-night after such a hot d-day." He smiled at her and turned to look up at de Clare House, then back at the carriage at the curb.

"You are j-just returning?" he asked curiously.

It was unusual for her to be out, especially after dark, with no chaperone. Emerson quickly racked her brain for a reason she was just coming home. Her mind was blank.

...

Dammit, completely empty...

...

The front door opened just then, saving her from having to answer as they both turned at the sound. Hazel rushed out, her lovely blonde hair down and flowing freely behind her. She smiled widely at Mr. Brown in greeting, as her slippers skipped down the steps.

"Hello, sir, it is wonderful to see you. It was such a beautiful day, was it not? We all went for a ride in the park to enjoy the coolness. Are you taking the night air as well?" she chattered brightly to him.

Emerson nearly sagged in relief at seeing her best friend rushing toward them. It was obvious she was being a deliberate distraction for her.

"Oh, y-y-yes, I-I-I am." Mr. Brown smiled shyly, and a flush came to his face as he bowed to Hazel. As usual, his stutter appeared to get worse as she got closer.

Hazel turned to Emerson and put one hand on her arm, surreptitiously slipping something into Emerson's hand. The one on the side away from Mr. Brown.

"Did you get the ribbon you forgot?" she asked happily, looking meaningfully toward the hand she just touched.

"Yes, of course," Emerson smiled at her appreciatively and lifted the ribbon up and showed them both as it unraveled in midair. She recognized it as the one Hazel had used to tie her hair back that day when they left to go riding, and she knew her friend must have taken it out only moments before.

She really is brilliant!

"Well, it was wonderful seeing you again, Mr. Brown, but it is getting late, and we really must get inside before Lady de Clare comes back out to search for us," Hazel chattered lightly as she looped her elbow through Emerson's, and they made their way through the wrought iron gate.

"Will we see you at Lord and Lady Milner's party next week?" she asked over her shoulder as they got to the front steps and Giles, the de Clare family butler, opened the wide walnut door almost immediately.

"Y-yes, m-most d-d-definitely, Miss Atwood, Lady H-Haven. G-good evening to you b-both." Then he put his top hat back on and walked away. Though he did look doubtfully back at the carriage once more before he turned the corner and went out of sight.

chapter four

After they got through the door, and returned Giles's unusually kind greeting, Hazel pulled Emerson up to their rooms quickly. It was not empty, however. Leighton was standing near a window, looking out over the square.

"Phew, that was close!" she exclaimed as she turned around, "I thought Mr. Brown might never leave!"

Next to her, Emerson breathed a heavy sigh.

"Yeah, that was unfortunate, but I think Hazel managed him quite well. I do not think he realized I was out alone."

"Forget about him. He is a nice enough fellow and not prone to gossip. I have literally never heard him say a single bad word about anybody. I do not think we need to worry," Hazel rushed, grabbed Emerson's arm again, and led her to the sitting area.

"We have been positively anxious and worried over what happened after we left Nox House. Please, sit. Tell us everything."

Emerson sat on a pretty, light blue velvet chair and ran her hands along the silken material. Hazel and Leighton also sat, leaned forward, and waited with bated breaths for her to begin.

"I am not sure what to say," Emerson began honestly.

Hazel watched Emerson closely, as sadness and pain crossed her face, wishing she could do something to help her.

"Just start at the beginning. Or, rather, when we were made to leave." Leighton suggested.

It was Leighton who overheard her brothers and Lord Warwicke as they discussed where Marien was secreted. When the men left to get to her, Leighton rushed to share what she learned, and then all three of them had followed.

I suppose it is only natural for her to want to know what happened after they were gone. As Hazel watched, Emerson seemed to be warring with herself, but eventually a resolute look came to her eyes.

"Well, once you both left—"

"Once we were forced to leave, you mean!" Leighton interjected crossly, obviously still upset by the whole affair.

"Well, yes, after that." One side of Emerson's mouth lifted in an attempted smile and she reached over to pat the younger girl's hand. "Your brother, I mean His Grace—"

"Call him Lathen, please." Leighton interrupted Emerson again, but with an answering grin, "I think we are all close enough now for that, at least. Especially when it is just us."

Emerson took another deep breath and began again.

26

"Yes, Lathen. He took me up to where Marien was. That woman is...well, she is insane."

"What do you mean?" This time it was Hazel who asked.

"Well, she was Kit's mistress, as you suspected. He was never planning to marry her, as she suggested. But worse, when he went to leave her for good, she lost all sense and..." Emerson stopped, and braced her hands on the chair arms, closing her eyes tightly. As though the next words were too difficult to say out loud.

"It is okay, take your time." Hazel told her softly and Emerson opened her eyes. They held a deep pain, turning them nearly violet.

Hazel already suspected the dark truth, ever since Lennox mentioned Marien earlier that day. But she knew Emerson needed to tell them, to let the truth be free.

When the words finally came out, it was in a rush. "She killed him," Emerson cried, her voice breaking. "She pushed him down the stairs at the pub where they met for their affair!"

Leighton gasped, covering her mouth with her hand as Hazel rushed over and enveloped Emerson in her arms, holding her tightly. After a time, Hazel realized Emerson had calmed. So, she squeezed her again and returned to her chair. Everyone was quiet for a while as they absorbed the information. It was Leighton who eventually broke the silence.

"But that was hours ago. It took that long for her to tell you this?"

Emerson's eyes widened, and she looked quickly to Hazel for help. For her part, Hazel knew right away there was more to Emerson's tale, and she understood it had to do with Lathen and the things he and Emerson had been doing together in secret.

"I am sure Emerson just needs to rest," Hazel stood, trying to distract Leighton with a gentle tone, "it has been a long day, after all."

Leighton looked at them. Back and forth. Then she narrowed her eyes and snorted indelicately.

"Please. If you want me to leave so you can talk, just the two of you, you only have to say so." With that, Leighton stood as well and made to leave their sitting room. Her face was pinched with barely suppressed sadness, and Hazel felt bad for her.

"Wait!" Emerson tried to stop her.

"No, really," Leighton raised her arms and crossed them to protect herself from her hurt, "I understand. I am not part of your special club. I am too young, right?"

"Please, Leighton, wait, really. I promise, it has nothing to do with your age. Truly!" Hazel grabbed Leighton's arm as she was rushing off toward the door.

Leighton stopped. She looked down at Hazel with a pained expression.

"It is something, though. I am not a dunce. I can tell when I am being put off. But Emerson was my sister, my friend, before she was sent away. We grew up together. She taught me how to climb trees, and I taught her how to embroider. Not that she was ever good at it. Now, she is yours. You can say things to each other that I am not part of. If it is not because I am a mere year and a half younger, then what is it?"

Hazel sighed. She knew Leighton was struggling to not be part of the season, but this was something else. Yet, as she thought about it, Hazel could understand why Leighton was so upset. Lathen had separated the two of them two years ago, after Emerson had convinced Leighton to go on a midnight ride through Hyde Park with her. Since then, she had been at school with Hazel, and the two of them had become the best of friends. It was never their intent to exclude Leighton, but they obviously had. Hazel looked at Emerson, and they came to a mutual, silent agreement.

chapter five

"Leighton, we are very sorry. I guess we just thought that we should not talk of things that are outrageous and potentially compromising," Emerson apologized before continuing, "Especially if it has much to do with your brother."

"Posh," Leighton frowned and responded with a wave of her hand, "everyone seems to think that I am too young to know anything. For goodness' sake, I have not one, but two older brothers. And one of those brothers is Lennox, who is always off meeting with some new mistress! Of course, they always think they are being discreet, but they still talk about their affairs. It is not my fault they are loud, and I happen to have overheard many things I probably ought not to have."

"All right, well, I guess you should know that Lathen and I have been..." Emerson paused and thought. She did not know how to explain the last few months in a delicate way. Even if Leighton had managed to learn a lot from overheard conversations, she was still barely seventeen and surely any part of what she and Lathen had done would still shock her. "Well, we have been intimate."

"I knew it!" Leighton exclaimed and slapped her hand to her thigh, making Emerson's eyes widen. "I just knew that he cared for you. I could see it this season. He always looks at you when he thinks no one, especially you, is looking."

"He does?" Emerson raised her brow, and her mouth formed a circle. She thought their relations had been circumspect, but perhaps they were not as secretive as she supposed. If Leighton noticed, who else might have witnessed Lathen observing her. Or all the times she searched for him with her gaze. Let alone the times they thought they were alone, and he touched her.

And I let him.

"Yes, of course," Leighton waved a hand in certainty, but with a distracted tone. Then she gasped as if something had occurred to her. "Actually, I think I saw it the first time two years ago. Remember, when you and I came to town, and we got into that small bit of trouble? Right before you left for school."

"Oh, yes, I remember. But I certainly never noticed him looking at me. Not two years ago."

Except the moment when he looked at me and I felt the first stirrings of desire in my belly. I was so naïve back then, not even seventeen yet. I did not even realize what was happening to my own body.

"Well, it was more subtle then. Like he was not even sure who he was seeing. But this season, it has been quite obvious. He went to your coming out ball, too. Trust me when I say that he *never* goes to those sorts of things." Leighton nodded matter-of-factly.

Hazel had kept silent until this point, content to just let Leighton and Emerson talk and renew their bond. Yet she was curious.

"Do you think maybe he sent her away, back then, because he was beginning to care for her?"

"Perhaps, but of course Lathen would never tell me anything like that. Perhaps Lord Warwicke. That is the only person he ever opens up to." Leighton looked thoughtful for a moment before she brightened suddenly and turned back to Emerson. "Wait, when will you two be married?"

Silence was her only answer.

Emerson blushed and felt more tears come before she let her gaze fall to her clasped hands, so she did not have to come up with something to say.

Huh, I suppose I can still cry.

Leighton looked back and forth between Emerson and Hazel again, trying to figure out just what happened. The tension was suddenly palpable. When she finally realized the issue, she started to sputter and got red in the face.

"You do not mean you two will not be married, do you? After he has compromised you, he must! My brother always does the honorable thing."

Emerson felt a sharp pain spearing her heart. How could she explain that she could not marry Lathen, especially given his reluctance to marry. The reasons were unfortunate and unsavory. It was impossible. She decided not to get into the specifics but still be truthful.

"No, we are not to be married. I am sad about that, but it is not something I can discuss the particulars of. So please, do not ask me more. I only know one thing for sure, and that is that I absolutely must take some time away. I must."

Emerson knew she needed to leave de Clare House. It had been her plan before she went to confront Marien, and now she was even more determined. Even if her reasons had changed.

I need to get away from Lathen. I cannot imagine having him walk through the front door and seeing him again after everything. Especially knowing where he has been after I left him! He probably went to that naked redheaded witch we saw earlier! Visions of Lathen and the other woman floated in her mind, with her hanging from the beam as Lathen moved around her. Her breasts lifted toward his mouth. Her cries as he did all the things he wanted. She had to close her eyes and shake her head to clear it.

When Emerson opened them, she noticed that it was Leighton and Hazel's turn to exchange a quick glance.

"I will not be dissuaded, so please do not try. I am going." She uttered firmly and began walking toward her bedroom without waiting for her friends to talk her out of leaving.

"Oh, darling," Hazel followed her to her door, "we are not going to argue with you."

Emerson opened it and gasped in surprise. When she left earlier that afternoon, to follow Lathen to Nox House, her room was a complete disaster. She had thrown everything she owned onto every chair and across the bed, in a vain attempt at packing her things in a hurry. Someone had clearly been in and put it all back in order. Nothing looked amiss. She turned back to Hazel and Leighton, who were both grinning at her.

"You picked up?"

"Of course, it would not do for poor Alice or Mrs. Jaymeson to find it the way it was," Hazel explained.

She is right, of course. It was quite rude of me to leave such a mess for the maid. And I am far too grown to have my governess picking up after me. I

*suppose it is a testament to how upset I was that I did
not even think about it when I started throwing things
around. Or when I went running out of here.*

"And we already packed a small trunk for you,"
Leighton interrupted Emerson's thoughts. She looked
like she was happy to have been able to play a part.

"You packed for me?" Emerson asked. She
would be grateful if that was so. It would save her
quite a bit of time, as she was hoping to be gone
before Lathen returned and could stop her.

*I will have to leave on horseback. It is the only
way since I will not have a carriage at my disposal.*

"Actually," Hazel answered, "we packed for all
three of us."

"Because we are going with you!" Leighton
added quickly. Her smile widened even more.

"Oh!" Emerson was shocked. "But you really
cannot. Hazel, it is your season, too. You need to stay
and keep looking for a husband. And Leighton, there
is no need for you to get into any more trouble with
your brother on my behalf."

Emerson knew Lathen would be angry with her
for leaving without an escort. To do so with his sister
would make him livid. She did not want either of her
friends to have to deal with the consequences of
leaving London.

"No, the decision has been made," Hazel told
her firmly. "We already set the wheels in motion. Lady
Sutcliff was by earlier, and we let it slip that it is the
anniversary of your father's death, and you were
planning on going home to Havenfield to lay flowers
for him and your brother. Of course, that means the
entire *ton* will have heard the news by tomorrow."

"But I have never marked his passing. You
know we were not close." Emerson looked confused.
Her father was a drunkard and had never paid her
any mind when she was a child. As she grew older,

she realized that it was probably because her mother had died giving birth to her, and he somehow blamed her for that. Regardless, what she had said to Hazel was true. She did not choose to mourn him.

"Oh, I know, but that does not matter. What does matter is that Lady Sutcliff thought it was sad and terribly romantic. Half the *ton* will think the same and our leaving will be understood. The gossip will be of how tragic your loss was, and how you are a good daughter to remember your father."

Emerson thought about it for a moment before responding.

"What about the other half? They will still gossip and make up other reasons for our being gone."

"Let them try. We are taking two footmen and a well trusted driver, and we have no intention of stopping at any inns along the way. As far as anyone knows, there is no reason for us not to go for a quick trip." Leighton answered.

"But your brother is going to be furious, Lettie." Emerson used the younger girl's childhood nickname. It seemed appropriate considering their renewed closeness.

"Posh," Leighton frowned, and her face grew determined, "I am positively furious with Lathen right now, and I refuse to worry about his anger. He can live here alone in his over starched shirts and ledgers filled with numbers, for all I care. If he thinks he can compromise my friend and still have the moral high ground, he can stuff it!" She waved her hand as if she was turning a page. "Now, no more trying to talk us out of this. If you are going, we will be going with you."

Hazel nodded her agreement before turning back to Emerson.

"She is right, we all go, or no one goes," she reiterated. "No more arguing, Em. It is only wasting precious time. If we are going, we must leave soon."

Relief flooded through Emerson. She was going. That had not changed. But she did not realize how good it would feel to have her friends going with her. To not be alone on the road, on horseback, for days as she went north.

"Okay, I accept. But how will we get out of here?" Emerson asked. "It is not as though your Aunt Lillian and Giles will simply let us walk out without any questions. Plus, we need to get our horses and provisions. I would not know how to do all of that without Giles's help."

Leighton grinned again.

"I have already taken care of all of that. The large coach has been prepared to take us all to Havenfield, and we just need to get a footman to bring our trunks down. I have spoken to everyone, even Aunt Lillian, and they all understand. Giles and Lennox have been especially helpful in getting everything organized."

Emerson decided to do as her friends suggested. She would not worry about the details of how Leighton had managed to secure everything without getting approval from Lathen. She was merely glad to be going. It was not going to solve her problems. Lathen would probably send someone after them as soon as he realized they were gone. Or at least a letter demanding they return to London. Yet the thought of going home, even for a single day or two, was a relief. It was even worth whatever punishment Lathen might have for her when she returned.

I am finally going home. Back to Kit.

chapter six

Lathen woke as the sun was coming in through delicate white lace curtains that did absolutely nothing to hinder its early morning rays. He cracked one eye open before reaching for a pillow to block the blinding light. Unfortunately, the fabric smelled of orange blossoms and brought him to his senses. Long enough that he realized where he was.

He was in the Blue Room at Nox House, sprawled across the bed. It was where he had carried Emerson after she fainted, overwhelmed by meeting Marien and discovering the woman had murdered her brother. He had laid her gently on the chaise, flung open the very window now tormenting him, and later, after heartfelt words, they had made love on that same chaise.

When they were done, she fell asleep on his chest. He remembered lying there with her in his arms, stroking her dark hair that smelled of orange blossoms. He had felt a sense of contentment for perhaps the first time ever.

That peace did not last long. A small wisp of fear and guilt began to twist through him as he realized he could not have Emerson without her knowing all of him. It was just not possible. Too many secrets had wedged them apart for years.

That certainly did not turn out well. She left. She left me. Another searing pain stabbed at him, and he remembered the rest of the evening.

Desperate to purge his anguish, he went back down to *Noir*. It was with the specific idea that he would wear out his own disappointment and pain by hurting Marta. She came down to the same room he had taken Emerson to, but that was where it all went wrong.

When he turned to Marta, ready to order her to undress and to stand over by the cantilevered beam, he saw her kneeling down with her head low. Her black curly hair trailed down onto the stone floor, nearly enveloping her entire body. It instantly reminded him of Emerson.

How many times in the last two years have I imagined her just like that? Kneeling before me, with her long dark hair trailing down her back and over her naked shoulders. Her sighing softly and calling me "Master." Too many. But Marta is not Emerson. Not even close.

He ordered Marta to leave. When she got up, he saw disappointment pass over her face, before her usual serene features fell back into place. Lathen had to catch himself as he almost apologized for his brusqueness. But that would have been too out of place with his anger. Plus, the Master never apologized.

"Yes, Master," she answered softly and, without any questions or even looking directly at him, she got to her feet and left quietly. She took the cane and flogger with her.

Lathen lingered in the Cantilever Chamber for quite some time, sitting alone at the small table. He kept going over the discussion he and Emerson had there, seeing her face as he explained what he wanted. The way it turned from excitement and attachment to fear, then disappointment, and eventually, sadness. Each shift in her expression haunted him, a silent rebuke he could not escape.

When he finally left, it was not to go home. Nor was it to fetch another to take Marta's place. Instead, he went back up to Nox House, found a full bottle of brandy, and took it upstairs to his room. There, he hoped the liquor might dull the ache of his regret.

His pounding head told him he must have drunk the whole bottle before passing out. Which, in hindsight, was probably a good thing, as it was the only thing that kept him from heading straight home, climbing the stairs to Emerson's rooms, and dragging her back to his own bedroom. Or back down to *Noir*. Down to the Cantilever Chamber. To show her how wrong she was to leave. To show her she was meant to stay with him.

But that would not do, would it? I need to gather my strength and learn to live as I always have. I will simply get up, get dressed, and go home and act like nothing has changed. Emerson still needs a husband who can make her happy. I still need to make sure she finds someone worthy of her.

His resolve faltered as dizziness forced him back onto the bed with a groan. He draped an arm over his eyes, blocking the sun.

Perhaps later, when the room stops spinning. Damn brandy...

He drifted into a light, snoring slumber, his worries over Emerson thankfully floating away. But her eyes still haunted him.

It was nearing teatime when Lathen finally staggered into de Clare House. When he walked in, he immediately understood something was different. It was still. Yet there should have been multitudes of servants running around, completing their duties. Even Giles was silent when he opened the door.

Giles was always a bit reserved, like all good butlers who pride themselves on properly servicing their families. But as Lathen walked in, he was downright frosty as he gave the barest of nods. In fact, Lathen barely made it through the door before it closed firmly behind him, and Giles said nothing as he practically snatched Lathen's hat from his hand and walked away.

Lathen almost asked the older man if all was well, but Giles was gone without looking back, so he merely shrugged and turned toward the stairs. He did not have it in him to worry over the strange behavior. It would have to wait. All he wanted at that moment was a proper bath, fresh clothes, and a meal that did not include brandy.

And perhaps a few more hours of sleep.

"Your Grace," a call came from the morning parlor.

Lathen stumbled and came to a stop as he recognized his aunt's voice. He did not have the strength to talk with her either. However, he had resolved to return to his usual self, which unfortunately meant he needed to remember his manners. With a heavy sigh, he turned and walked to his aunt. It took all his effort to keep his back straight and not to drag his feet.

Lillian was not alone. With her were Mrs. Jaymeson and Lennox. Like Giles, Aunt Lillian and Mrs. Jaymeson were both staring at him coolly. Though his brother was grinning, as if he was deriving great enjoyment from whatever was going on. Or just from seeing his older brother so disheveled and coming home at an inappropriate hour.

I am sure he is pleased with the role reversal.

They were all sitting in a small circle of four chairs, with a tea tray on a cart near them. Lathen went to the cart, made himself a strong cup with one sugar, and grabbed a plain biscuit before he sat in the last chair near them. He raised his brow in expectation.

"Lathen, I thought we had an understanding about our responsibilities regarding Lady Haven and Miss Atwood this season. Especially since our conversation after the Queen's Birthday."

Aunt Lillian referred to the night of the debutante ball. When the girls had been introduced to the Queen and the rest of the *ton.* Much later that night was the first time he kissed Emerson.

She had come down to his study, and he had been unable to resist the temptation of her standing in front of the fireplace in her thin nightgown. Of course, her asking him to teach her how to kiss was not at all helpful to his reserve. He nearly lost all control and took her right then and there.

He did not. Instead, he summoned all his strength and sent her away. After he kissed her, of course. His aunt found him soon after and warned him away from Emerson. He was still not sure how she knew they were together, or if she knew anything at all. Perhaps she was simply shooting in the dark after he made the mistake of going to the ball. All because he was enamored after seeing Emerson in her finery before she left. Either way, he had agreed to her request.

Well, to be fair, she first suggested that I marry Emerson. Then she told me to stay away from her. I absolutely tried my best, I really did. But I guess she must know I failed in my efforts.

He was not sure how she could possibly know what happened last evening. Looking at his brother, it was clear he was enjoying watching him get raked over the coals, but it was unlikely he would tell their aunt anything. Even if he had known of everything that had gone on between him and Emerson. After all, it was an unwritten rule that they were to keep their liaisons with mistresses, or anything of that sort, from their aunt and sister. To always be discreet and keep any scandal from their family.

Perhaps it was Emerson. Maybe she was so upset when she left Noir that she told Aunt Lillian what happened. Or, more likely, she told Mrs. Jaymeson, who then shared it with his aunt. I suppose it would be what I deserve, even if it is disappointing to think she would share our intimate secrets.

"Well?" Aunt Lillian's foot tapped with impatience.

Lathen nodded his head, in lieu of answering her. Even that was a lot for him, and he hoped she did not expect more. At the moment, he was struggling to keep upright in his chair, instead of sliding, boneless, to the floor.

"Okay then. So, why is Lady Haven so ready to abandon her efforts to search for a husband? I mean, even these one or two weeks of them being gone could be the difference between both girls getting proposals or not. It is a crucial time. The second half of the season is about to begin!"

Baffled, Lathen's eyes widened. His whole brain was misfiring in spurts, making everything she was saying hard to understand. He even opened his mouth to speak several times before closing it again.

What does she mean by a week or two of Emerson being gone? She cannot leave now. I would never allow it, and she needs my permission to go anywhere. Why is this even a conversation I am being forced to hear?

"I am sorry, my dear lady, but I am confused by what you are referring to. Why would you think that Lady Haven and Miss Atwood are going away? I have made no such plans for them." He finally answered, holding his temple from the effort.

Lillian and Mrs. Jaymeson looked at each other. It was their turn to look puzzled. For his part, Lennox was covering his smile with his hand. Somehow it had grown even wider as he listened to the conversation. As though he knew the joke, but very much enjoyed watching Lathen stumbling to figure it out as well. It was Mrs. Jaymeson who broke the awkward moment.

"But Your Grace, Lady Haven, Miss Atwood, and Lady de Clare, your sister...they have already gone north."

Lathen stood up abruptly, dropping his teacup onto the floor in his haste. His aunt and Mrs. Jaymeson both looked down and gasped in surprise. His aunt also had to yank her skirts out of the way to avoid the tea that was making a spreading puddle on the beautiful carpet.

Like my time with Emerson. A beautiful thing left stained by me. He thought offhandedly.

"How?" he shook his head to clear it and shouted, then lowered his voice when he realized how loud it had come out. "When did they leave? And where did they go?"

"They left last evening to go to Havenfield. We thought you knew." Aunt Lillian explained. She was now looking flustered and unsure, instead of irritated. Obviously, someone had misled her.

"Of course I did not know. I was out all afternoon and the whole of the night. How could I have possibly arranged for such a journey?"

She did not just leave me at Noir. *She really left me. And what the bloody hell, she took Leighton and Miss Atwood with her! Somehow, they also managed to convince Aunt Lillian that I gave my permission. But how did they get a coach and a driver to do their bidding? It is not like they asked to go shopping on Bond Street.*

Lathen was still trying to process everything when he looked over and saw his brother had stopped smiling and was now avoiding his gaze. That was when he knew exactly who helped Emerson leave.

Lathen bowed quickly to his aunt before he started to walk out of the morning room.

"Lathen, wait!" his aunt raised her voice, "what are we to do?"

"I will go and get them and bring them all back. Everyone else will stay," he answered coolly before he looked over his shoulder to glare at Lennox and continued tersely, "A word, brother, in my study if you do not mind."

He then continued walking away, expecting that he would be followed.

chapter seven

Though the sky was morose and heavy, the weather was holding, and the coach was making excellent time. Unfortunately, such speed made for a very bumpy ride. The three girls took turns lying across one seat to nap while the other two sat together on the opposite side. But between rolling off the upholstered bench seat whenever they went over a large rut or being woken each time they stopped at an inn to exchange for fresh horses and provisions, they were all overtired and barely speaking. The initial excitement of their shared adventure had long since worn away.

Yet they did not dare to stop and rest at any of the inns they passed. Not only was there the danger of being seen and recognized by someone from London, but they also did not want to waste any time. It would take them nearly two days of constant travel to reach Havenfield. They had already been on the road for a day and a half.

It was Leighton's turn to try to sleep, but she lay on her back, legs pressed against the window, staring at the single lamp swaying from a hook above her. Her expression suggested she was deep in thought. If Emerson were not so tired and preoccupied with her own memories, she might have asked her friend if she needed to talk.

I wish I could convince myself that leaving Lathen was right, but I still ache for him. Both my body and my heart burn. Maybe I should have stayed and tried.

Flashes of that night filled her mind once more. Lathen kissing her all over her body. Nipping at her neck and ears. Sucking at her nipples, pinching them tightly. Giving her the pain he said she liked. Her begging him to continue. To take her. The climax she experienced when he finally entered her. He filled her completely, until he pressed against the very end of her womanhood. How it burned with white light during every deep thrust, heightening her pleasure.

He tried to explain, but I could not hear it. It all seemed harsh and unreal, and she ran. Yet she missed him. The thoughts spun around in her mind. *I really miss him.*

"Oh, Em, are you okay?" Hazel asked softly.

As she was thinking of him, Emerson started to cry silently. Hazel reached over and placed a clean handkerchief into her hand.

"No, I guess I am not doing so well," Emerson replied with a weak smile. She did not know how to explain. There was a lot she had not been able to tell Hazel. It was still too much to talk about in front of his sister.

I would not want to know about Kit's prurient interests, no matter what they were. Certainly not about the women he was with or his preferences with them.

Hazel nodded to her with sympathy, but she did not push. She understood that Emerson would tell her more when she was ready.

"Well, maybe it would help to sleep a bit more. I know it is rough, but we are all exhausted."

"Yes, take your turn to lie down," Leighton agreed as she sat up, "I cannot sleep anyway."

Emerson smiled gratefully and traded places with the younger girl. She doubted she would be able to sleep either, but it was still good to stretch her legs out. She yawned and grunted as they went over a large bump that lifted her body in the air and slammed her back down.

There is no possibility of going to sleep...

Lathen reached for her with his large hands. He gave her a slight, secret smile that brightened his eyes. She never wanted this moment to end. As she reached to hold his hand, he grabbed her wrist instead and placed a leather cuff over it. When she looked up to ask why, she realized he had encased her limbs in leather straps. No longer standing, she was tied with intricate knots, attached to chains hanging from a large wooden beam. The straps held her upright, with her arms and legs spread wide. Like a phoenix, ready to take flight, or burn. Shockingly, she was not scared. She was curious and waiting with wide eyes, desperate to know what Lathen was going to do next. When he next came to her, he was undressed. She did not even bother to look down at herself to see if she was also unclothed. She knew she was, but she was more interested in

47

watching Lathen as he prowled toward her. He was all muscle and sinew. Each step made his thighs tighten and release, his arousal evident as he approached. Her mouth began to water, and she realized she wanted to taste him again. To let him grab her face and control his entrance while she hung there. She knew he would be just gentle enough to hit her limits without going past them.

In his left hand was something long and black. It hung by his leg, its ends dragging on the ground. When he lifted it, she saw it resembled a riding crop but with a shorter, silver handle and multiple black strands falling from it, like a large bouquet of leather strings just for her. Without a word, Lathen began to drag the long tendrils over her shoulders and down her spine. He circled her, as if studying her body to decide where the flogger would land. His hand lifted above his head and the strands floated in the air as if a breeze was blowing through them. Emerson could not look away. It felt as if he were about to play a musical instrument, and she awaited the first note eagerly. When the leather strands came down, it was with a low whistle. They struck her bottom, curling around one cheek to grasp her hip. She gasped at the sensation. But not because it hurt her. It felt glorious. As if his strong hands were grabbing her, pulling her toward him. She tried to arch her back. Not to get away, but to get closer. However, all the straps were holding her in place, and she could not move. She could only take everything he was giving her. She looked at him, longing to beg for release. She wanted to touch him. He grinned even wider and lifted his arm again, only to drop the leather tendrils onto her upper back. This time they swirled around her side and grasped at her breast and arm, tweaking her nipple and making it harden at the tip. She wanted to tilt her hips as she felt a familiar wetness welling out of her core. She wanted him to stop. Or go harder. It was difficult to tell. But she did not have a choice either way.

Lathen was in charge. He was going to do what he wanted with her body. And he did. He whipped her all over. But it did not hurt. It felt like a warm bath enveloping her. Consuming her. Never in the same place twice. The straps felt like strong hands pulling her and holding her still for him. Until he felt she was ready. She was. She was dripping down her thighs. As she looked down, her dark curls were glistening around her secret entrance. He dropped the flogger without ceremony and moved closer to her so he could pull at the various ropes to change her position. She was suddenly upright, as if seated in an invisible chair. Her legs were pulled apart at the thighs and held wide at her ankles, her arms raised high and angled toward the ceiling. As though her body was an exploding star. She was open for him with her pelvis tilted up at the same height as his, a triumphant look on his face. Then he raised his fingertips to her face, touching her cheek with reverence. As Emerson looked into his eyes, he stepped closer. His manhood was straining to reach her. A small droplet at his tip reflected the candlelight. He came closer. Closer. Resting at her entrance. His hands gripped her hips and pushed, swinging her backward. The momentum brought her back forward. To him. His hardness started to pierce her, stretching her entrance, as his fingers tightened around her hips—

A loud noise and shouting woke Emerson with a jolt. She sat upright in the coach, her face flushed, realizing the yelling came from outside. The driver pulled to a hard stop, forcing her to grab the seat to avoid crashing into Hazel and Leighton.

"What is going on?" she asked, looking over at them with alarm.

Hazel had a strained look on her face, and she was lifting one of the curtains to peek outside. Leighton was doing the same on the other side. It was completely dark now, and Emerson realized she must have been asleep for some time.

"I do not know," Hazel whispered back to her, "but I heard a crack that sounded like a pistol shot, and then someone shouted at us to stop."

"I think," Leighton whispered back in a strained voice, "it is a highwayman!"

chapter eight

Emerson's tiredness vanished in an instant, her heart pounding with fear.

This! This is why we are not supposed to travel without a proper escort. Lathen will be so angry with me. That is, if we manage to get through this!

From outside they heard a gravelly voice ordering their driver and both footmen to come down and stand before him.

"I am certain now," Hazel answered, still in a whisper, "I just hope they only want our purses and do not wish to hurt anyone."

The coach door opened suddenly, and all three jumped and let out frightened shrieks. Heavy clouds obscured the moonlight, but the small lamp cast a stream of light, illuminating the covered face of the man standing there. He was dressed roughly in fraying woolen clothes and an old workman's cap over his long greasy hair. What they all noticed most was the rusty flintlock pistol that he was pointing at them.

"Oy, well wut do we 'ave 'ere?" he asked no one in particular, in a decidedly coarse northern accent. He smelled strongly of stale spirits and unwashed body, and as he pulled his mask down to get a better look, his grin revealed several missing teeth. Those that remained were dark and smelled of rot.

"Ya birds, out!" he barked and gestured with the pistol.

The girls recoiled. It made no sense that this one uncouth man, with nothing more than an ancient pistol, managed to overtake their coach driver and both of their well-armed footmen. Then, another voice rang out from beyond their sight.

"Is it some nabob? Shoot 'im in the leg if 'e does no' wanna part with 'is purse."

So, there was more than one of them. This was worse than they supposed.

"Nah, it be a trio o' feathered birds. They sure do smell nice," the man before them replied, his grin widening.

"Oh, bloody hell. Ladies? Step back, you fools. You two are going to scare them," snapped a third voice. His tone and accent were decidedly more refined.

He sounds like any one of the gentlemen we have met throughout the season! Emerson's mind was reeling. *Perhaps I am still asleep, and this is all just another dream. My subconscious's way of pulling me away from Lathen. Or of pushing me back to him.*

Another man stepped into view, pushing the first aside before looking at them. Peering into the coach, he recoiled in shock, then bowed deeply. Respectfully.

"Yes, I guess he was correct. Ladies indeed." The lower half of his face was also covered, but instead of a rough cloth, he wore a silk scarf. He also wore well-tailored black satin breeches, a finely woven blue greatcoat over a pressed lawn shirt, and a cravat tied with a flourish. He removed the top hat covering his blonde hair, but he was also holding a pistol. It was a newer and far more expensive model, and he at least had the good grace to point it at the ground and not at them.

"Well, my dear ladies, I am terribly sorry that we have hindered your travels. I hope my eager colleague did not frighten you too much, but I am sure you know what we desire. I trust you will part with the contents of your reticules. Then you can be on your way."

Leighton scoffed at him and made to stand. It was difficult due to the coach's low ceiling and her height. It was also quite obvious that she was now furious instead of scared.

"Sir, do you have any idea whose coach you have stopped?" she demanded, moving toward the door as if to climb down.

Hazel grabbed her arm and tried to pull her back. Leighton shrugged her off and stuck her head out of the door. She could see that all three of their servants were there, lined up and on their knees, with their hands intertwined behind their heads.

"And those men," she pointed, "you must let them go at once. They work for my family." She stepped to the ground and turned back to the man she was telling off. He was her height or slightly shorter, allowing her to lean forward and glare into his obscured face.

"I am devastated to say that I do not know to which family you belong. Pray tell, my dear girl, as I would love to know," the man answered her with a chuckle and a gleam of humor in his green eyes. He did not seem perturbed by her outburst. In fact, he appeared to be enjoying himself immensely.

Emerson was the one who bravely jumped out next. She also tried to grab Leighton and pull her back inside the coach. She understood it was safer for them not to tell this stranger who they were. Both she and Leighton came from wealth and titles, while Hazel was the daughter of the de Clare family barrister. If these men knew that, it could entice them to do more than simply steal their purses. They could easily kidnap them and hold them for a large ransom. More than they could ever hope to get by robbing a few carriages.

"Come on, get back in the coach, now!" she hissed under her breath, trying to sound firm as pulling on Leighton was proving futile.

"Oh, ho, I must admit, my dears, I much prefer you down here with me. It is a better view, after all." The man had watched as Emerson came down. He clearly enjoyed what he saw.

Emerson's cheeks were still flushed from her dream and the excitement of the robbery. The glow was noticeable even with the meager lamp from the coach.

"Sir, please, take this," she reached down and pulled her reticule off her skirt and shoved it toward him, "it is all I have, I assure you. And you can have theirs as well." She nodded toward her friends.

Hazel, who had wisely stayed inside the coach, reached for her own purse and handed it out. Leighton, however, jutted her chin stubbornly and crossed her arms over her chest. Emerson sighed, took Hazel's purse, and reached down to pull Leighton's off as well.

"Hey, Em, stop!" she shouted petulantly and tried to block Emerson. It irked her to give the ruffians anything. But to give her purse to a gentleman? That was simply too much!

Emerson gestured to silence Leighton and handed all three purses to the man. He took them with another short bow and slipped them into the pocket of his greatcoat.

"Well, thank you, *Em*," he added politely, emphasizing her name as if he was delighted to learn it. "I am in your debt, my lady. Truly I am."

"Can we go now, please, sir," Hazel asked softly from inside. She was focused on getting everyone out of there without injury.

"Of course," he gestured to the open door.

Emerson practically shoved Leighton up the running board and made to follow her. Before she could pull herself up, the man grabbed her arm and turned her to face him. A shriek escaped her, and Leighton made another angry shout above.

"I do believe that I require one more thing before you leave." With that, he pulled her away from the door and closed it despite Hazel and Leighton's protests.

"Sir, I have nothing left to give you. I swear to you, I gave you all our money. We will not even be able to buy breakfast." She tried to explain to him, fighting against him as he continued to drag her toward the back of the coach, out of the view of his companions and the de Clare coachmen.

Is this what Lathen has always tried to explain to me? About the dangers of breaking his rules.

"Oh, I do not believe that is true, Em," the man chuckled. "Besides, what I would like has nothing to do with money. In fact, here." He reached into his coat pocket, pulled out her reticule, and held it up. "It would devastate me to know you were hungry because of me."

Emerson was unsure what to do. She reached for the small bag with trembling fingers. Before she could grasp it, the man laughed again and bent down close to her.

"You can have it back, but first, I require a kiss!" Then he swooped down, pulling the scarf from his face, and covered her mouth as she gasped in shock.

Emerson had never been kissed by anyone other than Lathen. Not once. Not even a peck. The irony was that she had once thought of asking one of her suitors to kiss her so she would have something to compare to Lathen. So that she might stop craving his kisses so much. She certainly never imagined a stranger would kiss her.

And a scandalous gentleman highwayman at that!

It was not unpleasant. His breath tasted of mint and sweet summer wine, and he deepened the kiss, his tongue stroking hers. It was clear the man had experience in kissing. He held her in strong arms and pulled her close to his chest. His lips slanted across hers. First one way, then he turned his head for better access. It went on for more than a few heartbeats, but it did not move her. Not the way Lathen did. She felt a slight warmth flush through her, but her belly did not flutter, and she did not feel any urge to reach up and pull at his shoulder to keep him closer.

She waited patiently for the man to finish, then she reached up and slapped him across the cheek. As was proper after a gentleman had taken such liberties with a lady.

"Sir, how dare you!"

"Oh, I think you would be surprised at what I would dare, my dear lady," he chuckled, pulling his scarf back up to hide his face. Then he took her purse and tucked it into her dress. He slipped it deep into her bodice, between her breasts, grazing them.

She gasped and tried to swat his hands away, but he merely laughed gleefully as he grabbed her arm again. He led her to the coach door, opened it, and helped her inside. He shut it firmly, without another word.

"Come on lads," they could hear him shout, "let us be off. I would like to be in the next parish before the magistrate happens to pull himself from his cups and show his face."

The sound of the other men grumbling in their rough voices was muffled. As was the pounding of hooves as they all rode away.

When the coach door opened again, they again screamed in surprise. But it was only their driver, MacDuff, looking anxiously at them.

"Lady de Clare, Lady Haven, Miss Atwood. Are you all alright? I am so very sorry, but they put a tree across the road, so I had to stop. Then they were on us before we knew they were even there. As they were all armed, it seemed wiser not to engage in a pistol fight." The poor man was standing there, with his head lowered in shame and his red hat twisting in his hands.

Leighton leaned forward and patted his hand. She had known the man since she was a child and knew he would have done all he could to protect them. And he was correct. Getting into a shooting match would have been dangerous for everyone.

"Oh, please do not worry, Mac! We are all unharmed. But perhaps it is best if we discuss this later. We should be on our way in case they decide to come back. Stay on guard and keep your pistol ready. Oh, and tell the footmen to do the same, please."

The coachman dipped his head, tugged abashedly on his forelocks, and slipped his hat back on as he closed the door. He shouted at the other men to keep their eyes open, and they were soon back on their way, even faster and bumpier than before.

Inside, all was silent for some time. For her part, Emerson was bewildered. To be woken up so abruptly from the dream she was having...to all of that! Unsure if it was real, she needed confirmation.

"Did that really happen? Were we just robbed by highwaymen at gunpoint?"

Leighton looked at her for a moment before she broke into a crooked grin. Then she began to laugh nervously. Hazel stared at them both like they were crazy before she too started to laugh. Soon all three laughed so hard, clutching their sides, that tears streamed down their faces. When their giggles began to wane, Leighton finally answered her.

"Yes, I believe that is exactly what happened. Though I am baffled it was a gentleman with them. Oh!" she paused, realizing something. "Em, are you okay? We were so worried when he took you, but then you came right back. Did he try to take your jewelry?" She glanced at the delicate earrings still hanging from Emerson's ears and the small purple pearl around her neck.

Emerson blushed again. She did not know how to explain that a thief had kissed her. Or that she did not try to stop him, nor mind too much if she was honest with herself. And how, even now, she had her own purse nestled down in between her small breasts. It was not uncomfortable sitting there. Even if it were, she was not about to tell them how she had gotten it back. Much less how it had ended up there.

"Yes, I am fine. He just wanted to scare me, that is all. To ensure we would not report them," Emerson explained softly, feeling a little guilty at the fib.

"Well, I am sorry he manhandled you. The beast! I wish I had a pistol on me." Leighton could not get over the fact that anyone would dare to stop her family's coach. The fact that it was a gentleman was beyond her comprehension.

Such is the life of the daughter of a Duke, I suppose. And a sister of the current Duke, of course. Nothing untoward has ever happened to her. It makes sense she is so upset. Emerson reached over to pat Leighton on the arm.

"I am sorry I pushed you out there," she added, "but I did not want him to know who you were. You would be worth far more to them if they simply took you and sent a demand to your brother for money to get you back."

Leighton froze. Her eyes widened as she realized what Emerson was saying. Her mouth formed an 'oh' and her hand rose to cover it.

"You are right. I did not think. I was just so angry. How thoughtless of me. I could have made everything so much worse."

Emerson understood. Her own mind was struggling to process everything. She had acted on instinct to stop Leighton, but now she was also starting to appreciate just how much trouble they could have been in, and how lucky they were to have escaped relatively unharmed. Only lighter in their purses and one stolen kiss.

"Well, I do know one thing," she began, bringing Hazel and Leighton's attention back to her, "absolutely no one is to talk of what just happened. If Lathen or your Aunt Lillian were to hear of this, we will never leave the house again!"

They all grinned because it was true to a certain extent. Though Emerson knew Lathen would probably punish her in other ways. Something she was not as afraid of as she once was.

Or perhaps he would not. Not after I left him. He was obviously ready to move on and find someone else. After her dream, the thought of Lathen being with another left her feeling empty, her hand moving absently to her abdomen.

chapter nine

Lathen was saddle sore. He had been riding on horseback for more than a day and had only stopped three times. Once to catch a few hours' sleep and another to grab a hot meal. The last was merely to rest his horse. As it was, both he and Umbra, his stallion, were exhausted and ready to sleep.

Luckily, Lathen was beginning to recognize his surroundings. He was getting close to his destination. Probably no more than another hour or two.

Havenfield.

Even in the moonlight, the countryside was idyllic, fragrant with spring blooms, but an ache in his chest dimmed its charm. He had not been back to Havenfield since he brought his friend's body home more than eight years ago. After becoming Emerson's guardian, he hired a manager to oversee the estate. He ensured he received regular reports from Mr. Atwood, his barrister, on its management. After all, he wanted things to be ready for Emerson when she eventually married and moved her new family back to her home.

Of course, the idea of her leaving him now, to run back here, made him livid. The long ride had not dulled his feelings. The fact that she took his sister, that they lied to Aunt Lillian about his consent for them to go, and his brother had helped them...all of this made his jaw clench each time he thought about it.

After Lennox had come to his study and almost immediately started to make excuses, Lathen had wanted to punch him. Still reeling from drinking too much the night before, Lathen bristled. He had to listen to nonsense about how vital the trip was for their sister and Miss Atwood. How Lady Haven needed to go and mourn for her father. Lathen had scoffed. No matter what excuses they gave Lennox, he should have known better.

Worse, he found out Giles had helped them as well. It was he who arranged for the coach to drive them. Giles explained this to Lathen shamelessly, his tone cool and disdainful.

His scorn is only for me. As though he knows what is going on and blames me for Emerson wanting to leave. Perhaps he does know. Giles always seems to be around. I swear he never sleeps.

Regardless of how they had managed it, he could not get over how fuming he was at the thought of the three girls out by themselves for two days in the countryside. Anything could have happened. Luckily, he knew they had made it unscathed at least as far as the last inn he stopped at. The girls did not stay to rest as he had, but their coach did stop for fresh horses and one of the footmen came in to buy refreshments. It was the same at one of the other inns where he stopped.

I suppose I should be grateful that they were wise enough not to go inside.

Not that knowing they had been cautious made him any less furious. But beneath his anger, a flicker of guilt stirred. Had he been too absorbed in his desire for Emerson to notice her need to reconnect with this place? Or was this just her disgust over discovering who he was? His thoughts swirled in his tired mind, too convoluted to find any answers.

He had assumed that riding horseback would let him catch them on the road. Even with their nearly full day's lead. That was not the case. Because they had only made quick stops, they were probably still a few hours ahead of him.

They likely arrived a little while ago. I hope they get some rest, because I plan on dragging them right back home! My sore arse be damned.

With that thought, Lathen flicked his reins, and his horse picked up speed from a light trot to a weary canter.

"Good boy, we are almost there," he leaned forward and patted his horse's neck, "then you can rest and get some well-deserved oats."

Make that in less than an hour.

chapter ten

Emerson was suddenly alert, her eyes wide, heart After wrapping a light shawl around her shoulders, Emerson walked out of the wide arched double doors of her family home. Though it was dark when they arrived, she was still able to see how well-kept Havenfield was. It looked better now than it ever had when she was a child.

It was not as if my father ever took the time to notice anything beyond the apple orchards. He certainly did not bother with the whitewashing or making sure fences were mended, let alone getting new furniture or refreshing the wallpaper.

Not that she ever minded. As a child, she felt more comfortable playing outside, covered in dirt and climbing trees, than in a well-appointed parlor or dining room. And she was more likely to have been sleeping in her small cottage or in the hayloft than in a frilly bedroom with a featherbed. She had to admit, seeing those improvements in the house now was pleasant. Not to mention the fresh coat of whitewash on the manor house and the beautifully maintained gardens and pathways.

Someone has taken great care to make sure Havenfield has not fallen into disrepair. Hell, I should not fool myself. Obviously, Lathen has done this on my behalf. Or at least arranged for it to be done.

It warmed Emerson to think of him taking care of what was hers, just as if it were his own property. She took a deep breath to clear her mind, and a gentle smile came to her face at the familiar scents. The cool air had a heavy suggestion of rain that had yet to fall. The sweet alfalfa nearly ready for the first cutting. The warm lemon green scent of the blooming geraniums planted along the drive. It all reminded her of the years she spent here. Especially of the summers she spent with Kit when he was home from school.

Though she was drained from the long, two-day drive from London, she was wired and not yet ready to sleep. Leighton and Hazel, shown to their rooms by a welcoming housekeeper, collapsed on their beds after washing and donning nightgowns. Emerson decided it would be a good time to go for a walk instead. After all, the moon was nearly full overhead, and even though the clouds were heavy and shifting, she still knew every pathway and every stone. She would be fine.

She began walking toward the pond, but it held too many memories of her brother. She had been there the day Lathen brought his body home, and she had not gone back there since. Not even during the whole year she had lived there afterward. She turned right at a fork in the path and walked out toward the apple orchards instead. The Winesaps and Pearmains her grandfather planted long before she was born were heavy with sweet white blossoms. The canopies had grown outward since she last saw them, promising an excellent harvest this year. She raised her fingertips to brush the flowers. There were no fruits yet, but she knew they would sprout, small and green, in the coming months. Then they would grow plump and begin to blush red, and their lush scent would fragrance the entire valley. In autumn, workers would come from miles around and pick them all over several weeks. Some would end up in the old stone cellar to be made into pies during the long winter. Others would be dried in the sun and sealed in glass jars to be added to the pork or pheasant stuffing. Most would make their way to the cider house to be pressed and put into wooden barrels.

My father would have been pleased at how healthy the trees are, Emerson thought with a derisive snort.

Her father had been an alcoholic. Kit once explained to her that he was not always that way, but she had never known him as anything else. To a certain extent, she supposed it was her fault her father had fallen to the evils of the drink, as it was her birth that had caused her mother's death. It was that loss he was always trying to forget with his drinking.

Emerson sighed and shrugged. It did no good to think of such things. There was nothing she could do to change them. She kept on walking toward the east hills and came out on the other side of the orchard.

A forceful breeze lifted several tendrils of hair that had fallen from the simple twist at the top of her head. She laughed freely and patted her temple. She wanted to feel her hair in the cool wind, so she pulled out the pins, letting it fall down her back. Raising her arms, she spun in the breeze, her skirts whipping like a flag.

Goodness! She laughed aloud. *I must look like a hoyden, but I simply do not care. It is the first time tonight I have not felt like a visitor!*

After traveling for two days without a maid, Emerson had taken to doing her own hair. She never realized before that she was not very good at it. She was also wearing a simple white dress that only had a few buttons at the back.

Thankfully, Hazel did the packing and thought of such things. If it was left to me, I would be running around with nothing that matched and having to ask someone to do up rows of tiny buttons. Or leaving the back open in the breeze. That thought made her giggle even louder. It reminded her of how she used to run around Havenfield as a child. Back then, she never worried over her appearance.

A rustle came from her left, and a red fox darted from the field onto the path. He froze when he saw Emerson.

"Oh, hello there, little one," she murmured.

She stayed still, hoping he would not flee. The fox lifted its nose to sniff the air and tilted his head as she spoke. Then he slipped under the fence into another field and disappeared.

Emerson sighed again. *I suppose it is good to be home. If this is my home...* She kept walking as she mulled over the thought, past a field of strawberry clover ready to be turned into the soil. She wondered offhandedly what they would plant there next. In the past she would have known, as she had always been very involved in helping their tenants with their planting. Now it felt slightly foreign to her. After all, seven planting seasons had come and gone without her.

As she passed the waiting field, she turned toward the wide gravel drive. With no particular destination, she headed toward a high point near

Havenfield's main road, where she could view her home from afar. Maybe then the feeling of restlessness would ease, and she could go back to her room and sleep.

She began getting tired as she walked up the hill, but decided she could make it to the top, get at least one glance, then walk back to the manor. Her efforts did not disappoint. She reached the top and turned. The heavy clouds parted, and moonlight illuminated the entire Havenfield valley. From the wooded dale in the north, she saw the orchards on a gentle slope, positioned to catch the southern sun and windbreak. The main house stood centrally, with the barn and horse pastures to one side, while fields stretched endlessly eastward, and the creek and pond were to the west, with the cider mill nestled below. She had witnessed this view at least a thousand times, but it struck her in a new way now.

Is this still my home? She missed it and felt familiar with it, despite the changes. Yet something was discordant, like listening to an orchestra with one instrument out of tune. A faint prickle crawled up the back of her neck, not quite a chill, but enough to make her roll her shoulders as if to shake it off.

Is it Kit? I have waited so long to come back to him, but he is not here anymore. His ghost is free. Or maybe I have let him go.

Emerson turned around, away from the view of Havenfield, and rubbed a sudden soreness between her breasts. She realized absently that her small purse was still there, and the highwayman's kiss skipped through her mind.

Perhaps the attack is making me nervous?

But the encounter already seemed so far away, and she could not understand why she was feeling so unsettled. She stared absently across the road, remembering each tree and shrub, and laughed at her apprehension.

I am probably only worried over what Lathen will do when I see him again. Or what I want him to do.

Still her pulse ticked a little faster, her breath catching before she forced it to steady. She turned to her left where an ancient elm tree stood, marking the main road. Its gnarled trunk twisted up to widespread branches reaching like comforting, strong limbs toward the sky. She stepped over, ran her fingertips over the rough bark, and stared up. She must have climbed this tree more than a thousand times as well, waiting for Kit to come home. She would climb as high as she could and remain for hours. Often it was for naught, but she still climbed anyway.

I was climbing it the day I met Lathen...

From afar came the soft clop of a horse approaching at a slow trot on the road. Emerson scrambled to hide behind the tree until whoever it was passed by. It was quite late, and she had no wish to be seen. Havenfield was not London, and she was not worried about the gossip, but she had no desire to talk with anyone. Especially not a crofter who would want to welcome her home and ask her a lot of questions.

As the horse came closer, Emerson held her breath while she waited for it to go by. But when it reached the tree, the horse slowed and stopped. There was nothing to break the windy silence except a heavy snort from the horse.

"Are you planning on climbing that tree? Or are you just going to hide behind it until you jump out to scare my horse?"

chapter eleven

Lathen spotted Emerson from nearly half a mile away, her figure radiant under the silver moonlight. Her white dress gleamed, a stark contrast to her long, unbound dark hair, both billowing in the restless breeze heralding an approaching storm. Once, he had likened her to *Nyx*, the night goddess, when she stood before a glowing fire, her silhouette fierce and divine. Now, she seemed even more ethereal, as if woven from enchantments, a creature born of earth and heavens rather than mere flesh, her presence pulling at something primal within him. The urge to spur his horse and gallop toward her surged within him, but his weary mount, hooves dragging, was too exhausted. So, Lathen approached slowly, savoring the sight of her, each step heightening his anticipation. At some point she must have heard his approach, for she startled like a fawn in the woods, darting behind the massive elm that marked the lane to Havenfield.

That tree stirred memories. It was where Lathen first met Emerson, years ago, when she was just a girl. Dressed in oversized, tattered boys' clothes, she had looked like a London street urchin, clambering up that same elm. With a mischievous leap, she had startled his horse, sending it rearing. Her laughter, wild and unapologetic, had echoed through the glade, marking the start of their tangled history.

Now, both grown, they stood worlds apart from those first days. The years had carved new lines into their story. Shared moments beneath the London streets, dark secrets leaving silences too heavy to break, and a quiet longing they could not ignore. The elm, ancient and unyielding, seemed to watch over them still, its gnarled branches whispering of time's passage and bitter secrets. As Lathen drew nearer, the storm's first raindrops, light and born on the wind, kissed the earth. In that moment, the weight of their past and the promise of the storm collided, leaving him to wonder what fate awaited them.

A gasp escaped Emerson's lips. She would have recognized Lathen's deep voice anywhere, but to be certain, she twisted around, peeking from behind the tree. Slowly, she stepped into the open, mesmerized by his sudden presence before her.

He sat astride a dappled, dark grey thoroughbred, its coat gleaming almost black under the moonlight. It was not the same horse from eight years ago, when their paths first crossed beneath this very tree, but she knew it was sired by that stallion.

As she watched, Lathen swung his leg over the saddle and dismounted with the fluid grace of a panther she once saw prowling at the Royal Menagerie. His movements were deliberate, predatory, as he stalked toward her.

Emerson's breath caught, her body frozen, her heart skipping in her chest. A small voice in her mind urged her to flee.

Like I am the little fox, caught on the path. But is he a friend or foe?

He stopped several paces away and waited. His gaze searched her face, as if seeking a sign, a silent permission to bridge the chasm between them.

A warmth kindled in Emerson's belly, swirling like the gathering storm. It spread, molten and insistent, rising to her chest and cascading down her legs. His nearness was electric, vibrating in the air like the approaching tempest, prickling her skin with unspoken promises. As if in cosmic accord, a jagged bolt of lightning tore across the sky from the north mount of the valley, illuminating the world. Seconds later, thunder rumbled, cascading as it approached, shaking the earth beneath them.

The sound snapped Emerson from her trance. Casting aside the myriad reasons to hesitate, she let her shawl slip to the ground. With a surge of reckless abandon, she closed the gap at a run, leaping into Lathen's arms. Their lips met in a kiss that was its own clap of thunder, fierce and consuming.

chapter twelve

Lathen did not hesitate. He pulled Emerson close, one hand on her bottom to lift her, the other woven into her hair to hold her steady. Their mouths met in a wild frenzy, tongues twisting, teeth grazing each other's lips in a rhythm that mimicked lovemaking and set his pulse hammering. Her hands grasped at him. His shoulders, his hair, the back of his neck. Clutching tightly, as if to pull him even closer.

Sensing her need, Lathen carried her several steps, her weight light in his arms, until her back pressed against the rough bark of an elm tree. The wood's texture bit into her, he could tell, but she only pressed harder against him.

He tugged at her long skirts, freeing her legs. Emerson wrapped them around his waist, her thighs tightening as he rolled his hips into her core. Through her lace undergarment, he felt the heat and pressure of her, a glorious ache that stoked his own desire. She broke their kiss, throwing her head back with a loud moan, baring her throat. Lathen seized the chance, trailing soft kisses and small nips down her exposed skin, from her neck to where her demure dress covered her bosom.

With one swift motion, he grabbed the top of her white muslin dress, along with her chemise and stays, and pulled them down. A slight rending noise sounded, but Lathen barely registered it, his eyes on her taut breasts as they sprang free, the fabric settling beneath to push them toward him. His mouth latched onto one peak, drawing it deeply inside, savoring her sharp gasp.

Emerson arched against the tree, her fingers twisting into his hair, tugging at the strands to pull him near. Her breathless encouragement stirred something deep in him. He had been with many women, all eager to please, but Emerson met him with a raw, unguarded passion that set her apart.

"Lathen, please!" she begged, her voice raw with desperation. "I need you inside me, now!" Her hips tilted into him, a frantic arch pressing her core against his straining arousal. Her heels dug into his backside, urging him closer, her body trembling with a hunger that seemed to crackle in the air.

Lathen's body surged with desire, his erection throbbing against the confines of his breeches. He tried to temper her wildness, to hold her steady, but Emerson was a tempest, fierce and uncontainable. His lips crashed against hers, a searing kiss that swallowed her gasps as he gripped her hips, fingers digging into soft flesh. He set a relentless rhythm, grinding against her through the maddening barrier of fabric, each movement a torment fueling their shared fire.

Her kisses grew fiercer, all teeth and tongue, matching the primal urgency of her rolling hips.

Lathen sensed her nearing climax, her breaths turning to sharp, keening moans, her body tightening beneath him. His hand slid upward, finding her breast, and he pinched her nipple hard, rolling it between thumb and forefinger with deliberate pressure.

"Come for me," he demanded, his voice rough with need.

Emerson's scream shattered the night, raw and unrestrained. Her nails raked down his shoulders, the sting piercing through his lawn shirt, marking him with her intensity. She surged forward, her teeth sinking into his neck, a bite that promised a bruise by morning. The pain only heightened his desire, a sweet agony that made his own unfulfilled need pulse harder. Yet to witness her surrender, her moans, her body shuddering against the tree in ecstasy, was a glory that eclipsed his own denied release.

Suddenly, the storm above them mirrored her fervor, lightning splitting the sky in a blinding flash, followed by a thunderclap rattling the damp earth. The air grew thick with the sharp bite of ozone, as wild and electric as their passion.

The sky broke and cold rain poured down, no longer a drizzle but a deluge, as if buckets were tossed from the heavens. Emerson shrieked, the sound sharp in his ears, and Lathen gently lowered her feet to the ground, her skirts falling back into place. Turning, he saw his horse, Umbra, bolting into the darkness.

"Damn it," he shouted, voice rough with frustration. "Umbra, come back here!"

chapter thirteen

Emerson giggled, her eyes sparkling, seemingly amused by his frustration. Lathen watched her straighten her dress and bend to retrieve her sopping, heavy shawl from the ground.

"Do not worry, he is heading toward the barn. I am sure he will scent the other horses and wait there. Come," her hand reached for his, "we can go down and make sure he gets a good rubdown before he finds his bed."

Lathen looked at her outstretched hand, then back to her cheerful face, still flushed from passion. It all seemed right. Even with the rain. He still needed to address her leaving London, but he did not want to ruin the moment. Taking her offered hand, they ran through the torrent toward the barn. Together.

Emerson was correct. Umbra stood outside the barn's tall double doors, under a slight overhang that kept most of the rain off him. He was making small noises of greeting and nickers answered from inside.

Emerson went right up to Umbra and patted him softly on the neck. His flank shivered in response.

"Shhh, you are all right. It is just a storm. Soon you will be safe and warm, and inside with new friends. Do not worry, darling boy."

She pushed open one of the doors and Umbra followed her inside without any sort of lead, his nose nudging her shoulder for more affection.

Even my horse is enchanted by her, Lathen mused with a wry smile.

"Ho there!" Emerson called out brightly, "is there anyone around?"

From above, shuffling sounded, and bits of hay floated down as a russet head peered from the hayloft railing. It was a young man barely out of his teen years, and he smiled shyly as he saw Emerson.

"My Lady Haven?" he asked tentatively, his eyes wide as he took in her disheveled state.

"Yes, is that Timothee?" she remarked happily when she recognized him.

Lathen kept a good eye on Havenfield. He knew Tim O'Brien was now in charge of the stables, having been a hand to his father as he grew up. He also knew that Tim often slept up in the loft, to be near his charges, instead of walking the two miles to his mother's cottage. Lathen watched the young man climb down and approach Emerson.

"Yes, my lady," he bowed awkwardly as he tried to straighten his rumpled shirt, "it is most pleasurable to have you home. We all hope you will stay. Can I help you with your horse?"

Lathen snorted as he took in the deep flush and hesitant smile on Tim's face.

Yet another man who has fallen to her charms. Though one could hardly blame him. With that thought, he strode forward and handed Umbra's reins to the stable hand.

"Timothee, is it? Give Umbra some extra oats and a good rubdown. He had a long ride from London to get here."

Tim flinched, obviously having not noticed Lathen, but he quickly recovered, nodded his head, and took the reins.

"Yes, of course, my lord. Right away." He tugged his forelock and scurried off to do Lathen's bidding.

After he was gone, Lathen noticed Emerson looking at him curiously.

"What?" he asked her.

"Do you ever say please?"

"Excuse me?" Lathen's eyes widened.

"Well, you always speak as if everyone must follow your orders without question. I was wondering if anyone ever tells you no. Or if you ever thought to say please instead of demanding."

Lathen was stunned. No one had ever asked him something like this. He always strove to be moderate and calm in how he dealt with his staff or family. He did not believe he was overly demanding, but he did expect everyone to do as he asked. When he asked.

So, does anyone ever question me or refuse my requests? Yes. Yes, someone does.

"Well, *Nyx*," he leaned close and lifted a hand to tuck a wet tendril of hair behind her ear, "I must admit, you are the only one who dares to tell me no. Or defy me. But I must say, I will work on the please."

With that, Lathen grabbed her hand and pulled her back toward the door. It was still raining hard, but with no empty stalls available, they needed to make a break for the manor house.

"Wait, Lathen! Perhaps we should stay here," Emerson shouted over the rain while she looked dubiously at the sky, "at least until this slows!"

Lathen looked back over his shoulder at where Tim was rubbing down Umbra. Then he leaned down to Emerson and whispered again, "If we were to stay here, I suspect we would be depriving your Timothee of his bed. Plus, I could do with a hot bath, a good meal, and a much softer bed than the hay loft would provide."

Emerson glanced back at Tim as well. With a nod of agreement, she returned Lathen's grasp, took a deep breath, and ran with him. It was cold, but Lathen felt a freedom he had not had in years. Laughter escaped as they sprinted through the rain, splashing through puddles. It was not far to the manor, and they soon reached the front portico, stepping out of the rain. Water streamed down their faces, and Lathen reached forward to wipe droplets from Emerson's chin and nose.

He wanted to kiss her again. But softly, without the frantic urgency of before. He still ached painfully from not having her, yet a tenderness he could not explain speared through him. Tomorrow, he would need to be angry at her again. To be fair, he would have to chastise all three girls. Tonight, he just wanted to kiss her.

So, he did.

chapter fourteen

I must not hurt her. I must not!

To mar such beauty would certainly be a sin, an unforgivable desecration of the divine. But she let him kiss her!

Again!

The word sears through my mind like a blade, slicing deeper with every repetition, a relentless echo threatening to shatter my skull. I had to sit here, cloaked in the suffocating darkness of the underbrush, and witness that vile spectacle as de Clare met with my woman.

My woman!

He pressed her against the stupid elm like she was some harlot peddling her wares on the London docks. Like some whore! Leaving invisible marks where his hands roamed, oblivious to the sanctity of her form.

And she...she let him!

She did not scream for him to stop, nor did she shove him away or strike his groping hands. Instead, she yielded with a hunger that twisted my stomach into a knot of rage and despair. She begged him for more, her cries drifting through the night air like poison, words so brazen they would make a sailor blush and turn away. Those words clawed at me, urging me to surge forward, to clamp my hand over her mouth, to shake her until she remembered who she truly belongs to.

Me. Only me!

I wanted to shout until my throat bled, to demand she stop this betrayal, this mockery of our unspoken bond.

I cannot fathom what I saw and heard tonight, this nightmare unfolding under the cold gaze of the moon. She must know she was made for me, sculpted by some celestial hand to fit perfectly within my life, my arms, my soul. How dare she scatter her favors like cheap trinkets, tossing them to a swine like de Clare? Especially when she knew I was here, watching her every move, my eyes burning into her from across the road. Did she not glide toward me earlier, her silhouette swaying in the silvery light, and smile directly to where I crouched? She waved her arms, her movements a dance meant for me alone, a silent vow that tethered us together.

She knew I was there! She had to!

It was our secret, our game, a thread of fate pulling us ever closer, a journey we have been taking together.

But my journey to this wretched moment was no small feat. It was a grueling chase over two long days, switching horses whenever Lady Haven's coach stopped. With no rest. I saw when her coach was halted by highwaymen, their pistols glinting in the moonlight as they barked demands. I watched, heart pounding, as they took the ladies' purses, their coarse laughter grating against my ears. I could have acted, could have drawn my pistol and scattered them like rats. But to reveal myself would be folly. I am no fool to risk capture or a ball in my gut for heroics. So, I stayed hidden, my breath shallow, gripping my own pistol, watching as one of them kissed her.

My woman!

Her lips met the stranger's with little resistance, a sight that burned. I suppose he was lucky I am capable of restraint, as I nearly broke free from the shadows and killed him.

Then I was forced to remain here, across the road in the tangled, thorn ridden brush, the sharp points pricking my skin like accusations. My fingers traced the pistol in my coat, stroking its cold metal over and over, a ritual to soothe the beast within. I whispered to it, soft as a lover, promising that now was not the time, but soon.

Soon I could aim at de Clare's smug face, watch his arrogance dissolve into blood and bone, and no one would know. After all, he is the one who deserves my enmity. My true rival. To destroy him would be the only solace for what I have endured. The thought sends a shiver through me. Not of fear, but a dark, intoxicating thrill that coils tight in my chest, begging for release. Yet, tonight is not the night. Patience is my cruel ally, gnawing at my sanity with every passing second.

If I killed that arrogant bastard now, under this starless sky, I would have to flee through the night, praying no one saw me galloping across these unfamiliar lands. It's nearly impossible as these damn roads twist like serpents, leading to places I cannot name. I do not even know where I am, the countryside a maze of shadowed hills and whispering woods after trailing her in my delirium. My horse, as weary as I am, is sleeping in a thicket over the hill. Even if I could whip him into standing, returning to London tonight without asking for directions would be madness. It would expose my face to strangers who might remember the wild-eyed man fleeing in the dark. No, I must bide my time, let the rage simmer until the moment is right.

As for my dear Lady Haven...

Her name is a melody laced with venom, sweet and deadly on my tongue. She must be punished for this betrayal, for tarnishing what is mine, for no longer being pure. But later, when the red haze of fury cools into precision, when I can teach her without leaving permanent scars. I know how to inflict pain that lingers only in the mind, bruises that fade like whispers. Lessons she shall carry in her heart. The thought of her eyes, wide with realization, pleading for my forgiveness, stirs a hunger that battles my anger, a twisted dance of love and wrath.

So, I waited, the rain falling in heavy sheets, drumming against the leaves like mocking laughter, failing to douse the fire in my veins. It soaked my coat, chilling my bones, but the inferno within burned brighter, unyielding.

After they left, I stood by that cursed tree, the one they defiled with their animalistic rutting. I watched them go into the barn, only to leave moments later, running through the rain. I watched him kiss my beloved once more. I watched them slip into the manor house, her hand in his, swallowed by the warm glow of candlelight. What are they doing now behind those stone walls? Tangled in sheets that should be ours? Her laughter echoing in halls I will one day claim as mine? The images torment me, each one a fresh wound that bleeds inside.

My frustration overwhelms me, and I strike the tree with my fist, the pain in my knuckles a sharp relief, a reminder of my own existence. In my fury, I kicked something half buried in the mud, its jingle cutting through the rain's drone. Bending down, I retrieve it, shaking off the muddy water. It is a lady's reticule, delicate and embroidered, heavy with a few coins that gleam faintly. It must be hers, dropped in her reckless abandon as de Clare's hands roamed her. I lifted it to my nose, inhaling the faint scent of orange blossoms. I recognize her essence, a perfume that haunts my dreams and fuels my obsession. I tuck it into my coat pocket, close to my heart, a relic of her I shall keep until she is my own.

I will return it to her. Later. When she kneels before me, understanding the depth of my devotion, the lengths I have gone to claim her.

All will be settled later. Lady Haven, de Clare, their sins piling like kindling awaiting my spark. The night whispers it, the rain chants it, and my pistol hums in agreement.

Soon.

chapter fifteen

Madam Irina glided through her bedroom, humming to music only she could hear. Nox House, always cloaked in shadow, murmuring secrets in its narrow corridors, was a stark contrast to the bright opulence of her bedroom. Here, pink silk wallpaper bloomed with swirling roses and gilded filigree fit for a Russian noblewoman's dreams. Her long silvering blonde hair, braided over one shoulder and tied with a crimson ribbon, swayed as she sipped the last of her vodka, its fire steadying her against the late hour's chill. Her matronly nightgown, heavy with embroidery, brushed her ankles as she set the glass on a lacquered bedside table.

She leaned toward the lone candle on the table, its flame dancing across the pink walls, casting shadows that made the roses grow. With a soft breath, she blew it out, the room sinking into darkness, pierced only by slivers of moonlight through the sash windows. Irina turned to her canopied bed, its rosy drapes cocooning her, when she heard something.

A low, scraping sound, like stone on wood, rumbled from the lower floor. Then silence.

Her heart stuttered, curiosity warring with a crawling unease. *Old homes creak*, she reasoned, yet her feet drew her to the hall, the cold floor biting her bare soles.

Irina descended the narrow stairs, her braid swaying like a metronome. From the back of the house, a single candle burned in the small library, its glow spilling faintly, painting the dark walls with writhing shapes. She scanned the shadows, finding nothing but empty air.

She tilted her head, held her breath, and listened. The only sounds were a carriage going past outside and the clock in the sitting room, its ticking a comfort slowing her heart. She let her breath out and sighed, deciding to go back to bed.

At the front door, she paused, then unlatched it, revealing London's fog-choked night. The street was quiet, the air heavy with damp. No one. Just the void of the city's slumber. A wry smile flickered.

I am a foolish old woman, out here chasing phantoms. She shut the door, the bolt snapping closed.

Then it struck. A force, swift and savage, crashed into her from behind. Her knees buckled and pain flared as her body slammed against the gray marble. Unseen hands seized her shoulders, pushing her down. Something sharp tore into her lower back, a hot sting blooming. She writhed, but a heavy weight crushed her, her braid snagging, the ribbon ripped free. Irina struggled to draw in breath, and the library's candlelight dimmed to a speck in her vision.

Darkness claimed her.

chapter sixteen

Birds woke Emerson. Dozens of warblers, finches, thrushes, and robins were all greeting the dawn and one another. Each with their own distinct melody. Memories of thousands of mornings hearing the same music came back to her and made her smile. Even her time spent at Windemere was not like this, because the great house there was twice as big as Havenfield, set back among an enormous grassy park. The birds had no large trees to roost in every night. In London, the birds in the square were quieter and not as prone to this symphonic cacophony.

Likely they would not dare to disturb the sleep of the gentry for fear of being evicted!

Emerson giggled at the silly notion. Then she rolled over onto her back and lay there for some time, staring at the ceiling. Listening to the birds. And thinking.

He came for me! Her grin widened, energy suddenly coursing through her. *I knew I was running away, and I thought he would send someone to escort us back to London, but it never entered my mind that he would come himself. He must have left soon after and ridden nearly nonstop. In a saddle the whole time!*

The idea of Lathen inconveniencing himself to chase her baffled Emerson. She could not seem to wrap her mind around the why of it all.

To think of him arriving when he did, when I was alone, not expecting him. He did not yell or punish me. No, we practically made love out by the road. We likely would have if the storm had not caught up with us!

Instead, after stabling Lathen's horse and making it to the manor through the rain, he again kissed her softly, tenderly, and without urgency, before they went inside together. They found an empty room for him to fall into, and she made her way back to her own bedroom. She had half hoped Lathen would come to her, so they could finish what they started, but she fell asleep once her head hit her pillow. As if her restlessness from the last couple of days had vanished, allowing her to finally relax.

Now, in the bright light of day, there was much to consider. Why had Lathen come? Did he realize she could not do what he wished at Nox? Was he willing to abandon those desires and marry her? To be with her as she needed him?

What do I need? Emerson wondered, as visions of herself hanging in the Cantilever Chamber were curling around in the back of her mind. She shook her head to clear it.

She was unwilling to reflect on the dream she had in the coach and consider if it was her who had changed. Maybe she wanted what he did, but that was simply too much for her to ponder now.

Her door flew open, and Emerson sat up in surprise, grasping her blanket to her neck.

"Em, you would not believe who is here!" Leighton, dressed in a yellow morning gown trailing behind her, rushed in and leaped onto Emerson's feather mattress.

Hazel came in after her, also already dressed in light blue muslin, but her face was twisted in concern as she closed the door and walked over slowly. She glanced at Emerson with a lowered brow and wrung her hands, as though she felt the news was going to upset her friend.

Emerson leaned over and patted the bed beside her, the side Leighton was not kneeling on, and grinned encouragingly at Hazel. Hazel sat and took a deep breath.

"Let me guess," Emerson said brightly, "you have just discovered His Grace arrived last evening."

Hazel's eyes widened, and Leighton gasped.

"Wait!" Leighton interjected with a small pout over having her news spoiled. "How did you know?"

"Because I met him when he arrived, and I showed him to an empty room."

Hazel watched her shrewdly, and Emerson blushed, realizing her friend suspected more had happened. Even if she did not know everything, she could certainly tell that Emerson was not upset at the idea of Lathen being there.

A kitchen maid arrived, thoughtfully bringing a tea tray for them. She set it on a low table in the sitting room and left quietly after Emerson's thanks. None of the staff, except Tim, were people she recognized. She might wonder at that, but she had to admit the house was much better kept, and the servants were a lot more attentive than when she was a child.

"Well, let me up, and I shall dress and join you in a few minutes." She pulled the coverlet back and swung her legs over to the side to stand.

"Okay, but you are not getting out of this that easily," Leighton warned her as she too stood, "we expect to hear what happened last eve. Do we not, Hazel?"

Hazel narrowed her eyes at Emerson and nodded in agreement.

"Indeed, Lettie."

Emerson rushed to the dressing room and came back with a resolved expression. She decided to be honest. Or at least as honest as possible. After all, Leighton knew something of what was happening and would be hurt if left out again.

"Well, I could not sleep when we first arrived, even exhausted as we all were," she began as she bent to add sugar and milk to her tea. "So, I went for a quick look outside. I went up to the top hill by the main road, and as I was taking in the view, Lathen approached on horseback."

"He rode the whole way here? Instead of using a coach?" Leighton seemed to also be astounded and impressed at the idea of her brother experiencing such discomfort.

"Yes, and let me tell you, he looked positively un-ducal! His hair was everywhere, and his clothes were mussed and wrinkled. He was not even wearing a coat or a cravat!"

"Was he angry?" This was from Hazel, who still looked anxious.

Emerson could not blame her friend. After all, while Lathen had responsibilities for both her and Leighton, he could ask Hazel to leave at any time. He could literally end her season with the barest of thoughts or words. Emerson realized she had not considered that enough before they left London.

Sometimes my impetuousness is detrimental. I love these girls so much. I must do better.

It was already done, however, and all she could do was try to assuage her friends' concerns with the truth. Even if it might shock them.

"No, he was not upset with me. Or he did not show it. In fact, he ummm..." she trailed off, considering how to share without too much detail, "well, he kissed me when he saw me."

"Out there? On the road!" Leighton exclaimed and clapped her hands together near her chest. She did not look shocked. Her eyes were lively, and she seemed happy.

"Yes, but it was quite dark, and of course very late. I am certain we were not seen."

"Oh, that is so romantic. He pursued you all the way up here, by himself, and by horseback. And the first thing he wanted to do was kiss you! Perhaps you were wrong. Maybe we all were, and he does wish to marry you, Em!" Leighton was flushed and gleeful at the idea of her brother and Emerson ending up together.

"Well, to be truthful," Emerson murmured, "I suppose I kissed him first. But he certainly did not push me away. He pulled me closer and made the kiss last much longer."

"Oh, Em, that is even more romantic!" Leighton let out a gentle sigh.

Hazel remained silent, her thoughts a tangled weave of concern pressing heavily on her chest. Her worry was not for herself, as Emerson might have assumed, but stemmed from a deeper, selfless fear. She knew all too well the punishments Lathen had inflicted on her friend in the past. Hazel had no desire to see Emerson endure such again, not when she had already borne so much. Moreover, Hazel's keen intuition had pieced together fragments of a story Emerson had not fully shared. She suspected Emerson and Lathen had shared an intimate moment at Nox House. Perhaps it was not a matter of Emerson surrendering her virtue, but something significant had transpired. Something that caused Emerson's words to falter when Leighton pressed for details. Hazel did not prod, respecting her friend's reticence, but the unanswered questions gnawed at her.

If Lathen and Emerson had indeed grown close, and yet no proposal followed, what could have shifted to prompt one now? The logic eluded her, and as she studied Emerson's flushed cheeks, the rosy hue betraying a blend of excitement and unease, Hazel grew certain there was far more to the events of last night than her friend was willing to reveal. A happy ending seemed elusive.

The room fell into a prolonged, awkward silence, the weight of unspoken thoughts settling over the trio. Leighton's expectant gaze flickered between Hazel and Emerson, her curiosity palpable, but it was Emerson who finally broke the quiet, her voice laced with hesitation.

"Well, romantic or not, I am far from certain that anything has truly changed between us," she admitted, her words carefully chosen, as if testing their truth against the uncertainty in her heart. "There is still much to discuss, and I suppose those conversations will have to wait until Lathen wakes up." A fleeting frown creased her brow, a shadow of doubt that vanished as quickly as it appeared, replaced by a determined glint in her eyes. "In the meantime, how about we seek out some breakfast? After that, I would love to show you both my home. So much has changed since I was last here. Even the air feels different. Truth be told, I am eager to explore it myself in the light of day!"

Murmurs of agreement rippled through the group, a shared sense of purpose easing the tension of the moment. The three rose from their seats in Emerson's room, their footsteps soft against the polished elm floor, the wood gleaming under the morning light that streamed through tall, arched windows. Outside, the morning was breathtaking, a stark contrast to the tempest that had raged the night before. The air carried a crisp sweetness, infused with the scent of dew kissed grass and climbing roses, as if the world itself were offering a promise of hope and renewal.

Hazel's mind, however, was far from settled. Questions swirled around, but Emerson's infectious excitement softened her desire to press her for answers. Perhaps the truth could be uncovered another way, through careful observation or a well-timed conversation.

Emerson might not even know His Grace's true intentions, Hazel reasoned, *especially without family to guide her through the complexities of such matters.* A new thought struck her, sharp and clear. *Perhaps I need to go straight to the source, to the one who holds the answers.*

The duke, with his imposing presence and guarded demeanor, could be the key. Hazel would need to tread carefully, but she was determined to unravel the mystery for her friend's sake, to ensure Emerson's heart was not left vulnerable.

chapter seventeen

Lathen woke with a low groan, and he sat up on the side of the bed. His legs, back, and arse were all screaming at his foolishness in riding up to Havenfield the way he had. Worse, he had gone to bed naked after stripping off his wet clothes, leaving them in a messy pile by the door. Now he had nothing to wear. He wrapped a sheet around his waist and pulled a cord near the bed to summon help. Then he opened a large window for fresh air, gazing outside while he waited.

From that vantage, he saw Emerson, his sister, and Miss Atwood as they walked away from the manor along a pebbled path. They headed toward the orchards, followed by a gaggle of geese honking and wagging their white tail feathers. The girls tossed bread crusts to them.

Even as far away as he was, he could hear the girls' laughter as the geese waddled after them, nipping at their hands for more treats. Emerson threw her head back, revealing the delicate arch of her neck and her dark hair flowing in curls down her back.

I have never seen her this carefree and full of joy. Not once, in all the time I have known her. Not when she was a child. Not when she was living at Windemere. Not even when I touched her or when we made love.

Lathen had an epiphany. He realized Emerson belonged there. Havenfield was a part of her and gave her happiness he and his darkness never could. He could insist that his desires, his actions at *Noir*, would bring her ecstasy. He believed she wanted it as much as he did. Indeed, last night showed him they were still compatible physically.

But would it bring her joy? Would being with me make her smile and laugh out loud the way she is now? Likely not. In fact, it might smother her brightness and drag her down into my darkness.

The thought made him miserable in a way her leaving him had not. It was not just a mental pang but a deeper, physical throbbing throughout his body. A pain separate from the ache of travel. As if his entire being suffered from the realization that hope of having Emerson was lost forever.

I must take her back to London. She still needs to marry. But I have no reason to remain there and watch it happen. The temptation of being close to her is just too much for me.

He had thought of leaving before, but had to put the idea aside as he was too busy dealing with the Marien situation. Now that Marien had been found and was safely held at Nox House, awaiting arrangements for India, he had no more excuses. He might as well be the one to take Marien away. Then he could ensure she was placed where she could never escape. More importantly, to never return to England and bother Emerson ever again.

She has been through enough because of that despicable woman.

He would never let Emerson be hurt by her again. Or anyone else.

Including me.

An efficient knock came at the door, and he walked over with the ends of the sheet trailing after him. He opened the door and saw a young maid carrying a tea tray.

"Yer Grace," she squeaked out in her northern accent, seeing his state of undress, "I brought ye some breakfast."

"Oh, yes, thank you." Lathen opened the door wider for her. She tried to avert her gaze as she walked in and placed the tray on a table. Then she attempted to scurry out with her head turned away, but Lathen stopped her.

"Wait!" He bent down, grabbed his still wet pile of clothing, and held them out to her. "I was caught in the storm last night. I am afraid my other clothes are still in my saddlebag. Do you think you can find someone to fetch them from the stables?"

"Yes, Yer Grace, I will go straight away." She gave a clumsy curtsy, grasped his clothes, and held them close, letting them soak her dark dress. Rushing out, she nearly tripped and dropped half his things in her haste.

Lathen figured it would be a while before the servant returned. He made a cup of strong black tea, grabbed some crusty bread and bacon, and returned to the window to watch Emerson while he waited.

The three girls had walked into the orchard, so he could only see flashes of their hair and clothing through the blossom covered branches. But even from where he was, their laughter kept drifting softly to him. He liked the sound of it, not just of Emerson, but all of them, and decided he would not make them leave for another few days.

A break might do them all good, even if Aunt Lillian disagrees. Besides, it might be the last time I get to spend time with Emerson. Unfettered, without the ton's *eyes upon us. Before she marries another.*

The pain hit his body again, but this pursuit of her, chasing her all the way from London, had made him realize he had to let her go. He had his shot. He tried. He showed her who he was, and she ran away.

It is time for me to release her.

chapter eighteen

Emerson gazed at the long table in Havenfield's ornate dining room, feeling a strange twinge strike her. It was not painful, but it tightened her chest.

Perhaps regret? She guessed. *Yes, I think I regret never experiencing this before. Not here anyway.*

She was referring to the cheerful discussion and all the happy smiles. Her friends, Hazel and Leighton, sat together at one end of the table. Lathen was also there, and though he laughed and talked less than the others, his countenance was not its usual brooding reserve. He even smiled occasionally, his eyes glimmering indulgently as he listened to the chatter.

Emerson also realized Leighton had been correct. Lathen did look at her. Often. He tried to turn his gaze away as soon as she noticed, but she kept catching him anyway.

They had not been alone since she left him at his room the previous night. At lunch, he informed them they would stay to rest for three more days before returning to London together. He even smiled when he told them.

It was more than what she had expected after he had pursued them all the way to Havenfield. She had assumed he would insist they leave today. Or tomorrow at the latest.

Instead of packing back up, they had an enjoyable day exploring her home. She took her friends to the woods and showed them her old cottage. It saddened her to see how it had fallen into disrepair during her absence. Hazel, with her brilliant mind, insisted it only needed a thorough cleaning and a few hammered boards, and devised a short list of materials they would need. They gave the list to the housekeeper, who kindly assured them a footman would fetch everything from the village by morning.

That was their plan for tomorrow, and Lathen listened as they discussed their hopes for the project. It was amusing, considering none of them were skilled with a broom, let alone a hammer and nails. Not that they had ever tried.

"You will help us, will you not, Lathen?" Leighton asked out of the blue. Though he had probably never held a tool either.

He smiled indulgently and turned to Emerson with a raised brow, as if he were seeking her permission before answering his sister. Emerson smiled back shyly with encouragement.

"Of course. Someone must be there to ensure you do not fall off the roof, kitten," he teased. "Aunt Lillian would never forgive me if you came back to London with a broken limb."

"Posh!" Leighton snorted and threw her napkin at him. "I have scaled more things than you ever have. I am especially adept at climbing trees. I had Em to show me how, after all."

"Yes, you are likely right, as I am not sure when I last climbed one. And I certainly did not have as fine a teacher as you did," he murmured, glancing at Emerson again. This time he did not look away when she returned his gaze.

Emerson felt the now familiar warmth in her belly and an answering clenching, deep in her core. She blushed as she kept his gaze and refused to be the first to look away. But Hazel tapped her arm, and she turned to her questioningly.

"Shall we play some music? I saw the pianoforte in the drawing room," she insisted firmly. Hazel was trying to keep her word and help Emerson from falling into the trap of Lathen again. Though Emerson was slightly annoyed with her at that moment.

"Hazel, you know I do not play. I never have. It was my mother's, and no one has touched it since before I was born."

"Yes, I know. But I do. And I happen to know you have a lovely voice. Also, I walked by and played it earlier and it not only works, but it has been tuned recently." Hazel was not going to take no for an answer, and she stood, pulling at Emerson's sleeve to join her.

Leighton stood as well and clapped, then turned to her brother with a smile and held her hand out to him. He pushed back from the table and went with her.

"Oh, yes, we will all go. I would love to listen, though I can barely carry a tune. But you two should hear Lathen sing. He is simply marvelous." It was clear that Leighton had her own plans and had no wish to keep her brother and Emerson apart.

When they walked into the drawing room, Emerson was astounded. It was not the same room she had seen as a child. Then it was dark and dusty, and smelled of long dead flowers sitting in dozens of vases. The furniture was always covered, and the drapes were permanently closed tight. As were the double doors. She had only ever sneaked in, because her father would rage if he saw the doors open or anyone inside. Even the maids avoided it.

Now everything was clean and bright. The furniture was the same, but it was uncovered and repaired with new fabrics. Even the vases were dusted and filled with fresh flowers. The ebony wood of the pianoforte, polished to a shine, sparkled in the light of lamps and candles placed throughout. The room had a new purpose and was meant to be used.

Emerson crossed over a thick Aubusson carpet and came to the fireplace that was lit with a small cheery fire. Above it was a portrait of a woman and a little boy, sitting in a field of English lavender. Both had dark curly hair. The woman had lavender eyes, and the child had bright blue.

A gasp came from behind her. She did not turn to see who it was, as she was too enthralled by the painting. It had always been covered in a black cloth, and she had never tried to lift it.

"Oh, Em," Hazel whispered, "is that your mother?"

Emerson did not answer. She supposed it was. It made sense. The boy must be her brother, Kit. He looked like he was about five years old in the portrait. So, it would have been painted several years before she was born.

"Wow," Leighton leaned forward to get a better look. "She looked just like you. Everything. Even your eyes are the same."

Emerson felt a prickling in her eyes, and she blinked rapidly to stop the sensation. She did not wish to cry in front of her friends. Not when they were all having such a good time. She looked one more time, seeing how her mother held Kit and the loving gaze she was giving him. The small smile that revealed a dimple on her cheek, in a nearly identical placement to her own.

I will not pretend I do not wish I could have had that. To be held and loved by my mother. But at least I know Kit did. And he did his best to give me that same love.

She took a shuddering breath and turned. The first person she saw was Lathen. Both of her friends were still looking up at the picture in wonder, but he was staring at her. His gaze was filled with compassion. As though he knew what she was feeling and wished he could help in some way. Again, she was a bit taken aback by how he was allowing himself to show his emotions. She smiled to give him assurance she was all right.

After all, it is silly to miss something I never had.

The moment was broken as Leighton suddenly turned and put her arm through Emerson's and then Hazel's.

"Well, darlings, someone promised there would be music!"

Together, they walked to the piano and Hazel lifted the lid of the leather seat to look for sheet music.

"Wow," she whispered softly as she sifted through the fragile papers, "some of these are quite difficult pieces, and there are others I have never seen before."

"Well," Emerson answered as she too looked at the sheets in awe, "I imagine they have been here for a long while. They must have been my mother's. Kit told me she was the only one who played."

"Oh, Em." Hazel looked up and put a hand on her friend's shoulder. "Are you alright? Should we leave them here, unbothered?" She made a motion to shut the lid.

Emerson stopped her and smiled again.

"No, I think it is well past time someone played them. And this pianoforte! Someone has taken great care to make sure it is playable. It would be a shame for it to continue to be ignored."

"All right, then. If you are sure..." Hazel hesitated, looking into Emerson's eyes for a moment, then she picked a song from the pile and delicately opened the sheets, spreading them out along the music rest. Emerson closed the bench lid, and they sat down together. Leighton came and stood behind them and looked over their shoulders.

"Wow, you were not jesting. This is very complicated," Leighton breathed, amazed as she pulled the first page toward her. "But who composed it? There is only the title. *Mon Enfant Bien-aimé.*"

Leighton put the page back and Hazel's brow furrowed in concentration. As she looked over the notes, her fingers were working in the air above the keys, in imitation of what was to come.

Across the room, Lathen moved to the stocked bar and lifted the brandy as though he were going to pour himself a glass. Then he seemed to change his mind, and he pulled out three small tulip glasses. Then one more. He chose cream sherry instead and poured four glasses. He carried three to where the girls studied the music.

Well, Leighton and Hazel were. Emerson was watching him, though she was trying to pretend she was not. She saw him approach. When he stopped before them, all three girls noticed the drinks and reached to help him.

"Wow!" Leighton exclaimed, "I never thought I would see the day you made me a drink, dear brother."

"Yes, well do not expect it to be a habit, kitten. Oh, and do not dare tell our aunt. She would skin me alive for contributing to your downfall."

She grinned happily at her brother as she took a small swallow.

"Do not worry, my lips are waxed and stamped. I promise."

Emerson had a tiny sip as well. She could not help but remember the first time she ever tried sherry. It was Lathen who gave it to her then as well. She vividly recalled how young and small she felt as she sat before him, but it was the first night Lathen had treated her as an adult. It was also the first time he kissed her. It seemed like it was a lifetime ago, but really it was only several months. Much had happened since then, and she had grown and learned so much.

Next to her, Hazel took a small drink and then turned to place the glass on a small table behind them. She took a deep breath, straightened her back, wriggled her fingers, and placed them on the keys. She was ready to play.

The first notes were soft and sweet, and they moved gently from one to another. Like a hummingbird hovering over a foxglove that was bending in a summer breeze. It was a cheerful and moving piece and, as Emerson listened, she closed her eyes to feel the sound.

When she opened them, Lathen was there again. He was sitting on an overstuffed leather chair and holding his glass of sherry, twisting it gently with its delicate stem. Looking right at her. She stared back at him again and realized she wanted to go over and touch him. She longed to sit on his lap, place her hand on his chest, unbutton his lawn shirt, and run her fingers through the sparse hair across his torso. Then she could kiss him. Bite his lips softly. Wrap her arms around his neck and pull him close.

Closer.

It began to get hard to breathe, a flush spreading across her cheeks.

Lathen smirked, and she realized she was still staring back at him. She nearly gasped in embarrassment but managed to stop herself.

He knows what I am thinking.

Instead of turning away from him, she suddenly felt bold. She took another drink and swallowed while still staring in his eyes, the tip of her tongue darting out to lick droplets from her lips. It would have been easier if she were not blushing so much.

Perhaps tonight? Maybe tonight we can finish what we started last night. This idea was to herself, but she willed it to him, eager for him to understand her. To nod his acceptance. To change her desperation to anticipation. To agree to touch her.

The music ended, and the last note drifted off in a cheerful twinkle. Leighton leaned forward and clapped, breaking through Emerson's thoughts and drawing her eyes from Lathen's. She stood up and rubbed her arms, hoping her desperate need would go away.

"Wow, it was absolutely stunning!" Leighton exclaimed as she reached for the pages again and turned the paper gently. "I have definitely never heard it before, but it deserves to be played at Hofburg or Covent."

"Many of the others looked to be written by the same hand," Hazel explained as she stood and lifted the lid once again. "Perhaps there is a signature on one of them," she suggested as she began to sift through several piles.

From outside, they could hear a horse galloping on the gravel drive and the echoing call of the rider under the portico. Mrs. Goode, the housekeeper, rushed past the open drawing room door, obviously flustered, mumbling to herself about the late hour, as she went to open the front door.

She came back and entered the drawing room with a sealed letter in her hand.

"Your Grace, I hate to intrude," her voice wavered as she bent her generous body into a curtsy, "but a rider has just come from London with a missive. He said it was urgent."

Lathen stood and reached for the letter and gave his thanks. Dismissed, the housekeeper rushed out, closing the door softly behind her. He glanced at the address, snapped the wax, and unfolded the paper.

"Damn it," he swore softly as he finished.

"What?" Leighton rushed over, worried it could be something about their family. "What is it?"

Lathen glanced at his sister, "It is nothing you need to worry about."

"It is not *nothing*," Leighton scoffed as she emphasized the word. "*Nothing* does not show up by rider near bedtime, brother dear."

"Yes, well, perhaps I should have clarified. I should have said it is none of your business." With that, Lathen walked off briskly, leaving the drawing room door open behind him, and rushed up the stairs to his room. The sound of his door slamming resounded down the stairs soon after.

The girls exchanged worried glances.

"I wonder what that is all about," Hazel said softly. She still had her hands full of sheet music, but she put the pile back carefully and closed the lid. The idea of discovering the mystery composer suddenly seemed unimportant.

The sound of Lathen descending the stairs faster than he had gone up made them turn toward the door. He came back into the drawing room with his saddlebags over his shoulder.

"Listen, I must rush back to London. I must leave Umbra here, but if I change horses a few times, I can make it in less than a day. You all may stay for another few days and return at a slower pace. I am going to arrange for the housekeeper to go with you, so you can stay the evenings at a couple of inns, instead of trying to sleep in the coach."

"Wait! Why are you leaving in such a rush?" Leighton grabbed him by the arm when he turned to leave.

"I told you not to concern yourself." His voice was clipped, and his jaw was clenched.

Yet even as he said this, Lathen looked to Emerson, and wavered, as though he wished to tell her something. He took a deep breath, closed his eyes for a moment, and made up his mind.

"It is Marien."

Emerson gasped and she reached out to grasp Hazel's arm to steady herself. She had hoped to never hear that name again. To hear it now, when they had all been having such a lovely day, was nearly a physical blow.

"What about her?"

"Apparently, some thugs broke into Nox House last night, roughed up Madam Irina, and took Marien away. She has escaped."

chapter nineteen

"Come now, Lathen, you need to lighten up. You cannot still be mad at me about helping Lady Haven and Leighton. Are you?" Lennox stood beside his brother, nudging him to emphasize his point.

Lathen turned to scowl at him because, yes, he was still irritated with his brother. He had been home for nearly a week and had a team of investigators looking everywhere they could think of for Marien. To no avail. He could not help but think that if he had not run off after Emerson, then Marien would have already been gone to India. Certainly, it was not Lennox's fault that someone had helped her escape, but Lathen could still be annoyed with him. It was his prerogative as the older brother.

"Well, puppy, if you would rather, I could pop you one in the eye, and then we can be even."

"Ha, like you could catch me," Lennox smirked, "I would dance around and tire you out, old man." He knew it was a good sign that his brother was offering fisticuffs. It was much better than if he continued to brood in silence.

Lathen snorted and waved his hand in dismissal.

"I will let you dance like a court jester and wait for just the one hit. With a crystal jaw like yours, that is all it would take."

"Och, yer both blathering like a couple auld maids and there are pretty fillies out there." Lord Greyson Warwicke gestured past the railing where they stood, toward two beautiful yearling mares being walked in the dirt oval of Astley's Amphitheater. They had come for a horse auction to find new blood to add to the de Clare breeding program.

Lathen really did not want to be there, but the appointment had been on his calendar for months, and it had to be done. No matter how much he would rather have been at home. He was expecting Emerson back from the country today. With his sister and Miss Atwood, of course.

Lathen was sure Emerson would want to hear about his success with locating Marien. Or rather, his lack of success. While he was not looking forward to telling her, he did want to see her. He could admit that much to himself.

In fact, he had been thinking of her nearly every moment of the ride back, and every second since he reached London. When he left Havenfield and told Emerson of Marien's escape, he watched her crumble. To his mind, he lost her trust as well. In a moment, she went from smiling and giving him secret looks of longing to turning away for comfort from his sister and Hazel. He had hoped that finding Marien would make up for the error. That she would at least look at him with faith again. Even if she no longer desired him.

As far as his brother...he would forgive him. Eventually. For now, he would do his best to pay attention to the horses. That way Greyson would not knock their heads together. He had done it before, so there was precedent.

"Sorry, Grey," he grumbled to his friend, "my mind has been elsewhere."

"Nae bother, but I figure ye need at least three new fillies and one new stud. I hear that Brainewhite has a stud coming up with impressive lines. Best we keep our minds on what is important fer the moment."

"Yes, though, I trust your instincts. They have yet to lead me astray." Lathen clapped his friend on the shoulder. It was true, Greyson practically ran the de Clare racing program. When he was not off traveling on the continent, that is. It was not something Lathen cared much for, and he was strongly considering letting Lennox have the reins, so to speak. Greyson could continue advising his brother on stock. But it was not something he could decide on that day.

Nor do I wish to give him the responsibility while I am still cross with him.

"Aye, my sense on cuddies is usually spot on. Lassies, not so much."

"Oh, ho! Are you having trouble with your newest mistress?" Lennox quipped, "I thought she was doing pretty well for you. Not too much drama and whatnot."

"Aye, Mrs. Nichols is a bonny lass, and she does nae ask fer tae much of my time. But I have tae admit she is starting tae bore me a wee bit."

"Ah, so too little drama then." Lennox chuckled.

Greyson grunted and leaned forward to look at Lennox who was on the other side of Lathen.

"Perhaps, but I am nae looking for a lass who is feisty as that filly," he pointed to the young mare being led into the ring. She was prancing and snorting, and she put her head down several times to nip at the shoulder of the man leading her.

Both Lennox and Lathen leaned forward as well. Their eyes took in the mare's sleek auburn coat and fiery determination.

"She is magnificent though," Lennox spoke with hushed admiration. The mare was at least sixteen hands tall, with an elegant form and a high step.

"Yae, her dam has bred some lovely foals. I have been waiting tae see her for a few months."

"Now that you have seen her, do you want her?" Lathen asked.

"Aye," Greyson breathed, still watching the young mare canter around the ring. Lathen could tell, in his head, he was already running her in a baby race at the end of the season.

"Very well," Lathen took out a notebook from his coat pocket, jotted down something, and tore it off. He waved over to a passing stable hand and handed it to him.

"You know we are here for an auction, right?" Lennox chuckled. He knew his brother had just bought the horse outright and likely paid too much.

"Yes," Lathen retorted, "but I lack the patience to wait. I would like to go back to de Clare House."

"Ah, I see. Is Lady Haven to return today then?" Lennox feigned nonchalance that made Lathen want to punch him again.

"Yes, but that is not the reason I wish to leave," he lied, "I have a meeting with the lead investigator this afternoon. I am hopeful they might have some positive news for me."

Greyson snorted and Lathen turned away from his brother with a raised brow.

"Lathen, ye know we understand how upsetting it is the tart got away again. But ye cannae fash yourself over it. She is either run off fer good, and we will nae be bothered with her nonsense anymore. Or, more likely, the stupid chit will pop up somewhere and be found. Tae be so wearied is nae good fer ye."

Lathen knew Greyson was right, but it did little to relieve his mind. He wanted Marien found, and out of their lives for good. He still needed to get Emerson married, which was hard enough for him to do, and he did not need this loose end waving in the wind, distracting them.

"Listen, you two can decide on what horses will do best. I am not of a mind to be here. I am terribly sorry, but I must go." Lathen knew it was rude, but he turned and made to leave anyway.

Greyson grabbed his arm and stopped him. Lathen looked up curiously at his friend. It was not often anyone touched him, and Greyson was probably the only one who would ever dare to do so when he was obviously upset.

Well, except Emerson. But that is likely over too, he mused with a heavy heart.

"Lathen, remember what I said," Greyson said to him softly, "there is nae reason why yea cannae just marry the lass." He did not name Emerson, but Lathen knew who he meant. They had talked about her several weeks before, and he told his friend then he could not marry her because of his own dark secret.

And I was right.

Once he told her, she left him. He decided to say so.

"Grey, I appreciate that," his shoulders dropped, "but I already tried. I showed her, and she could not handle what I am. I do not blame her. She deserves to marry someone uncomplicated who can take her back to the country where she belongs."

Greyson held his gaze, his deep-sea eyes sympathetic and understanding. Nodding, he let go of Lathen's arm and went back to join Lennox at the railing once more.

As Lathen walked away, his mind was full, but he heard his brother comment to Greyson.

"You say I blather like an old maid, but I swear you two are worse."

chapter twenty

The rooms at Almack's were filled with members of the *ton*. It was congested, overwarm, and hard to move about without running into someone. Wall to wall, there were young ladies with their mothers and men, young and old, who were there looking for new wives or simply new conquests. Still others were just there to be part of the London social scene. After all, Almack's was the best place to be seen. If you could score an invitation, that is.

It was just past the height of the season, and a fever had taken hold. Many families were growing anxious over not receiving offers of marriage for their daughters. None of the ladies wanted the horror of a second season. Or worse, no one wished to be put on the shelf and be labeled an old maid. For ladies like Emerson, options were still open. Her fortune and title made sure of that, even if she did not have her unique beauty and charm to recommend her.

For Hazel, it was getting more difficult to pretend that time was not running out. She had many suitors who still wished to dance with her, and they continued to call on de Clare House to pay respects after their return from the country.

A couple even asked after when her father might be coming to town. Which led Hazel to believe they were interested in meeting him, possibly with the intention of asking him an important question. Possibly just to be polite.

The most persistent gentleman was still Mr. Brown. He attended every ball or party Hazel and Emerson attended, and he called every afternoon at de Clare House. Still, he had not asked for her hand.

No one had.

She was pretty enough. Even objectively, Hazel understood this. Men, young and old, had glanced her way since she began developing bosoms at age twelve. Her mirror explained not much had changed since then, except her clothing was of better quality, and her shared lady's maid was an expert at styling her hair.

Unfortunately, it was well known that she did not have family connections or even a small inheritance to bring to a marriage. The de Clares were generous enough to sponsor her season, but that meant little as far as prospects. She had yet to express her growing worry to Emerson, because her friend had her own concerns. But if something did not happen soon, she was going to have to lower her expectations dramatically.

Perhaps marry a man of the church, a second or third son, or maybe a gentleman farmer with a small cottage. There is no shame in those options. Hell, maybe I should marry a barrister like my father. At least she would know what to expect, even if it meant he was often busy or away. *My only hope is to live close enough to Emerson to visit regularly, and I can afford to buy my books.*

These thoughts were running through her head as she walked next to Emerson through the rooms that evening. Many heads turned toward them, but Hazel understood they were mostly focused on Emerson.

If it were not for her friend's kind heart, and the fact Emerson did not even realize her appeal, Hazel might have felt a twinge of envy. Yet Emerson was blissfully unaware of everyone's stares. She was just as nervous as Hazel was about not having found a husband. Especially after the last couple of weeks. Her friend also had her mind filled with worry over Marien's escape, and of the duke himself, of course.

When they were still up at Havenfield, Emerson finally told Hazel everything that had occurred the evening she went to Nox House to speak with Marien. To say Hazel was shocked was an understatement. She considered herself a worldly woman after all her reading, but she never realized what was happening under their very feet. Literally, even now. *Noir* was practically a den of ill repute.

It might as well be down by the docks with harlots flipping their skirts for coins. Yet it is run by a duke of all people.

No wonder innocent misses like herself were not worth as much as they once were. The men of the *ton* could get more without marrying.

Look at Lennox for example. He only comes to these things to please his aunt. He does not wish for any connection with these young girls who stare after him. Each with the barest hope he might look their way or dance with them. Let alone marry one of them. It is the same for all these men, I would swear on my life.

Hazel shook off the dark thoughts and grabbed Emerson's hand, squeezing it tightly for reassurance. They were both going to need it. Emerson turned and smiled back, her lips trembling slightly.

"My dear friend, it will be alright. We shall have a lovely time tonight," Hazel told her warmly. She was not sure if she was trying to boost Emerson's morale or her own, but she knew they both needed encouragement. It was going to be a long night, as both their dance cards were full again.

From behind them, Lady de Clare put her hands on their backs to lead them. "Come, girls, let us find somewhere to be seen by all."

Hazel knew she was also aware of the season's second half. Having been a spinster herself, she was conscious of needing to get both her charges well situated. Soon. Before hushed whispers started as to why they were not yet engaged. Hazel was surprised she had not heard them already.

Lady de Clare led them to a set of chairs near her good friend Lady Sutcliff. Lennox had of course come with them, but Hazel watched earlier as he bowed to his aunt and then went off to find his own refreshments as well as a game of cards. Many of the other ladies, both the mothers and their daughters, observed him leaving as well. There was a moment when the ladies stood taller, batted their eyes, and waved their fans to move their hair, followed by barely hidden sighs of disappointment and downcast glances as their efforts went unnoticed.

Hazel would have rolled her eyes if it would not have been impolite, and if she did not feel sympathy for them.

The poor girls still believe they have a chance, Hazel thought cynically, having realized the futility herself.

Since they had returned from the country, Hazel had deliberately avoided being alone with Lennox. Mostly because of what happened the night they left, when she had gone with Emerson and Leighton to Nox House.

The absolute nerve!

He had forced her to leave by tossing her in the carriage. The grin on his face, as though her anger was amusing to him, still irritated her.

Hazel was not sure what was worse. Lennox mocking her fury, or the feeling she had when he picked her up. Emerson once explained how her body would betray her just by looking at His Grace, and now she understood.

Even now, my skin tingles at the knowledge that he is near. It makes no sense. The music began, and Hazel was reminded of what was important. *A proper gentleman, to marry.*

She and Emerson were led to the floor for the first dance. For her, it was much the same as every other ball and party they had been to thus far. The same conversations. The same lords and gentlemen on her card.

Almost all of whom are completely uninterested in an attachment to a nobody like me. Of course, they still like to be seen dancing with a pretty girl.

Hazel went along with her first several partners by habit, lost in her thoughts. She barely realized what music she was hearing, or which steps she was supposed to be making. Luckily, her muscle memory came through and she danced adequately, if not beautifully. She also managed to give the right answers to all the small talk her partners insisted upon. When Mr. Brown came to claim the fifth dance, she was grateful for a friendly face. He bowed low to Hazel and tried to speak with her.

"M-miss Atwood, it is a p-p-pleasure to once again s-see you."

Hazel blushed and nodded to him as she took his hand. He led her away toward the dance floor but could barely look at her, his gaze mostly trained toward the floor.

It is such a shame that Mr. Brown still gets flustered after all this time. She thought he would likely suit her as a husband. He was bright enough, and he liked to read. Not as much as she, nor with as wide a variety, but it would give them something in common to discuss at least. He was not wealthy, but he was not poor either. *It would be a comfortable life.*

Their dance began and Hazel did her best to do most of the talking. It was that way during all their dances, as well as when he came calling.

"Mr. Brown, I have missed seeing you in the last weeks. I suppose you heard that we went for a quick jaunt to the country to get some relief from the hot city. It was nice to have some fresh air and quiet solitude. You have a house in the country, do you not?"

"Y-yes, a small house with a little property to the n-north. N-nothing g-grand. N-not l-like Havenfield."

"Oh, have you been to Havenfield, then?" she asked.

"N-n-no," he blushed and ducked his head again in embarrassment, his cheeks flushing, "b-but you know how p-people talk."

Oh yes, I know. The ton *loves to gossip more than they love drinking illicit French wine. More than having air to breathe! If they had a hint of why we truly left town, or how we did so without a proper escort, it would be an actual scandal.*

"Yes, well, Lady Haven's home was lovely. I enjoyed visiting the orchards and seeing her mill. We are planning on going back to pick apples in autumn. After the season is over, of course."

"Th-that sounds w-wonderful. M-my house is m-more of a c-cottage, really. Small but c-cozy. B-but it is n-near the c-coast. And I d-do so love the sea."

Hazel brightened and smiled widely at him as she realized they finally had something else in common. Mr. Brown blinked back, seemingly stunned.

"Oh, I too love the sea. We used to spend our breaks from school in Brighton. Lady Haven and I. We went sea bathing there as often as we could. There is nothing more invigorating than breathing in the salt air and listening to the waves crash during a storm!"

She chatted about the seaside until their dance ended. Hazel let go of Mr. Brown's hand, stepped back, and accidentally trod on another woman's dress hem. She jumped off immediately and turned to apologize.

"Oh, dear!" she exclaimed, "I am terribly sorry." She leaned down to inspect the light pink dress. Luckily there was no tearing or marks from her slipper.

"No, pardon *moi, mademoiselle*, it was I not paying enough attention," came the delicate reply as Hazel straightened.

Hazel immediately recognized the other young woman as Lady Sabine Rousseau. Her nearly white hair, translucent skin, and silver eyes glowed in the candlelight. Her soft smile was genuine, unusual for their surroundings and company. Neither she nor Emerson had ever been properly introduced to the lady, but they often wondered about the little French *émigré*, and how she was making do during her first season.

"*Bonsoir*, Mr. Brown," Lady Rousseau nodded politely, "how lovely to see you again, would you introduce us to your friend?" She motioned to Hazel and back to her own grandmother who was standing at her side and slightly behind, a shadow in her black dress.

"Y-yes, of c-c-course," Mr. Brown blushed even redder, "Lady Rousseau, and her grandmother, the Comtesse d'Orléans, may I p-please introduce M-miss Hazel Atwood."

Hazel curtsied. "I am delighted to meet you both."

"Oh, no, *mademoiselle*," Sabine said in her beautifully soft accent, reaching forward to place a gloved hand on Hazel's arm, "it is we who are delighted. We have wanted to meet you and your friend, Lady Haven, for quite some time. But alas," she motioned to the crowded room, "such is not always possible."

Lady Rousseau's grandmother squinted, as if trying to see Hazel's face clearly, but did not acknowledge her. She leaned up and said something to her granddaughter in a loud whisper instead.

"*Nous devons aller de l'avant. Vous savez qu'elle n'est pas aimée de* Lady Willoughby."

Lady Rousseau winced, blushed prettily, and replied to her grandmother. Her tone was still gentle, but firm.

"*S'il te plaît, Grand-mère, cette femme ne contrôlera pas avec qui je suis amie.*"

Then she turned back with a shy smile.

"Are you here with Lady Haven?"

"Yes," Hazel answered her brightly. She knew French quite well and understood Lady Willoughby must have expressed her dislike of her at some point. She barely knew Lady Willoughby, having met her only once before the season. Such limited contact hardly justified forming or sharing such an opinion. But it would not do to embarrass her new acquaintances, so she merely smiled as though she was unaware of their conversation and looked to see where Emerson was.

Thankfully, Emerson was walking toward them with Sir Richards, her last dance partner. Slowly, as the gentleman was not as spry as Hazel assumed he once was. Emerson smiled cheerfully and waited for a moment to be introduced. Hazel obliged right away.

chapter twenty-one

"It is lovely to meet you, Lady Rousseau, Comtesse d'Orléans," Emerson said sincerely, nodding to both in turn. Even though they had been to nearly all the same social events for the last several months, somehow, they had never met. Lately it seemed Miss Willoughby and her mother were constantly in the company of Lady Rousseau and her grandmother. The Willoughby ladies and their group of friends were best avoided. They were known to spread gossip and invent stories about other girls whom they saw as rivals. Emerson and Hazel had been warned at the very beginning of the season, by Lady de Clare herself, to keep their distance from both Willoughby ladies. So, they were delighted, and somewhat surprised, at finding Lady Rousseau alone, with only her grandmother, for a change.

"Sir Richards and I were about to sit for a few moments. Would you like to come with us?" Emerson asked, fanning herself, "It is awfully warm here tonight." She did not really need rest, but even now Sir Richards was practically hanging on her arm as they stood.

"Yes, that would be splendid." Lady Rousseau smiled and put her arm through her grandmother's as the older woman grumbled in French under her breath. Lady Rousseau merely sighed, gave her grandmother an indulgent look, and patted her hand kindly.

"Lady Sutcliff, Lady de Clare," Emerson said as they reached their table, gesturing to the two women, "I would love to introduce Lady Rousseau and the Comtesse d'Orléans. And of course, you all know Sir Richards."

Everyone exchanged polite hellos and nodded to one another. Lady Sutcliff asked if they would care to join them as she gestured to three open chairs and a low backed bench.

"Oh, yes, thank you very much," Lady Rousseau agreed with a bright smile, and sat in a chair at their table. She gently tugged on the skirt of her grandmother's gown until she sat as well with a stiff nod to the other ladies. The Comtesse still had a slightly sour look that contrasted with her granddaughter's cheerful countenance. Sir Richard sat down and sighed. His chin immediately dropped, and he was asleep before he fully settled.

"How are you enjoying your season, Lady Rousseau?" Lady Sutcliff asked. She seemed like a harmless little old lady, but Emerson knew that was not true. She was probably one of the biggest gossips in the *ton*. Though not a malicious one, thankfully.

"It is well, I suppose." She turned to Emerson and Hazel, "It is quite a lot though, is it not?"

They smiled back as they knew what she meant. All the parties, the dances, the theater... Every night there was something else and it was expected that every young woman, if they were serious about finding a husband, would attend them all. Also, they had gentlemen calling in the afternoon and had to drive or ride in the park. Through it all, they had to smile, dress for every occasion, and be proper.

It is exhausting to always be...well, on.

"Ah, young people are so dramatic!" Lady Sutcliff chuckled. "I remember my own season, even if it was long ago. It was such a wonderful time. All the beaus, the dances. Although, they were not always romantic, were they?" She grinned at Lady de Clare.

Emerson and Hazel laughed with Lady Sutcliff as she told them an amusing story from when she and Lady de Clare had come out. Something about a foppish lord who always belched loudly during every dance. And another who always smelled of onions and aged cheese.

Sabine giggled as well, and she lifted a gloved hand to cover her smile. On her finger was an enormous pink sapphire ring that caught the candlelight, as well as everyone's attention.

"Wow, that is stunning!" Emerson exclaimed, leaning forward.

Sabine glanced down at the ring and flushed brightly, seemingly uncomfortable. She covered it with her other hand.

"Yes, it is...something, I suppose. It is quite ostentatious, actually."

"Are you engaged, Lady Rousseau?" Lady de Clare asked quietly, her curiosity evident. Usually, young ladies experiencing their season were extremely happy to have a proposal and took great care to flaunt their engagement ring to anyone they could. Sabine did not have the same enthusiasm.

Sabine sighed and lifted her hand and stared at the ring, taking her time before she answered softly.

"I suppose I am. To the young Lord Willoughby. It was to have been announced tonight," she looked dejected for a moment before brightening, "but as he has apparently decided not to show up, perhaps not."

"*Ne dis pas de telles choses, ma petite*," Sabine's grandmother spoke with vehement eyes.

Sabine blushed again and turned to answer her even more firmly, yet still with a gentle hand to soothe her grandmother at the same time. It was obvious she loved the older woman dearly.

"I speak nothing but the truth, *Grand-mère*." Then she stood suddenly and looked pointedly at Emerson and Hazel. "I must go to the ladies. Would you care to join me?"

Stunned, yet recovering quickly, they nodded and rose to go with her. Her grandmother did the same.

"*Grand-mère*, why do you not stay and enjoy the company of these wonderful ladies? I promise I will not go elsewhere, and I will not be alone. And I will not be long." Sabine nodded to her new companions and, though her grandmother huffed and grumbled, she did sit back down.

The three of them rushed off before anyone else could stop them, weaving their way through the considerable crowd.

The ladies' room at Almack's was quite beautiful. There was a large, rounded sitting area stuffed with comfortable couches and chairs, with mirrors and benches on all the walls, and several smaller chambers that went off to the sides. The girls went into one of the smaller areas, so Sabine could use the facilities, and Hazel and Emerson remained by a large mirror to check their hair and fix any errant pins. They had not been there long before they heard the unmistakable high and nasal voice of Miss Millicent Willoughby coming into the central room. Her words echoed off the arched ceiling in the sitting area and made it easy to hear what she was saying.

"I swear, my poor mother is at her wit's end with Percival. I had to come with my father tonight, late of course, because my mother is off chasing my brother down, wherever he may be."

"Percy never comes to these things, so why is she so worried?" This was from one of Miss Willoughby's nameless friends who usually followed her everywhere. Each was dull, fairly unattractive, and unusually meek. Emerson often wondered why Miss Willoughby enjoyed their company, and vice versa.

"Oh, because we finally found a girl for him to marry," she snickered at this and there were several answering gasps from her entourage. "It is true!" she replied to their apparent disbelief, "it is to be announced tonight, and the banns should be posted after the weekend. They are to be married next month."

"Really, to whom?" A different nameless friend asked.

"Lady Rousseau accepted his proposal last eve. She does not have a penny to her name, of course. And she comes with her horrid, sour grandmother, who looks like she should have had the good grace to die long ago. However, she is of good aristocratic stock and has an impeccable family history that goes back eons. Even if she is French."

"Does she know...about..." another of her friends began but seemed hesitant to finish her question.

"Does she know about his *peculiarities*?" Millicent finished for her friend and then laughed nastily. "Of course not, but it does not matter. Her sole purpose is to give our family an heir. Grandfather insists upon it, and my brother understands his duty. If he wants any money at all, not just a useless title, he will marry the chit and bed her immediately. Then he can drop her off in the country, return to London, and do whatever he likes. With whomever he likes. Besides, the girl is flat chested enough that Percy may not mind. Or notice. In the right light, of course." At that, Millicent and her friends cackled, and the grating sound drifted off as they left to rejoin the crowded rooms.

Emerson glanced at Hazel, to see what she made of what they heard, but noticed Sabine had walked up behind them quietly. Her face made it clear she overheard much of the exchange. The poor girl's silver eyes were welling with angry, unshed tears, and splotches of red were brightening her unusually pale cheeks.

"Oh, dear," Emerson gasped and reached for a clean towel from the counter. She handed it to Sabine and stepped back. She could not fathom how it must have felt for the poor girl to overhear such unkindness spoken of her and her only family. But she could imagine.

"*Merci,*" Sabine whispered as she dabbed at her eyes, knowing it would not do for her to be seen crying or with red eyes for that matter. She took a shuddering breath and braved a slight smile. "I will be fine, *je vous promets.* I promise I have heard much worse. One does not grow up in London as the poor French girl during the war with Napoleon, without developing a thick skin."

Emerson wished to say something comforting, but as they had only met the other girl a mere half an hour before, it seemed forward. Then she realized she would want someone to help her if she were ever in a similar position, so she shrugged and came forward, gently laying her hands on Sabine's delicate shoulders.

"Listen, we know that Miss Willoughby does not have the kindest of hearts," Hazel snorted aloud behind them and Sabine's smile widened a bit at the understatement, "It is not something you should worry about. Miss Atwood and I are here if you ever need friends to talk with. And we promise to keep your confidence."

"Yes, we understand the difficulties of navigating the *ton*," Hazel agreed right away, a solemn expression on her face. Then she grinned and added, "I mean, have you seen her suitor, Sir Richards, and how he snores?"

Emerson's eyes widened before she broke out in a giggle and nodded, "Hazel is quite correct!"

Another quick smile lifted Sabine's lips. "You two are lovely, but I do not care about Miss Willoughby's words. Truly, I do not. To be honest, Millicent and her mother have vicious tongues and have said much worse to my face. It is the idea of getting married that has upset me so. I wish it was not a necessity, and I had the luxury of marrying for love. I waited to have a season, with the hope of doing just that, but as you have just heard, needs must." With that, she took another deep breath to clear the tears from her voice and patted her silvern eyes one more time. Then she straightened her shoulders and back.

"There, can I pass muster?"

Hazel and Emerson smiled kindly and nodded.

"You look simply lovely," Hazel told her, the honesty evident in her voice. Sabine had a fragile beauty that was somehow only enhanced by her melancholy and overbright eyes.

They walked out together and went back to where the older ladies were still waiting for them. Sabine stopped short and turned to Emerson and Hazel.

"I hope you will not mind, but I suppose I should go look for my future sister. After all, she is obviously excited to have me join her family," her open sarcasm made them all grin.

"I was sincere when I said that if you ever need to talk, or really if you need anything at all, please do not hesitate to call on us at de Clare House," she reminded her softly, shaking her hand in farewell. But, based on which family she was marrying into, Emerson realized this might be the only time they would ever have the chance to talk.

Such a shame. She seemed quite wonderful. Not at all someone I would wish the Willoughby family upon.

Sabine went to her grandmother, bent down and whispered in her ear, and the two of them left as suddenly as they had joined them. Sir Richards stirred, and his eyes opened, making contact with Emerson's.

"Oh, Lady Haven, how wonderful to see you again. It is wonderful to watch all the young people here at Almack's, but I must be off." With that, he stood and slowly made his exit. Emerson met Hazel's gaze and had to lift her gloved hand to her lips to keep from laughing at the sparkle in her friend's eyes as he left.

The musicians began re-tuning their instruments, signaling dancing would soon resume. Emerson shook off her thoughts of poor Lady Rousseau, preparing for the next gentlemen on her dance card.

chapter twenty-two

The evening was almost over when Emerson read Lord Virgil Farnsworth's name on her card. She was excited to dance with him as she had not seen him in some time. He had been one of the first suitors she met at her debut, and he used to come calling on her often. But one day, Lathen saw him grasping her hand and declaring his affection. He grew angry and forbade her from seeing the poor man again.

*Right before Lathen kissed me, laid me down on his desk, and caressed my womanhood...*The first time he showed her how her body could explode with color and come back together again. The very memory was enough to make Emerson breathe deeply as heat flushed through her body. She shook her head to clear it and waited for Lord Farnsworth to approach.

She believed Lathen had kept his word and banned Lord Farnsworth from calling on her at de Clare House. She thought once he might be jealous, but she could not see Lathen being envious of a man like Lord Farnsworth. She certainly did not have any strong feelings for him. Not as she did for Lathen.

"My dear Lady Haven," Lord Farnsworth claimed his dance with a respectful bow. His manners were impeccable as always. "I am very glad to have the opportunity to resume our acquaintance."

"Yes, Lord Farnsworth," she lowered her head demurely in response, "I am very happy to see you as well."

He led her to the middle of the dance floor, and a waltz began. He was an adequate dancer. Not fluid like Lathen, but he did not step on her toes like many of the other gentlemen often did. He also was only slightly taller than Emerson, so she did not have to angle her neck up to see him and they were able to carry on a conversation with very little effort.

"I heard that you went to your country home in the north. Did you have a good time?"

"Oh, yes, we had a lovely time," she smiled enthusiastically, "Lady Leighton and Miss Atwood had never been to Havenfield, and I enjoyed showing them my childhood haunts. It had been years since I last saw it as well."

"I am surprised His Grace let you go in the middle of the season."

"Yes, well, it was a short trip, coordinated as a remembrance for my late father. We wanted to get out of the city for a few days, and His Grace and his aunt, Lady de Clare, thought the fresh air would be healthy after so much time in the city." The lie was well rehearsed. She and Hazel had practiced being asked about why they had gone on the trip. It felt like it was almost close to the truth at that point.

"I am glad for you. Though we missed having you both here," he said kindly before he lowered his voice, "I hope you do not find me too forward when I say that I missed you in particular."

Emerson blushed and looked away. She still cared for Lathen and dreamed of him every night, but he had made it quite clear, since she came back, he still expected her to marry someone else. The day they returned, he summoned her to his study and reported his failure to find Marien. Afterward, he instructed her to resume her normal season activities. And she was to find herself a husband. Or else he would find one for her, as she once suggested.

She was shocked. After their meeting at Havenfield, she thought perhaps they could work through their differences. They could compromise. Maybe she could do some of the things he wanted. Maybe she realized how much she wanted some of those same things. Now they would never know. He slammed the door and locked it before she could open it more than a crack.

Since then, she had done as he asked. Gone back to the opulent balls, danced with those on her card, and sat in the morning parlor when gentlemen came to call. Through it all, she had barely seen Lathen, and she knew he was back to avoiding her.

He is probably down at Noir. Her grip tightened for a moment, and she had to force her mind back to the present.

Now she was giving consideration to every gentleman who had shown her any interest. Including the one dancing with her. She realized she needed to find out how he felt about her.

Does he care for me? Or is he just being polite? It is so hard to tell, as he is always a bit shy, and he is usually more interested in talking of poetry and things he has seen in the park, than of anything substantial.

Emerson supposed it meant he could be quite happy in the country, if they were to marry. She studied his thinning, well-combed, oiled hair and trim mustache, which he also seemed to comb, realizing she might never feel for him as she did Lathen. But maybe she could be content with him.

"Lord Farnsworth, I was wondering if I might ask you something. In the strictest of confidence, of course."

"Of course! Anything I can do to be of service to you," he kept dancing, but he looked at her curiously and with kindness.

"Well, I am sure it is known I have had several offers of marriage. But my guardian, in his effort to find what he considers to be a good match, has turned them all away." Emerson took a deep breath. She knew that it was no small thing she was about to ask. Ladies were not usually so forward, and she could only hope that Lord Farnsworth would understand and not be put off by her forthrightness.

"Yes, Lady Haven, it is known. I have heard many of your suitors are now afraid to approach His Grace. And I, of course, am turned away at the door when I come to call..."

Emerson lowered her eyes quickly before he might see the flash of anger in them. She assumed as much, but it still made her furious to hear it confirmed.

"Well, my lord, do you know of anyone who is not afraid?" She realized as soon as the bold question left her lips, there was no turning back.

Farnsworth raised his brow, danced for a few beats, before he finally responded.

"Well, I hope you know that I would be delighted and most happy to declare myself to you. I have thought many times about asking you for your hand. I believe we would be a good match." His voice was quiet as he proclaimed his affections once again and tried to keep everyone around them from overhearing.

There was also something else in his emphatic tone and gentle expression she could not place, but she reasoned could be love. It was not a sentiment she knew well. He certainly was looking at her in a way that showed he had feelings for her. Whatever it was, Emerson did not feel any responding sentiment, nor did it give her the heat she always experienced with Lathen. She did her best to ignore the comparison.

Perhaps affection will grow after some time, she hoped even though the thought made her feel hollow.

She was trying to figure out how they could move forward, how she could ask if he was willing to try, when Lord Farnsworth continued.

"But Lady Haven, certainly, you must be aware I would have the same problem as all your other suitors. Especially those that have been turned away. For some reason, the duke does not like me at all. Not only am I no longer welcome at de Clare House, but several other invitations have also been rescinded. Lady Sutcliff sent word I am no longer welcome at her weekend party. To be honest, there are many who say the duke is considering marrying you himself." The last was said in a low voice and Lord Farnsworth blushed in embarrassment and looked away.

Emerson was shocked. She had not realized there was talk of her and Lathen. As he was not willing to marry her, she knew such a rumor could ruin her chances of a good match, as many men would avoid crossing a powerful figure like the Duke of Windemere. She began to feel her hopes wane as the last chords of music were sounding.

She knew it made sense for Lord Farnsworth to be reluctant to press his suit since Lathen had expressed his disapproval and possibly had a claim on her. The lord was a slightly built man and held far less power within the gentry. It must be hard to even consider pursuing her.

Just as the song ended, Lord Farnsworth leaned down and whispered in her ear. She listened intently.

"If you are willing, however, I would love to meet with you at the Drury tomorrow evening, during the intermission. We would have more time to talk then."

Emerson thought about it for a moment. A Shakespeare play was opening tomorrow, and almost everyone in the *ton* would be going. It might be tricky to get time alone to speak with him, but she was willing to try if he was.

"Certainly, my lord. I will see you then."

chapter twenty-three

Lord Farnsworth was leading her back to Lady de Clare's table, when they came upon Miss Willoughby and Lady Rousseau. With them was another gentleman Emerson did not recognize. Emerson moved to one side to go past them without incident, but Miss Willoughby noticed and stepped in her path.

"Lord Farnsworth, Lady Haven, how wonderful to see you both," her tone was unctuous and grating, "I had heard you left town, Lady Haven, yet here you are. I also heard the duke went with you, but he came home by himself, soon after. I was able to dance with him at the Grafton Ball last week, you know. It was quite a pleasure to see him out and about again. It is said he is ready to find a proper lady to make his duchess."

Emerson did her best to put a serene expression on her face. After overhearing Miss Willoughby's cruel words toward Lady Rousseau, it was hard not to show her own dislike for the woman. Especially as she was bringing up her trip, likely so she could gossip about it.

And her bringing up Lathen like that. It was an obvious attempt to suggest that she held Lathen's favor now. *I wish I could just rip her overly coiffed hair right off her head. She would not be smirking so much then!*

Emerson suppressed her unfamiliar jealousy, realizing her best hope was a quick meeting without confrontation. Which was not easy since the woman was obviously looking to press the issue.

She deliberately blocked my path, after all.

"No, Miss Willoughby, we only left for a quick trip. It was lovely to get some fresh country air."

"Well, is that not just fantastic. I believe it has done wonders for your complexion." She gave a prim smile that did not reach her eyes and turned to Farnsworth. "It certainly looks like you are glad to have Lady Haven back, are you not, Lord Farnsworth. I hope we can look forward to hearing an announcement soon." Her hand gestured between the two of them.

Lord Farnsworth blushed at the comment. As he had no response to give her, he looked away uncomfortably. Emerson did her best to keep her face passive, pursing her lips together at the obvious inference that she and Farnsworth were soon to be engaged.

"Oh, pardon my rudeness. Do you know Lady Rousseau?" Miss Willoughby gestured to Sabine, who paled a little.

"No," Emerson feigned ignorance, "I do not believe I have had the pleasure." She gave a quick nod to the other women.

Sabine murmured back a polite but absent greeting and then remained quiet. Her grandmother, who was standing right behind her, was also silent and avoided looking at Emerson at all. Miss Willoughby did not bother to introduce her. Instead, she turned to the gentleman standing on her other side.

"Oh, and I suppose you have not had the chance to meet Lord Blackburn, the Viscount of Greaves. He lives near our country estate. Our families have known each other since we were children. He does not come to town often, but we are very happy to be hosting him." Miss Willoughby sounded quite proud to make the introduction.

Emerson gave a quick curtsy to the lord as she hoped she could leave afterward. But the gentleman stepped forward, grabbing her hand with unexpected familiarity, leaving her unsure how to respond.

"Well, well, *Em*, it is good to see you again," he began with a knowing smile even as Emerson looked at him with barely contained surprise. She still did not recognize the man, and his voice made gooseflesh run up her arms. She could not understand how he knew of the name only her closest friends called her. She attempted to pull her hand back, but he tightened his grip, and it would be obvious if she kept trying, so she pasted a polite look on her face.

"You two have met?" Miss Willoughby's eyes narrowed, and she sounded shocked and irritated in equal measure.

"Oh, yes. Lady Haven and I had the chance to meet only a couple weeks ago. When her coach had a problem on the north road from London. I believe you were with two of your friends?"

The room spun and Emerson had to contain her gasp as she suddenly recognized the man in front of her.

It is the gentleman highwayman! The man who kissed her and returned her purse. *To my bosom!*

Before escaping into the night with his two rough companions.

Of course, Emerson could not claim such an acquaintance with the man holding her hand. To do so would be ruinous. Not just to him, but to her, Hazel, and Leighton. She merely nodded her answer to him and tried once again, in weak futility, to pull her hand from his.

"Oh, and I forgot to get the name of your escort." This was said with a raised brow, its meaning clear to Emerson.

He is blackmailing me. All of us! He knows we were out without a chaperon. Not that having one would have saved them from being waylaid by three highwaymen. Nevertheless, it was still subtle intimidation. *No, I suppose it is a stalemate. A mutual secret that cannot be exposed.* She could not reveal how they met without letting everyone know she and her two friends were out without a chaperone.

"Mrs. Goode," Emerson blurted out, naming the Havenfield housekeeper who had come back from the country with them. "She was most grateful for your help, of course. We would have been stranded out there without getting a new wheel from the next village." She offered the most common excuse she could think of, avoiding any mention of highwaymen. She also made a mental note to inform Hazel and Leighton about the new lie they would need to maintain.

Just one more thing we must remember...

"Yes, of course, Mrs. Goode. She was quite the harridan. I would have wished to make a better acquaintance with you and your two friends, but she was very staunch in her duties." The lord's eyes twinkled as he lied, seemingly without worry or effort. "Perhaps we can take the opportunity to fix that while I am here in Lon—"

"I am sure we will be quite busy while you are visiting, my lord," Miss Willoughby cut him off before he could finish.

Likely she is hoping to snag the lord for his title. Ha, it would serve her right to marry a man who turned out to be no better than a common thief! Emerson had to work hard to smother her smile at the thought.

Lord Blackburn turned to Millicent with a slight frown, then back to Emerson. His lips lifted in a half smile and he shrugged, before he finally let Emerson's hand go, his fingers trailing familiarly from hers.

"Perhaps another time then. Oh, and do tell Mrs. Goode I hope we can meet again. She was such an amusing character."

A character whom you have never met and likely believe does not exist. You bloody cad! Emerson glared pointedly at him, hoping he could feel her annoyance. His answering grin indicated he did.

Lord Farnsworth, watching from the sidelines, finally regained his composure. "I really must get Lady Haven back before her next dance partner arrives," he said, thankfully offering an excuse to escape.

Miss Willoughby narrowed her eyes again as if she still wondered about Emerson and Lord Blackburn, but she finally moved to the side to allow them to pass.

When they got far enough away, Farnsworth leaned down and whispered to Emerson. "Miss Willoughby has quite the sharp tongue, does she not?"

Emerson had no wish to get caught gossiping about the woman, and her mind was still whirling from meeting the highwayman again, but a bubbling laugh left her before she could stop herself.

"I think, perhaps, it is safe to say that. But maybe, like all sharp things, it is best to practice avoidance. Or at least to take great care when you are around them." Emerson felt proud of her diplomatic answer and smiled mischievously to him as they stopped.

They had arrived back at Lady de Clare and Lady Sutcliff's table and Lord Farnsworth took his leave with a polite bow and a knowing glance toward her. Once again, Emerson found herself considering him as a possible suitor. He was certainly not the most exciting of men, but he was kind and considerate, and she could hardly find any fault with him. And he helped her get away from Miss Willoughby, apparently recognizing her spitefulness.

Yes, he is slightly uninteresting, but at least I would have a chance at a mellow, pleasant life. Perhaps that is better than the darkness and tumult I would have with Lathen. Echoes of their passion filled her mind, reminding her of what else Lathen brought with him, but she did her best to ignore them. Instead, she focused on the best way to create a future with Lord Farnsworth. *But can I do that to him? Marry him knowing I might always be thinking of another man?*

Emerson let that thought sit, upset over whether she could handle such deceitfulness, even as her last partner of the night arrived, and she left to dance with him. She soon forgot Lord Farnsworth altogether and her mind continued to worry over two things.

Lathen...always Lathen. And now, the gentleman highwayman. *Lord Blackburn.*

chapter twenty-four

Oh, those dimples, twin crescent moons carved upon the alabaster canvas of her divine countenance! They ignite a celestial glow, bathing her in an ethereal radiance that could shame the heavens themselves. When her lips parted in that fleeting smile this evening, directed at me alone, it was as if time unraveled, spiraling back to that fateful moment we first met.

An angel, surely, descended from the empyrean heights to bless her with an aura so sublime it cloaks her delicate form in a halo of otherworldly light. Her lavender eyes, those orbs of amethyst fire, sparkle with a brilliance that outshines the trembling candlelight, each glance a dagger to my soul, both wound and balm. Her spirit, so pure, so singular, radiates a warmth that could thaw the iciest heart. The scent of orange blossoms clings to her, a fragrance so intoxicating it haunts my every breath, binding me to her irrevocably.

Her smile almost, almost, tempts me to absolve her of her grievous sins, to erase the torment of witnessing her profane dalliance with that bastard de Clare, their bodies entwined in shameless abandon against that cursed elm tree, a mockery of her sanctity.

Almost, but not quite.

For how could I, her destined soulmate, her fated lord, overlook such a betrayal? Her actions, so base, so perilously close to the common, sully the divine pedestal upon which she belongs. She is no mere mortal, no creature of fleeting whims. She is to be my wife, the sacred vessel of my lineage, the mother of my heirs. Her name, her very essence, must remain untarnished, a beacon of virtue above the sordid fray of this decadent, devious world. It is my solemn duty, my sacred charge, to guide her back to purity, to ensure she rises above the vulgarity of her missteps.

What kind of husband would I be, nay, what kind of man, if I allowed her radiant smile or the sweet perfume of orange blossoms to sway me from this righteous path? Her beauty and grace demand a fierce and unwavering protector, one who will not falter even in the face of her angelic charm.

Yet, oh, how tonight tested the limits of my restraint! It was the first time since that accursed night at Havenfield that I stood so near her, close enough to breathe her presence, to feel the warmth of her existence mere steps away. My blood roared with fury, a tempest barely contained, as I watched her glide across the ballroom, her silken gown whispering secrets to the polished floor. She danced with them, those unworthy suitors, those hollow men who dared to bask in her light. And worse, she bestowed upon them her smiles, those precious gifts that should be mine alone! Each curve of her lips, each flash of those dimples, was a betrayal, a lash upon my heart. Does she not know the torment she inflicts? Does she not sense the agony of a man pushed to the precipice of his endurance? Of course. She must know! But a heart like mine, so vast in its devotion, can only bear so much before it shatters or strikes.

I nearly lost myself tonight. The urge to seize her, to grip her delicate shoulders and shake sense into her, was a fire in my veins. I wanted to demand why she cheapens herself, why she allows these lesser men to orbit her divine star, their presence an affront to the sweetness that should be mine to cherish. But I held fast, my resolve a fragile thread against the storm of my passion.

For her sake, I must remain composed, a guard of her honor, until the day she is mine in truth. Even now, as I trail her carriage through the shadowed streets, my heart thrums with purpose. It is my duty to ensure her safe return, to guard her from the perils of the night, as only I can. The horses' hooves echo like a dirge, a reminder of the distance that still separates us, but also of the inevitability of our union.

And then, there is my house guest, a wretch, a means to vent the seething frustration that festers within me. Tonight, I shall visit them, and in their shadowed company, I will purge the rage that threatens to consume me. It is a necessary release, a way to spare my beloved Lady Haven the full force of my turmoil.

For her, I must preserve the sanctity of our future, keep her smile unmarred, her spirit unbroken. That smile, oh, it is a treasure beyond price, a beacon that guides me through this torment, perfumed by the delicate orange blossoms that linger in my dreams. I will protect it, cherish it, even as I mold her into the paragon she was born to be. She will thank me one day, when she stands by my side, radiant and pure, her heart beating only for me.

Until then, I watch, I wait, and I burn.

chapter twenty-five

When the carriage stopped at de Clare House, Lennox opened the door and stepped out before a footman could get there. He was running late and trying to move the ladies in his care inside as fast as possible. However, he still had to do his duty. He lifted his hand and helped his aunt Lillian down, then did the same for Emerson. When he turned back, he saw Hazel and felt a stir in his groin as she grinned at him, her blue eyes sparkling in mirth. He was so distracted he almost forgot to help her as she descended. He quickly realized his mistake and grabbed her by the arm.

It was not the first time he had felt a growing desire as he looked at her, but he knew he dared not indulge in any fantasy he might have about her. She was not one whom he could love and leave. Things would be expected of him. It was best he left the house and met with his mistress. To that end, he dropped Miss Atwood's hand as soon as was appropriate and moved to help his aunt up the stairs. Giles, as usual, opened the door for them as they reached the top.

"Welcome home, my lady, my lord." Then as Emerson and Hazel came in behind them, "Lady Haven, Miss Atwood, I hope your evening was well." Giles had returned to his usual self after the return of the three young ladies from the country. If anyone had bothered to notice, he was as close to a smile as he had ever been as he welcomed them home.

Once everyone was safe inside, Lennox bowed quickly and bid good evening to them all.

"Oh, dear boy, are you going out again?" Aunt Lillian's tone carried a hint of surprise, but also exasperation.

"Yes, Auntie, I have plans at the club," Lennox answered offhandedly as he turned his top hat in his hand and looked down at the ground. He was slightly embarrassed to have to explain where he was going to his aunt. It was one of the reasons he disliked the season so much. It was more relaxing when his sister and aunt were in the country, with no one to question his late-night rendezvous. Or if he even came home at all.

Aunt Lillian sighed, her voice tinged with reluctant indulgence, and said, "Very well, but you must not stay out too late. We have plans to attend the theater tomorrow evening, and I expect you to be ready." She reached up and gave her nephew a quick pat on the cheek, perhaps with more force than necessary, the brief contact carrying a subtle reprimand. Then, with a graceful turn, she ascended the stairs, her footsteps resounding with purpose through the marbled entry hall.

Lennox watched her go until she vanished from view, and then he moved toward the door, eager to escape into the night. When he noticed Hazel gazing at him with a knowing expression, he paused. She narrowed her eyes and tilted her head slightly, her lips curving into a smirk. For a moment, he almost wanted to stay.

His club. As if I do not know what that means, even if his aunt does not. The thought made Hazel annoyed even though she knew it was irrational.

Lennox gave her his usual charming grin, put on his hat, and continued walking toward the door. Giles bowed, but his earlier hint of a smile had vanished, replaced by a disdainful look as he opened the door again.

"My lord," his tone matched his censure.

Lennox seemed not to notice, cheerfully waving to the butler as he walked out. He even whistled as he skipped down the steps and jumped into the still waiting carriage.

Hazel watched him leave with pursed lips and met Giles' knowing gaze for a moment. The normally gruff man risked a gentle look of encouragement.

Well, he knows too, and disapproves. But it matters not. Lennox is who he is. A rake, she thought to herself before she gave Giles a small return nod and turned to follow Emerson up the stairs to their rooms.

She had barely made it inside before Emerson grabbed her hand and pulled her over to the sitting area.

"Goodness, Em, give a girl a moment to get in before you accost her!"

Emerson waved off Hazel's words, a wild look in her eyes. Even if Hazel had not known her as well as she did, she would have known that Emerson had something important to tell her.

Emerson opened her mouth several times, then closed it, clearly unsure how to begin. She was given more time to think when Leighton entered their sitting room with a sleepy smile, her hair and nightgown already rumpled.

"Hi, ladies, how was Almack's?" As usual, Leighton had not been allowed to join them, but the renewed closeness of all three girls made them more conscious of including her as best they could.

"Oh, thank goodness!" Emerson exclaimed and walked back to close the door behind them, giving them privacy. "I have news. Something unbelievable!"

Emerson was not prone to gossip, but she knew she needed to tell them about who she met at the rooms that evening. And with whom.

"What?" Hazel asked as she sat expectantly.

"So, I was with Lord Farnsworth—"

Leighton interrupted with a scoff. She was not partial to Lord Farnsworth and thought him dull and unworthy of her friend. She had mentioned, more than once, she was not sorry he was no longer coming to call.

"We just finished our dance," Emerson rolled her eyes and continued as though uninterrupted, "and we were stopped by Miss Willoughby—"

This time Hazel groaned and made her stop her tale. No one liked Miss Willoughby, but after what had happened with Lady Rousseau that evening, she found her even more loathsome.

"Yes, I know, and we will tell Leighton about that in a moment," Emerson assured her friend before continuing with a frustrated sigh, "but first, this was far more important!"

Both of her friends stood up straight, realizing Emerson's seriousness, and they nodded.

"With her was a man who, at first, I thought I had never met. He was young and handsome, but his voice rang familiar. She insisted on introducing us. His name was Lord Blackburn."

"All right..." Hazel looked at Leighton. She did not want to interrupt again, but she did not know the name and wondered if Leighton knew of him. Leighton appeared to be just as puzzled.

"He called me Em!" Emerson blurted out finally as though that would clear up their confusion. It did not.

"Do you know him?" Hazel asked.

"Well, we all do..." she paused, worried about their reactions, but knowing she still had to tell them. "He is the highwayman!" she finally blurted out.

Hazel and Leighton gasped. Shock widened their eyes, but neither responded. There was so much to think about. If he knew Emerson, it would not be difficult to find out their names as well.

Emerson understood all their worries, because she had been thinking about it all evening.

"I do not think we need to be concerned over him telling the *ton* he met us and how." She tried to calm them.

"How can you be so sure?" Leighton cried.

"Because he let me know, subtly of course, that he will keep our secret, as long as we keep his," Emerson told them matter-of-factly, making them visibly relax. They might still face consequences for their unescorted travels, but perhaps not from Lord Blackburn revealing what he knew.

"Wow, what are the odds?" Hazel asked no one in particular.

"I know, I was thinking the same," Emerson answered. "Not to mention that he is an old friend of Millicent Willoughby."

"That is unbelievable," Leighton still sounded dazed, "what is he lord of?"

"He is the Viscount of Greaves."

Leighton looked baffled for a moment before a light of understanding came into her eyes.

"Oh, I believe I have heard of him. My friend Lady Trammel told me about meeting him while we were gone. I guess his father was a gambler and was shot in a duel over his debts. He only became the Viscount last year."

"Huh. I suppose that makes sense." Hazel said offhandedly.

"What does?" Emerson asked her curiously.

"Well, it explains why a gentleman, a *lord* at that, might be reduced to stealing. If his circumstances were reduced and he was not raised to do anything to keep himself. His options are almost as bad as mine."

Emerson reached for her friend to comfort her. She wished she had something clever to say that would refute what Hazel said. She did not.

I will always be here for her, of course, but I am not sure her pride would ever allow me to support her. Emerson wished Hazel could find someone who would make her happy and help her not feel like she was somehow less than. Just because she was born the daughter of a barrister and not of some lord. Heavens knew she was far more deserving and loving than others who were more fortunate. *Take Miss Willoughby for example!*

"Oh Hazel," Emerson gave her a hug, "you do not need to become a highwaywoman! I assure you of that."

She was trying to make light of the situation, and luckily it worked. Hazel and Leighton both laughed hysterically at the ridiculous idea of Hazel running around, trying to steal purses from wealthy travelers.

"Perhaps," Hazel wiped a tear of laughter from her eyes after catching her breath, "but I make no promises. I still preserve the right to resort to a life of crime if I end up an old maid. At least then I will be an interesting old maid! With exciting stories to tell both of your children!"

After they calmed down, and after Hazel and Emerson told Leighton about the rest of the evening, including what had happened to Lady Rousseau, they sat, contemplating in comfortable silence. It was Emerson who finally broke it.

"Well, I suppose we will all have to make choices that might not be what we were expecting. There might not be some handsome gentleman who will sweep us off our feet, marry us, give us children. Maybe our happily ever after is not something of novels. Maybe we should settle for pleasant enough."

"Well, that sounds dismal," Leighton sighed, leaned back in her chair and yawned, but she did not disagree.

"I once told you that you would marry for love, and I meant it!" Hazel reminded her. She still wanted the best for her friend.

"And I told you that I am not sure what love even is!" Emerson was just as firm. Not angry, but unyielding.

"You deserve to learn what love is. Just because you were not shown it when you were a child," Hazel stopped when Emerson bowed her head and looked hurt. Then she leaned over and grabbed her friend's hand and tugged on it until Emerson lifted her gaze. "You have love from me. And from Leighton," Leighton nodded emphatically to show her agreement, "but there is more, I promise. There is a man out there who will mend your heart and make it grow. We will renew our search for him tomorrow. Then someday, you will have your own children and give them all the love you should have had. Your life is going to be amazing. I promise you this."

Tears sprang unbidden to Emerson's eyes. She knew Hazel meant what she was saying, and if it was up to her friend, then love would be just around the corner.

But it is not up to her. Or me. Besides, if it was up to me, I already know who I want. But Lathen no longer wants me.

chapter twenty-six

The morning parlor of de Clare House was Lady Lillian de Clare's favorite retreat. In the early afternoon, it glowed with a soft light through tall southern windows. A vase of fresh-cut lilacs perfumed the air with their romantic aroma of honey and spice, mingling with the faint bitterness of her tea. Lillian sat in her usual settee, a delicate porcelain cup cradled in her hands, her gaze drifting over the diminished gathering of gentlemen callers.

Once, we could scarcely fit them all, she thought, her lips tightening.

At the start of the season, the clamor of suitors for Lady Emerson Haven and Miss Hazel Atwood was so great they had to throw open the grand drawing room to accommodate them. Carriages had lined the street, the hum of eager male voices filling the house. Now, only a handful remained, scattered across the parlor. The thought pressed heavily on her.

What has changed? She knew the answer, though she was loath to admit it even to herself.

Shaking herself, she turned to where Mr. Brown sat near Miss Atwood, his eyes soft with admiration as he leaned forward to watch her every movement. Lillian noted the way Hazel's cheeks flushed, though she was merely using a silver pen knife to sharpen quills, and neither was speaking, instead sitting in comfortable silence. Mr. Brown's speech impediment, modest estate, and unremarkable lineage left something to be desired, but his devotion was undeniable.

Hazel could do worse, Lillian mused, sipping her tea. *But she could also do better.*

Across the room, Sir Richards slumped in a high-backed chair in the corner, his chin resting on his chest, a faint snore escaping his lips. He was kind, gentlemanly, and possessed a comfortable fortune, but his interest lay firmly with Emerson. Lillian's eyes narrowed as she studied him.

He would suit me better, she thought wryly, not for the first time.

His advanced age, storied military career, and love of a good joint of beef were not a good match for Emerson's vibrant youth. But Sir Richards sought a young wife to bear him children, a prospect that made Lillian's stomach turn. As if on cue, Sir Richards stirred, his eyes fluttering open to fix on Emerson, who laughed brightly at something across the room.

"Such youth," he murmured, his voice thick with sleep and sentiment. He smiled faintly, then drifted back into his doze, snoring softly before his eyes closed.

Lillian did not bother to answer him, but her gaze shifted to the small table where Emerson sat with two suitors, Lord Dorning and Lord Bellamy, a deck of cards spread before them in a lively game of speculation. The cards turned up one by one, and Emerson's eyes sparkled as she placed a bold counter on a knave of hearts.

"I shall have it!" she declared, her voice lively with mischief. Lord Dorning laughed, tossing in two counters with a flourish. Lord Bellamy hesitated, his fingers lingering on his modest bid, as if weighing more than cards.

Lord Dorning was a minor baron with a crumbling estate and a charming smile. Lillian's critical eye assessed him. *His house may be falling apart, but his title is real enough, though Emerson does not need it. With the right management, he could be molded into something respectable.* She made a mental note to investigate his debts further.

Lord Bellamy, by contrast, was a study in ordinariness. Neither handsome nor plain, neither wealthy nor impoverished, he had been a constant presence since the season began. His persistence intrigued Lillian, but the rumors surrounding him gave her pause. Whispers of illegitimate children, several, despite his youth, had recently reached her ears.

A wandering eye is a burden no wife should bear, she thought. *Emerson deserves better than a lifetime of her husband's bastards knocking at her door.*

Emerson laughed again as Lord Dorning made a playful remark about her card playing prowess. Sir Richards stirred once more, his bleary gaze fixing on her.

"Such charm," he whispered softly. "I enjoy watching her."

Lillian nodded politely, though her thoughts were sharp. *He sees her as a spark to rekindle his fading years, not the woman she is.* As it was, Lillian was worried. She could tell Emerson's spark was struggling. She was still as beautiful as ever, still delightful, yet her laughter and chatter with her suitors seemed forced. *Perhaps she is only concerned by who is left as well, or merely worried about not being engaged.*

The paucity of offers puzzled Lillian. By now, she had expected at least one serious proposal for either girl, if not for both. The answer, she knew, lay with her nephew, Lathen. Gossip swirled that the Duke of Windemere intended to marry Emerson himself, securing the Haven wealth within the family. It was a falsehood, one Lillian could easily dispel, but she had not.

Perhaps because I still hope he might come to his senses, she admitted silently. Lathen's intentions were unclear, even to her, and until she knew his mind, she hesitated to quash the rumors entirely.

"Are you almost done defeating those poor souls, Lady Haven?" Hazel called out to Emerson, her voice teasing.

Emerson glanced up from the cards, her smile radiant but composed. "Oh, Miss Atwood, I only play to keep them entertained," she replied lightly. "A lady must let gentlemen win now and then, must she not?" Her eyes sparkled with mischief, betraying the calculated charm of her words.

"I suppose," Hazel tilted her head, as though deep in thought, before continuing playfully, "but were I in your place, I would have bankrupted them both by now!" Her laughter rang out, bright and cheery, drawing the gaze of the men at the table.

Their spirited banter drew chuckles from the rest of the room and Lillian's heart softened. Both girls were still radiant, with bright futures. If only she could steer them toward the right matches.

It is time to get serious, she thought, her fingers tightening around her teacup. The season was waning, and with it, her chances to secure their happiness. She would not let them slip away. *After all, no one better understands the difficulties of being shelved than I.*

chapter twenty-seven

Bees buzzed across the backyard, sipping from bluebells and black eyed Susans. They landed on tall purple coneflowers and vibrant orange zinnias before darting off to their hive. The early evening made it seem they were in a rush against time. Hazel watched absently, her book lying forgotten in her lap, her mind too full to read.

She was not sure what was worse. The highwayman who happened to be a lord was now blackmailing them. Poor Lady Rousseau having to marry into the Willoughby family for her own safety. Lennox running off to spend the night with his mistress. Or a room of suitors neither Emerson nor she wished to marry. *Yet we are like these bees, rushing before our season ends and everything has dried up and gone cold.*

A quick bark, followed by a fluff of black fur quickly passing her, jolted Hazel from her unpleasant thoughts.

"Hello, Dog," she giggled as she watched Dog romp through the garden, seemingly chasing something only she could see.

"She certainly gets crazy sometimes. I wish I had her energy."

Hazel gasped and turned. It was His Grace, and he was standing right behind her, watching Dog as well, a droll smile lifting one side of his lips.

"Your Grace," she said, setting her book down and moving to stand. He glanced at her briefly, waving his hand to indicate she should stay seated, before turning back to watch Dog.

Dog raced around the garden five times, at full speed, before trotting back, her tongue lolling, panting loudly, her tail wagging with glee. The duke leaned over and scratched her ears, then straightened, and moved to one of the other chairs near Hazel.

"May I?" He gestured, looking questioningly.

May he? Is he serious? It is his garden. His house. I am only a charity case, taking up space. Hazel did her best to keep her thoughts to herself and schooled her features into a serene expression.

"Of course, Your Grace," she nodded, slightly nervous at the idea of being near him, alone. It felt odd. In fact, she realized they had never been alone before.

The duke sat, and Dog went running off again, jumping over flower beds and chasing an orange butterfly.

Silence...

Hazel's mind struggled for a subject to break the awkwardness before a question finally came to her, "Your Grace, may I ask why you named your dog 'Dog'?"

Lathen actually grinned, something Hazel never saw him do. His face was normally a mask of indifference.

"I wish I could tell you there was some special reason, Miss Atwood. The truth is, I found her as a puppy, practically drowned in a storm, and I began calling her dog in lieu of anything else. Eventually, I brought her to Windemere, planning on giving her to Leighton and Emerson as a gift. Dog had other plans. She simply refused to answer to any of the names they tried. Though when you consider what they came up with, it makes sense."

"Oh?" Hazel's brow rose, "were they fanciful?"

A look of affection crossed the duke's face. "You could say that. Fluffelina. Puddlesby. Tippity-toes. Those were the top choices if I remember correctly."

"Ha!" Hazel chuckled and rolled her eyes. "That sounds about right."

"Exactly. So, you can understand why Dog had other ideas. When I eventually left, Dog followed me all the way back to London. No matter how many times I tried leaving her there."

"So, she decided her name was Dog?"

"I suppose that is true," Lathen answered and turned to watch Dog again.

Silence returned and Hazel racked her brain for another safe subject.

"Are you enjoying your book?" Interestingly, the duke broke the silence, sounding nervous as well.

"Yes, it is an intriguing novel. I hope you do not mind me borrowing it from the library."

"They are there to be read," he waved toward the house, "It is good someone has found use for them. I wish my sister would spend more time with novels, but she has always been more interested in talking than reading." The duke sighed. "Honestly, I wish I had more time to read as well."

Reading had always been Hazel's passion, and she never understood how anyone got on without a good book to escape with.

"Well, perhaps you just need to find the time, Your Grace," she suggested.

"Perhaps," Lathen murmured absently. He looked like he had something on his mind. Something that had little to do with books.

Hazel waited, to see if he was going to say anything else. It was several moments, but finally Lathen took a deep breath, and looked around the garden, as if to ensure they were truly alone.

"Miss Atwood, I was wondering if I might have a word with you," he began slowly before finishing in a rush, "about Lady Haven."

Hazel's mouth dropped open in surprise. She snapped it shut as soon as she realized. She knew so much about the two of them but never imagined it would be him coming to talk with her. Especially when she was still working out a way to find how he felt about her friend.

Perhaps there might be some way for me to help, though. I still believe they would suit, and I think Em loves him, even if she will not say so. If only he would come around.

"I suppose so," she glanced over at him apprehensively, waiting for him to continue.

"First, I wanted to thank you for being such a good companion for her. It is clear you get on quite well and you understand what makes her happy."

Hazel only nodded. She did not know how to explain to the duke that she and Emerson were more than close. That they might as well be sisters or something better than sisters.

"It is very important Lady Haven is married to someone who would also see to her happiness," he went on, "and I was considering several of her suitors

162

and wondered if she expressed any preference to you."

Is he serious? Hazel knew her brow was raised, and she did not care. *Despite all his unusual predilections, Em still wants him, and he has the temerity to continue pushing her away. He should be so lucky to have a wonderful woman like her. A wife who would suit him in every way.*

Regardless of her obvious irritation, Hazel realized this was an opportunity. It could be a way to help her friend.

Perhaps all he needs to hear is how much he and Em are right for one another. But how? It is not as if I can just tell him I know how they have been spending time together. Or where he has taken her. How he has touched her. Hazel decided she must be clever instead of direct.

"Your Grace, I am aware of the gentlemen you turned away. The whole of London has heard of them. As far as I know, the rest of the *ton* are a bit concerned about coming to you. They are afraid they will experience the same."

Lathen looked frustrated and he took a moment to school his features.

"Yes, well, I am afraid I had to say no to those proposals. They were not suitable. I thought, perhaps, you might know which of her other suitors would be better. For her. Has she expressed any affinity for one over the others?" His fingers wrapped tightly over the handles of the chair as he finished. It creaked in response.

Hazel's mind raced, working through a quick plan. *Maybe asking His Grace for his feelings about Em is the wrong tactic. Especially when he shows them so easily.*

"I think she is...*fond*...of several, Your Grace. But I believe she has especially liked meeting one gentleman and has talked of possibly accepting a proposal from him." Hazel had to turn her head when she saw the duke's eyes flash and heard the deepening protests of his chair as his knuckles went white.

See! He does have feelings in there, even if he tries to hide them. I only hope Em will forgive me for this. It was only an hour ago when Emerson told her she had no affection for any of the callers they spent the afternoon with. Though Hazel was not about to reveal such to His Grace. *So, who? Who would prick at the duke's armor?*

"Can you give me the gentleman's name?" Lathen was gritting his teeth, and a muscle jumped on his jaw.

"Of course," she stood giving Dog's head one final pat as she came bounding back, "she has become partial to Lord Warwicke." Then she walked away, working hard not to laugh as she watched the duke's anger turn to a comical expression of shock.

chapter twenty-eight

Lathen stomped back through the orangery. Dog followed cautiously, unaccustomed to such fury emanating from her master. Several maids jumped out of his way when they noticed his dark countenance.

Seriously? Lord Warwicke?

Lathen was dumbfounded. Greyson and Emerson had barely spent any time together. He was unsure how she could choose Greyson, who surely would have told him if he had feelings for her.

Especially since she is mine! His mind was reeling, and he was walking blindly down the hall of the east wing, just as someone walked out of the morning room, colliding with him.

"Oh, pardon me!" Emerson gasped and put her hands on his chest to steady herself.

Lathen felt her light touch through the heavy material of his jacket, scorching him, making it hard to breathe. He did not care. He had purposely managed to avoid being alone with Emerson since she returned home, and it felt like fate that she was here now. Unaccompanied. Right when he desperately needed to talk with her. Wordlessly, heedless of why he should not, he grabbed Emerson's elbow and pulled her down the hall, into the billiards room for privacy. He shut the door behind them. And locked it.

"Your Grace?" Emerson's voice was curious and shocked, but not angry.

Lathen had a moment where he just looked into her eyes, noticing the flecks of indigo amid her lavender irises. Staying clear of her had obviously been a good idea. Her closeness was already affecting him. All he could think of was the sounds she would make if he were to kiss her. The scent of orange blossoms reminded him of her sweet taste.

Lord Warwicke? How can she even think of him! Visions of his best friend with the woman he considered his flashed through his mind. He did not think of any consequences when he lowered his mouth, barely letting a shocked sound escape Emerson's lips before he captured them.

The kiss was wild. Anger and passion mixed with desperation. It took only a moment before Lathen realized Emerson was right there with him. She was not trying to push him away, but was instead pulling at his shoulders, her nails digging into them in her haste. Somewhere in the back of his mind, he remembered he was supposed to keep his distance, but it was an impossibility, a natural disaster he could not avoid. He stopped trying.

Lathen scooped Emerson up, one arm below her knees, the other at her neck, and carried her to a green leather Chesterfield sofa, managing to keep their mouths fused. He sat down with her legs hanging over one side of his, deepening their kiss. His hands dug into her hair, scattering hairpins and tugging at her scalp.

Emerson moaned, the slight pain exciting her, just as he knew it would. He would have smirked if he was not so involved in the kiss. He moved from her mouth, trailing his lips down her chin to the sensitive spot on her neck, right below her ear. Emerson tilted her head to give him better access. His right hand pulled her dress down from her shoulder, and his lips followed, leaving kisses and little nips along her collarbone.

"Lathen," Emerson gasped, and he lifted his head, smoldering passion in his amber eyes.

He was not sure if she was asking him to stop or asking him to continue, but he was too far gone to debate it in his head. His hand moved down even further to the hem of her skirts and then under them, searching for her inner thigh. He was rewarded when she widened her legs, giving him better access, and he slipped his long fingers below the edge of her soft underwear.

My lord, she is so wet!

His middle finger slipped inside, her slickness allowing him to bury it inside her completely.

And so tight!

A sharp sound of pleasure escaped Emerson, and she jerked her hips up to meet his hand. As a reward, Lathen added a second finger and went even deeper, stretching her sensitive tissues. Her uninhibited reactions made his already hard member swell to an almost painful degree. He had wanted her before. For more than two years, if he was honest. Now he knew exactly how good being inside her felt. How amazing a release was with her.

Plus, he had not been with anyone else since they were last together. He tried to tell himself it was simply because he was too busy, but in the back of his mind, he knew it was something else.

It has never been as good with anyone else. Perhaps it never will be. And this might be the last time I ever get to touch her.

He shook violently at the thought, withdrew his fingers from Emerson's core, and stood, bringing her with him. A moue crossed her face, but Lathen gave her no time to ponder the change. Instead, he led her to the felt billiard table and turned her so her back pressed against his chest. He wrapped his arms around her to hold her there. He bent down so his lips were right next to her ear.

"Bend over, *Nyx*. Grab the edge of the table and, whatever you do, do not let go."

Breathe. I must breathe!

Emerson's body was alive. Everywhere. Places that minutes ago felt frozen and numb were suddenly thawed, in the full bloom of spring. Her pulse raced and with a warmth that spread through her entire body. Lathen's words should have stunned her.

Hell, I should have been shocked the moment he pulled me in here and locked the door. I should have immediately demanded he open it and let me go.

Instead, it woke her. As if her very being had been waiting for this moment. The instant his lips met hers, it released the fierce part of her she only ever found with him, and now she wanted nothing more than to do what he asked.

When he touches me, I not only let him, I beg him. I should have the willpower to say no, but I do not want to. I want him. I crave him. It is simple.

Emerson did as Lathen asked. She bent at her waist, let her hands slide over the soft felt, and grabbed both edges, holding on tightly. Her head tilted to the side and, as she waited, she forced herself to breathe and looked at the red, white, and yellow balls. She had never played billiards and wondered offhandedly what each ball was for.

It did not matter. Especially as Lathen stepped even closer. She felt his manhood pressing hard against her backside and she had the urge to push against it. He distracted her by slipping one leg between both of hers and pushing them apart. Then he nudged them even wider. Emerson waited, still gasping for air, her cheek pressed against the felt.

Lathen ran his hands over her shoulders, leaning over her back, then down her spine, making her shiver. As if the inability to see him made his soft touch more intense. Lathen noticed, and he chuckled, the sexy sound resonating in her belly, making her core clench in anticipation. She had missed his closeness. It was more important than the air she could not pull into her lungs.

With one swift movement, Lathen grabbed the hem of her skirts and pulled them up and over her head. Emerson shrieked, but luckily the sound was muffled.

"Shh, *Nyx*," Lathen whispered as he used one hand to pull the skirts down just enough to look into her shocked eyes, "we would not want to be disturbed at the moment, would we?"

Emerson nodded, but Lathen kept looking intently at her, his amber eyes deepening as though she had done something wrong.

"I asked you a question." His tone was shadowed, and he was still staring at her.

Once again, that delicious clenching happened, but she could not feign ignorance. She knew what he wanted.

"Yes…" she whispered back, her eyes lowering, "…Master."

Triumph flashed in Lathen's eyes before he closed them and took a deep breath to regain some of his control. Hearing those words from her mouth nearly made him come.

Such obedience deserves to be rewarded.

Lathen fell to his knees and grasped Emerson's spread thighs, right above the tied pink ribbons of her silken hose. Her round, taut buttocks were right before his eyes, clasped gently in delicate French underwear. He had seen them before. He even had two ripped pairs in his locked office drawer.

They tear so easily, after all.

Lathen proved it. The material fell apart like paper as he pulled at the sides, near the gentle swell of her hips. Her womanhood glistened secretly near his face. He spread her upper thighs and leaned forward, eager to taste her. His tongue licked down her seam, finding the jewel of her passion. He swirled around it, pressing firmly, lapping up her glorious wetness as it flowed into his mouth. Emerson tilted her hips, pressing to his face, eager for more.

"Hmm," Lathen chuckled, stood and pulled Emerson's hair back from her face, tugging until her neck arched from the table. "My greedy *Nyx*. You need this, do you not?"

"Yes, Master," she gasped and pushed up on her elbows to relieve the tension from his fist in her hair.

Then she moaned as Lathen pushed up against her again, grinding against her exposed core, starting a rhythm that she soon joined. Lathen needed more. He needed to be inside her. He quickly unbuttoned his breeches, releasing himself, and used one hand to grasp his member. He stepped back a little, so that he could position himself at her opening, sliding his wide crest up and down her wet slit. Emerson panted and used her hands to push herself back, trying to get him inside her.

Lathen grasped her hips, stilling her, gritting his teeth from the effort. Yet he realized he needed her to want him. He needed her desperation. He needed her to feel what he was feeling. It did not take much before she let go of the table and tried to reach back for him.

"Oh, no," Lathen tsked, "I told you not to let go." He grabbed her wrists and forced her hands back to the table's edge. "Now, are you going to be a good girl?" he asked.

"Yes," she gasped hoarsely, licking her lips. Distracting him.

Lathen noticed she did not call him Master, but he no longer cared. He was so close to embarrassing himself by finishing before he even entered her. He dug his fingers into her hips again, let his cock barely spread her, then he slammed into her.

All the way to the hilt.

"Ahhhh!" Emerson garbled, turning her face so it was once again buried in her dress, biting it to keep quiet. Her knuckles whitened as she gripped the table tightly, her legs shaking. Lathen felt a quivering surround him as she climaxed almost immediately. Lathen was right there with her. He pulled back until he was nearly out, and crashed back in, pressing up against the end of her, stretching her.

And he came with her.

chapter twenty-nine

The theater at Drury was brightly lit with oil lamps as everyone made their way to their seats. The de Clare family had a box near the stage. It had sumptuous red velvet upholstery, and an unfettered view. Only a few others, such as the Royal Box, were closer. It was not only a great place to see the players, but it was also one of the best places to be seen. Which Emerson was certain was the main reason Lady de Clare insisted they go as often as they could.

Fortunately, Emerson enjoyed going to the theater. Even if she did feel a bit like an object on display. She supposed it was the fantasy of a life she might otherwise never be exposed to. This evening, they were going to watch a production of '*Much Ado About Nothing.*' She had read it but had never watched it acted out before. She was looking forward to it.

She was also anxious. Her entire world seemed upside down. She knew, now more than ever, she wanted Lathen. After their meeting in the billiards room, it was clear they both desired each other. Nothing in the world felt as good as when he was deep inside her. Making her whole.

But afterwards...

After our breathing and our heartbeats calmed, and even after Lathen was done gently stroking my hair from my face and he kissed me softly one more time, I watched his face change. From something I could swear was caring. Back to cool detachment.

Lathen had pulled her gown back in place, helped her stand upright, then stepped back from her. The air between them cooled just as quickly as his ardor, making her rub her arms from a sudden chill.

'*I am regretful that happened, Lady Haven. It was unconscionable for me to take you like that. I promise to do better. To keep my distance from now on. While you continue your season.*'

Emerson's heart dropped when he used her proper title, and she realized his meaning. He had not changed his mind. He still meant for her to marry another.

Lathen's decree shocked her, perhaps more than his touches had. But his resolve, despite his feelings, made her realize she needed to move on. There was no more hope for her and Lathen.

When she met with Lord Farnsworth tonight, during intermission, she was going to propose to him. It was beyond forward of her, and if the *ton* were to find out, it would be on everyone's tongue. She did not care.

I will move on. A stubborn glint came to her eyes.

Men in uniform went around and dimmed all the lamps, except those around the stage, letting the audience know it was time to stop wandering around and find their seats. As soon as the voices lowered as well, the curtain was raised.

Emerson sat between Hazel, who leaned forward to watch the actors, and Lady de Clare, who was also leaning forward, using her opera glasses to scan the crowd. She only wanted to see who else had come that night. She heard the Regent himself might attend, so she hoped most of the *ton* might show as well. On the way there that evening, she explained her wish for both girls to receive engagements within the next month. She ensured they were dressed especially pretty that evening.

That was another reason Emerson felt the pressure to propose to Lord Farnsworth. It would be good not to have to always be on or be seen at every party or ball. She could retire to the country and be done with it all.

Away from Lathen.

Emerson shrugged off a quick pang from the thought and tried to enjoy the play. She watched as Claudio and Hero fell in love. It was romantic and sweet.

How it should be, I suppose.

Then she sat up taller as she watched the masked party scene. She was reminded of the Masquerade Ball she attended with Lathen not that long ago. She found it ironic how even Shakespeare saw the trials and epiphanies that could come from anonymity. But it was not just the ball she was reminded of. She started to think of the underground darkness of *Noir,* and how everyone, including Lathen, wore a mask there. To keep their deepest vices a secret. She began to squirm in her seat as she remembered everything she saw there. Until Lady de Clare noticed and whispered for her to be still.

Emerson flushed and forced her attention to the play. Benedict and Beatrice were being tricked by their friends to believe that each was in love with the other.

If only it were that simple, Emerson thought with a soft sigh. *Especially when they are so obviously in love.*

When the curtain lifted for intermission, nearly everyone stood, including Emerson and Hazel.

"I believe I would like to walk around and stretch my legs, would you like to join us, Lady de Clare?" Emerson asked politely, though she knew Lady de Clare would decline, as she always did.

"No, thank you, dears," she said, lifting her glasses and scanning the crowd again, "I believe I shall stay and look around a bit."

Emerson linked her elbow through Hazel's, and they left the box. There were many fashionably dressed men and women in the hallway, and they had to weave around them as they moved toward the back of the theater. Emerson kept her eye out, beginning to feel a growing disappointment.

Lord Farnsworth was late. Minutes ticked by, and she worried they would have to return to their seats without her meeting. Then, just as she was about to give up, she saw Lord Farnsworth standing in a dark corner, talking with another gentleman she recognized, but could not recall his name.

Oh, bother, I was hoping to find him alone.

Luckily, Lord Farnsworth lifted his gaze and noticed her. He gave her a slight nod, showing he remembered their planned meeting. He must have excused himself, as the other man soon left, and he began walking toward her.

It is now, or never...

"Are you all right?" Hazel interrupted her thoughts. Emerson had stopped in her tracks and not realized it.

"Yes." She turned to her friend. "But can you please do me a favor? Walk over there with me, to Lord Farnsworth. I wish to talk with him. Alone."

Hazel raised her brow in surprise. However, after searching Emerson's determined face, she agreed without question. They moved toward him.

Lord Farnsworth bowed deeply and smiled. He looked genuinely happy to see her, and though Emerson still only felt ambivalence, knowing he cared was somewhat consoling.

"Lady Haven, Miss Atwood. Lovely to see you both again. I hope you are enjoying the theater tonight."

"Yes, definitely. This is one of my favorites." Emerson replied. She was unsure how to proceed and felt nervous, her heart fluttering in her chest.

What shall I say? Perhaps I should just blurt it out. 'Will you marry me, Lord Farnsworth?' No, I suppose that would not do.

Hazel withdrew her arm and took a step away from them. "I see Mr. Brown standing just over there," she said brightly as she tilted her head, "would you mind terribly if I went over and spoke to him?"

"Of course," Emerson smiled gratefully and squeezed Hazel's hand. "I shall meet you in a few moments and we can return to our seats."

Once Hazel left, she turned back to Lord Farnsworth. She realized she would lose her nerve if she did not get it over with. She lowered her voice to a near whisper and put her proposal to him.

It was not exactly romantic. She explained to Lord Farnsworth she wished to marry. Very soon. But she needed to do so without worrying about the duke's permission. Or waiting for the banns to be read. There was also the matter of her marriage contract. It was something she had written, with Hazel's help. It outlined her expectation of retaining control of her money. It also provided her husband with a generous stipend to spend however he wished. And children. She wanted them.

Lord Farnsworth listened intently. His eyes widened, and he was obviously shocked. Emerson did not blame him in the least. After all, everything she was saying was improper and forward. Not the marriage contract itself, as they were done all the time. However, they were usually handled by the father of the bride, or by her guardian. Also, her need for secrecy and how she wished to be married quickly were quite scandalous. It was only done that way if a girl were compromised in some way. Or if a babe was to be born less than nine months. Neither of which applied in this case.

Well, Lord Farnsworth has not compromised me, but he does not need to know what I have been up to with Lathen. And I can only hope I am not with child. It would be quite difficult to explain a dark-haired child with amber eyes. She ignored the sharp pang of regret she felt at the idea of a child with Lathen.

Emerson also felt regret over lying by omission, but she saw no benefit in revealing her lack of virtue to her potential husband. She decided not to tell Farnsworth, or anyone else for that matter, if he did not agree to her terms.

If he agrees, then I will tell him. Really, I will...Or perhaps I will tell him after we marry and our wedding night does not have the usual expectations. I am hopeful he will understand.

When she finished her proposition, it was met with silence. At first, Emerson worried that Lord Farnsworth would deny her outright, but he seemed to be pondering what she had said. Finally, just as the bells chimed, letting everyone know it was time to return to their seats, he leaned forward and whispered into her ear.

"I would be honored, Lady Haven, and yes, I agree to your terms."

Emerson gasped. She did not think it would be this easy.

I suppose I am engaged. Success should have made her happy, but it was hollow, and icy prickles formed at her nape.

Hazel was rushing back toward them, prompting Emerson to whisper urgently to Lord Farnsworth. He responded softly, and Emerson nodded her agreement.

"Hello," Hazel said as she reached them, "shall we return?"

"Of course," Emerson stared into Lord Farnsworth's watery green eyes one more time, willing herself to feel something for him. Anything. He was her fiancé now, after all. No, it was the same as always. Neither repulsion nor attraction. Just a friendly indifference.

A quiet life in the country with someone who I can hopefully learn to feel affection for, who at least cares for me. I just made a pact for that, I suppose.

chapter thirty

Hazel finally stopped her pacing, her golden blonde hair catching the candlelight as she spun to face Emerson.

"Em, this is madness! You are gambling your entire future on a man you scarcely know. Lord Farnsworth may seem charming now, but what if his promises are empty? What if he is only after your fortune?" Her voice trembled, and she clasped her hands tightly, her knuckles whitening.

Emerson set her brush down on her vanity, her fingers lingering on its cool surface, her chin set stubbornly. "Hazel, I have thought this through. I know it is a risk, a big one. But staying here...staying near *him*. That is a greater risk. My heart cannot bear it any longer." Her voice wavered, betraying the calm she tried to project. She met Hazel's gaze in the mirror, her lavender eyes fierce yet vulnerable. "Every time I see Lathen, it is like a knife twisting inside me. Then he brings me close, and I have hope, only to have it torn away once more. I cannot keep living this way, broken apart by feelings he will never return."

"But Em, marriage is forever." Hazel crossed the room and sank onto the edge of Emerson's bed, the silk coverlet whispering beneath her fingers. "You are tying yourself to Lord Farnsworth for the rest of your life. What if you wake up one day and regret it? What if you get bored?" Her brow furrowed, and she leaned forward, her voice softening to a plea. "I only want you to be happy. Truly happy. Not just...settled."

Emerson rose from the velvet cushioned stool, her delicate nightgown swaying as she moved to the tall window overlooking St. James's Square. The moon hung low, its silver light bathing the neatly trimmed hedges in an ethereal glow. She pressed her hand against the cool glass, her breath fogging the pane.

"Happy? I am not sure I know what that feels like anymore. But I need control. Lathen has it and I want it back. Control over my life, my home, my future. Lord Farnsworth offers me that. He has agreed to let me keep Havenfield as my own, to manage my inheritance without interference. He has even promised me children, Hazel. At least two, to secure my family's legacy. I believe it is enough."

"Enough?" Hazel's voice rose with frustration. "Emerson, you deserve more than 'enough.' You deserve love, passion, a partner who sees you as more than a means to an end. What if Lord Farnsworth changes his mind once the vows are spoken? A husband has rights, Em. He could take everything. Even your freedom."

Emerson turned sharply from the window, her long hair cascading over her shoulders. "I know the risks, Hazel. I am not naive. But I have spoken with Lord Farnsworth. Spent time with him this season.

He is...different. His interests are plain. He only cares for being in nature and poetry. And he offers me a simple life where I can be myself, not just a puppet of the ton, and not just someone's property." Her voice dropped to a whisper, almost as if she were convincing herself. "I believe he is the one for me."

"You are trusting a man's word over your own instincts," Hazel shook her head, closing her eyes in frustration. "Em, I saw how you looked at Lathen when we were at Havenfield. The way your face lit up. The way he returned your gaze. You cannot convince me you are ready to give up on him."

Emerson's shoulders stiffened, and she crossed her arms, her voice low but firm. "Do not speak of Lathen. Not now. Not ever again." The words carried a weight that silenced Hazel for a moment. "He does not want me, Hazel. He has made that clear. Whatever has happened between the two of us has been a mistake. Moments of weakness I cannot afford to repeat. Running off with Lord Farnsworth is my escape. Gretna Green is my salvation."

Hazel stood, her slippers silent as she crossed to stand beside her friend. She placed a gentle hand on Emerson's arm, her touch warm and grounding.

"Em, I am not trying to hurt you. I just cannot bear the thought of you throwing yourself into a marriage out of desperation. And His Grace...I do not believe he will let you go so easily. You know he will not."

Emerson's lips tightened, and she turned her gaze back to the window. Moonlight glanced across the tears welling in her eyes.

"I know," she admitted softly, her voice barely audible. "Lathen will chase me. He is too stubborn, too proud, to let me slip away without a fight. But once I am married to Lord Farnsworth," her whole body trembled, "once the marriage is consummated, he will have no recourse. No claim over me. I shall be free of him, Hazel. Free to live at Havenfield, to raise my children, to breathe without the weight of his presence smothering me."

Hazel's eyes widened, her hand tightening on Emerson's arm. "Consummated? Oh, Em, are you certain you can go through with this? To bind yourself to Lord Farnsworth in every way, just to escape the duke? What if you cannot bear his touch?"

"I will bear what I must," Emerson's expression hardened, though a flicker of doubt passed through her eyes. "Women have done this for centuries, and so will I. For Havenfield. For my legacy. For my freedom."

She stepped away from Hazel and returned to the vanity, picking up the brush once more. The bristles glided through her hair, each stroke steady and deliberate, as if she were brushing away her uncertainties. "Tomorrow night, when de Clare House is asleep, Lord Farnsworth will come for me. We will ride to Gretna Green, and before anyone can do anything to stop me, I will be Lady Farnsworth."

Hazel watched her friend, her heart heavy with unspoken fears. The room felt smaller. The tall windows rattled softly as a gust of wind stirred the trees outside, their branches casting restless shadows across the walls.

"And the *ton*?" Hazel asked quietly. "They will talk, Em. You know they will. They will say—"

"Let them talk," Emerson interrupted. "The *ton's* whispers will mean nothing to me once I am away. They will tire of the gossip soon enough, and I will be at Havenfield, far from their prying eyes and tongues."

Hazel sighed, her shoulders slumping in defeat. "I wish I could change your mind, Em. I wish you could see there must be another way."

"I know, Hazel. But there is no other way, I see that now," a flicker of gratitude softened Emerson's eyes as she resumed brushing her hair, the rhythmic motion a stark contrast to the turmoil in her heart. "I do not expect it to be a perfect marriage. But it will be mine."

chapter thirty-one

The hour was late, but Hazel lay tossing in her bed, unable to sleep.

This is all wrong.

She understood why Emerson agreed to marry a man she did not love. It was drastic, and impulsive, but that was her friend. Emerson was at her core a kindhearted soul, even when she tried her best to appear tough. But she often did things without thinking about all the consequences. Being raised as she was, she knew very little about human nature. Hazel could not get over her worry that Lord Farnsworth was willing to elope with her friend even though everyone would think terribly of them. They would talk and say they married because Emerson was expecting. On one hand, she knew her friend would not really care about the gossip. On the other hand, getting away from the duke was not worth being stuck. Forever.

Consequences. Hazel sighed. *There must be another way. There must!* She watched Emerson with Lord Farnsworth tonight and was certain her friend did not love him. *I do not blame her. He is perfectly fine, but he rarely has anything interesting to talk about.* She did, however, believe Emerson loved His Grace, the look on her face when she said not to talk of him was a confirmation. And, after their talk in the garden, she honestly thought he cared for Emerson. *Perhaps he even loves her, as well.*

With a frustrated sigh, Hazel finally jumped from her bed and yanked her robe over her nightdress. She knew Emerson was going to be angry with her for what she was about to do, but she had no choice. For her friend's sake, it made the most sense.

It was drafty in the hallway. She realized this at the same moment she remembered her slippers were still in her room. She went on without them, deciding she might lose her nerve if she went back.

His Grace's doorway was on the other end of the house and one floor down. She had never been there, except on the first day in London, when Leighton had given her a quick tour. Even then, it was only to glance through the door at the sitting area. She held her breath and knocked. It sounded overly loud in the darkness of the late hour. There was no answer. Hazel waited a few moments to gather her courage, then opened the door and walked inside.

"Your Grace?" she whispered softly.

There was no answer, but she heard soft snoring coming from another room. Past the sitting room and through another partially opened door, which she assumed led to the duke's bedchamber. In her bare feet, she walked slowly over soft carpet, her hands raised before her to feel any obstacles.

She bumped into an overstuffed feather mattress, and brushed a warm limb, just as a hand reached out and grabbed her arm tightly.

"You should not be here, Emerson!" came a deep growl as she was pulled onto the bed. A warm, bare chest covered her, and lips came close to hers.

"Wait! It is me, Your Grace!" Hazel squeaked as she pushed at his nakedness, blushing at the unusual intimacy.

"Miss Atwood?" Lathen leaned back, his confusion evident even in his sleep befuddled state.

"Yes, Your Grace. I am very sorry to disturb you, but I have something of great import to tell you."

Lathen let her up immediately and she scrambled to stand next to the bed. She stood there in mortified silence as she heard him rummaging around for something next to the bed, and she winced when he used a tinder box to light a candle. Hazel tried to avert her eyes, and she blushed. She had never seen a man shirtless and, judging by the sheet pooled at his lap, suspected the duke wore nothing beneath it as well.

"Well, Miss Atwood," he said evenly, "I assume this must be serious for you to come to my bedchamber. I am all ears."

Even in bed and naked, Lathen was commanding. It made Hazel pause for a moment. If she told him what Emerson was planning, there was no way to tell how he would react. Or if he might punish Emerson. It could mean that she was ruining her friendship forever.

Suppose she never forgives me? What if I am wrong?

Then she thought of Emerson being ostracized by the *ton*. Or worse. What if she got hurt in some way by Lord Farnsworth? She swallowed her trepidation and, in a rush of words, told His Grace the truth.

His anger was only evident in the stiffening of his muscles and his narrowing eyes. Otherwise, he was still as a statue while she explained the whole plan to him.

"When?" he asked with deadly softness.

"Tomorrow evening. Late. After the church bells stop. She is to sneak out of the back garden gate. He will meet her there with a hired coach. They are to drive nonstop, switching coaches, until they reach Scotland."

Lathen was silent for some time. Long enough that she began to wonder if he had heard her. Then he surprised her by thanking her quietly and sending her back to bed. She nodded and started to leave.

"Oh, and Miss Atwood," he said to her when her hand reached for the door to his sitting room, "I hope you understand when I request that you not tell Lady Haven that you have told me her plans. In fact, I wish for you to tell no one else about this. Am I understood?" This was said in a tone that brooked no argument.

Hazel glanced over her shoulder and nodded. She felt a pit in her stomach at the thought of deceiving her friend. Yet her instincts were still shouting. *Telling him was the right thing to do.*

She walked out without another word, nearly running to the stairs. Then she slammed into a hard chest. She would have screamed if the wind had not been knocked out of her. Strong hands grabbed her upper arms before she could fall.

"Well, well, well. What do we have here?" It was Lennox. Still dressed and obviously just coming back home after a night out. He looked down at her, then down the hallway toward the duke's rooms.

His brow rose.

"I have to admit, I did not see that one coming." His voice shifted from its usual cheerfulness to a disappointed, mocking tone.

"My lord, it is not what you think." Hazel whispered as she tried to pull herself from his grasp. She wished he would quiet his voice, but he did not seem inclined to do so.

"No? And what is it I think, Miss Atwood?"

Hazel did not know what to say. She could not explain what she was doing at that late hour, leaving the duke's bedchamber. Not without breaking her word.

Lennox leaned down. He was close enough that Hazel could smell the spirits he had been drinking, as well as the warm scent of expensive cigars and cinnamon, as well as the faint aroma of bergamot and honey. She mused to herself that it was not a bad fragrance. In fact, it made her belly curl. She breathed deeply and placed her hand on his chest before realizing.

"Miss Atwood, if you were looking to be someone's mistress, I would have been happy to oblige. You see, I treat my mistresses much better than my dear brother does his."

Hazel was shocked. Her mouth opened and closed, but no words escaped. Without thinking, she finally yanked one arm out of his grasp, reached up and slapped him. It was a lot louder than the last time as she was not wearing kid gloves, giving her fleeting satisfaction.

Lennox was still holding her other arm, and she felt it tighten reflexively as the loud crack sounded in the dark. In the deafening silence left behind, he let her go and stepped back.

"I apologize, Miss Atwood," was all he said, before he bowed and walked up the stairs to the third floor, where his own rooms were as well.

Hazel watched him go. Her shoulders fell at the thought of him assuming less of her, but there was no help for it.

She waited until she heard his door close, then climbed the stairs to her own bed. The sheets were still warm, and she mused at how much happened in the short time she was gone. The thought made soft tears fall until she fell asleep.

chapter thirty-two

Emerson dressed in haste, her fingers trembling as they fastened the clasp of her darkest cloak, its heavy wool swallowing her body like a shroud. The hood draped low, casting her face into a pool of shadow, a shield against watchful eyes. She stuffed necessities into a small travel bag, the straps digging into her palm, and slipped into the shared sitting room.

Across from her, Hazel's bedroom door stood sealed, a testament to her friend's disapproval. Emerson paused, her hand hovering near the knob, doubt gnawing like a wild animal at her resolve. Hazel had shunned her all day, her silence a rebuke of Emerson's reckless flight. She wished to walk over and knock. To make Hazel understand and give her blessing.

But time pressed, and she moved on, leaving the sitting room. Her slippers brushed the floor with ghostly softness, deliberately chosen to silence her descent down the grand staircase. Each heartbeat roared in her chest, a drum of dread pulsing through her mind, warning of discovery in the suffocating stillness. She was not just leaving, she was tearing herself free, and it meant she was choosing to forever end whatever she and Lathen were. In thirty minutes, she would meet Lord Farnsworth on the side street.

De Clare House had been hushed for hours, yet Giles remained a threat. He never slept, his presence a specter haunting her escape. Stationed by the front door, he waited vigilantly, for someone to return or for her to falter. If she could glide unseen to the east corridor, her freedom was within reach.

Lathen had departed earlier, his absence a cold fire that frayed her nerves. Her mind conjured him in *Noir*, entwined with another, his shadowed heart offered to a stranger's touch. The thought stabbed her, but she forced it aside, her jaw clenching against the pang of betrayal. Such emotions were fetters she could not bear.

His absence is my ally, she reminded herself as she neared the bottom of the grand staircase.

Across the main hall, she glimpsed Giles in the alcove by the front door. A book lay open in his lap, but his head tilted back, a low snore rumbling through the cavernous entry. Relief clashed with terror as she tiptoed left, past the open maw of the morning room, and rounded the corner to the breakfast orangery.

Moonlight fractured through the crystal-clear glass walls, casting jagged patterns across the marble tiles, like cracks in her resolve. She eased open one of the French doors, stepping into the gardens where the air was thick with damp earth and evening primrose.

She moved along the side garden, toward the back, until she saw the gate. Eyes seemed to follow her as she approached, but she saw no one and shook the prickling feeling away. Her hand reached for the gate latch, the iron hinges wailing as she nudged it open, the sound betraying her stealth. She winced, her breath catching, and peered around the fence.

The cobbles and sidewalk stretched, barren under the soft moonlight and a heavy mist. Down the block, a carriage hulked, the black horses snorting a promise of escape. It was exactly where Lord Farnsworth said it would be. York Street lay silent, the world holding its breath. She inhaled deeply, steeling herself to step through the gate, even as her body rebelled, frozen.

If I keep going, I will say goodbye forever to Lathen. Can I do that?

Then, from the back of her mind, came the vision of long red hair, twined about Lathen's body, whispers of *'Master'* with a French lilt echoing. Rough kisses and reverence. Ropes and whips. Red overtook her vision, blurring the edges of the dark night, and her foot lifted to walk away.

A hand clamped over her mouth, stifling her scream, as an arm coiled around her waist, yanking her back against a solid chest. Her jealousies vanished in an instant and terror took over.

chapter thirty-three

Lathen twisted Emerson around and his face caught the moonlight, distorting it in such a way that his anger was even more obvious. Emerson flinched, murmuring behind his hand for him to let her go.

"Oh, no, *Nyx*. Not this time," he leaned down to whisper in her ear. "I have done everything I know of to get you to behave. Now, you and I are going to talk, and we will come to an understanding. Now, be a good girl and keep quiet, or all the neighbors shall wake up and wonder why you are out. Alone with a man, at this hour!"

With that, Lathen picked Emerson up and roughly tossed her over his shoulder. He took long strides out of the gate Emerson had planned to leave through. Straight to the waiting carriage. The carriage he had hired for the evening.

"Take us to Nox House," he instructed the driver.

Lathen barely lowered Emerson into the carriage, pushed her inside, and closed the door before they were off.

Emerson shrank back in the corner, emotions fleeting quickly across her face. Fear, worry, even anger. He gave her a mocking look before he spoke to her with a barely contained sneer.

"In case you were curious, Farnsworth has been otherwise engaged this evening. I am afraid he is going to be unable to make your rendezvous." This was said coldly and Lathen watched her shiver. He imagined her worry over Farnsworth and his own rage grew, feeling palpable in the small carriage.

"Your Grace," she began timidly, "I know you are upset—"

"Upset?" Lathen raised his hand, cutting off her words. "Oh, Emerson, upset does not even come close. You have no idea," he growled, "you do not understand what could have happened to you! I am tired of alluding to the evils out there. I think it is time you see some of them for yourself."

Emerson remained silent, waiting for him to continue, as he struggled to keep a check on his temper. He realized every time he chose to punish her before, even when he was mad, he was collected. Especially when he touched her. This was different. Knowing she was trying to leave him was tearing his control apart.

The carriage came to a stop. Lathen hopped out, pulling her with him, only stopping to adjust the hood of her cloak to shadow her face. They barely made it to the top of the steps when the glossy black door of Nox House opened.

Madam Irina bowed as she stood back for them to enter. Lathen had to purse his lips when he saw the older woman's face. Normally naturally pale, it now bore the remnants of a blow struck more than a week prior. The bruise, centered on her left cheek, was a mottled blend of yellowish-green and pale blue. The discoloration spread lightly toward her temple, where it blended into her hairline. The idea of someone under his protection being injured, and he was not around to stop it, further tore at his tenuous restraint.

"Master," she spoke in her low Russian accent. She held out an object and Lathen grabbed it as he rushed past, murmuring his thanks. He strode toward the small library, pulling Emerson with him.

Lathen had a plan when he had first decided to bring Emerson here again. He was going to take her to the Black Room in the main house upstairs. They had been there before. He was going to restrain her with leather cuffs and rope, while she was standing before the mirror, and flog her until she cried for mercy and begged for forgiveness. His plan was to be merciless until she finally gave her word that she would never run off unescorted again. Until she promised she would listen to him. Until he knew he could believe her once and for all.

More than anything, he wanted to beat her for trying to leave him.

Again! She was going to leave me again!

Lathen was not particularly upset that it was Farnsworth she tried to leave with. Honestly, he had nothing against the other man. Other than he remembered how meek he was as a boy, and he could not see him as someone capable of protecting Emerson now.

Not with the way she manages to get herself into trouble at every turn.

Lathen wanted her married to someone strong. Someone who could take care of her even better than he could. He had no idea who that might be.

Certainly, none of the men who already came to him, asking for her hand, fit the bill.

*Yet she was running off with Farnsworth. And was planning to marry him...*Lathen realized he was not just angry. He was also hurt. *She tried to leave me!* Lathen's mind screamed again. He had never felt such a sting at the thought of losing a woman, a vulnerability gnawing at his heart, making his steps falter.

His anger began to melt away as the pain took over, leaving a raw, aching need pulsing through him. Ardent in its fervor, shadowed by its disquiet. He wondered if she could see the depth of his struggle. Would she yield to him, even as she was the one woman he could bend for?

Because of this, he changed his mind. All the reasons he always had for keeping his distance were still there. As well as the need to protect Emerson so she could not be compromised in the eyes of the *ton*. But, at that moment, none of that seemed to matter. He did not want to punish her. He did not want to hurt her.

Well, no more than she likes. The admission brought a dark, sensual tilt to his lips, even as his heart still raced with restraint.

All he wanted was to see her lavender eyes behind a mask, her rosy cheeks flushed with excitement, her body trembling when he touched her. He craved her nervous voice calling him 'Master'.

Everything about her turned him on. Even sitting in the carriage, livid and frustrated, he found himself getting hard just being near her. Which was a novelty he had not experienced in a very long time. Perhaps he had become too jaded after all he had experienced, but something about Emerson had always intrigued him. Now that she was a woman, he was no longer going to deny himself what he wanted. What they wanted.

There could be consequences, but Lathen no longer feared them. He simply wanted her more than he wanted any other woman.

Before any of that could happen, she had to understand what she was getting into and give her consent. She had to give herself to him.

Freely.

chapter thirty-four

Emerson's belly flipped as Lathen pulled her to the last bookcase in the library and lifted his hand to pull back the black leather binding of the third book from the left. The resounding mechanical noise of the lock opening and the secret door swinging inward made her shake. It was not in fear. Excitement flooded her body, a warm rush that prickled her skin before she even took her first step through the door. As she descended the ancient stone steps spiraling below the ground, the tingling warmth spread through her chest, tightening the tips of her breasts, her breath catching in anticipation of the unknown.

Lathen continued to hold her arm as he moved forward, his grip firm but not forceful, a touch that grounded her even as it sent sparks racing along her nerves, reminding her of all the times his control had both confined and liberated her. Emerson was not fighting him. She would have followed him willingly, drawn by the pull of curiosity and something deeper, something unspoken that thrummed between them.

Once they reached the vestibule at the entrance, Lathen handed her a black mask, smooth and cool to the touch. She took it wordlessly, slipping it over her face, the fabric settling like a second skin, hiding her flushed cheeks. Lathen donned his own mask and knocked on the heavy wooden door.

The small opening swung up, and a man's voice echoed into the entrance. "Yes?" That was it. You either knew the password, or the door would not open.

"*Obscurium per obscurius.*"

The man opened the door and let them inside. "Master," he said, bowing low.

Lathen murmured back to acknowledge the man but said nothing more as he grasped Emerson's hand and continued forward, his fingers intertwining with hers in a grip both possessive and tender, stirring the confusing warmth in her belly.

They moved from the dimly lit hallway into a vast amphitheater room, its high ceilings lost in shadow and ancient stone. Like any good theater, there was a show, and the air was thick with expectation, an electric hum that mirrored Emerson's knot of uncertainty, making her wonder if this was a glimpse of the world she tried to flee.

At the center of the room, on a large bed that dwarfed anything Emerson had ever seen, a woman lay alone. The bed was draped in rich, dark velvet, its edges gilded with intricate carvings that caught the flickering light of hundreds of beeswax candles. Surrounding the bed were chairs, arranged in a wide circle like an audience awaiting a performance. Emerson counted them quickly. Twenty, at least. Nearly every chair was filled, mostly by men, though a few women sat among them. All were dressed like her, in dark cloaks and masks that obscured their identities, their silhouettes blending into the dimness.

But the woman on the bed was different. She was on full display, her body bare and unapologetic, her skin glowing under the soft light that seemed to pool around her.

She lay like an offering on a stage, the center of a silent, rapt audience. The woman's movements were deliberate, her hands running across her body. Her fingers tracing slow, practiced circles at her core, each motion drawing a soft gasp from her lips. Emerson recognized the rhythm, the way it mirrored the sensations Lathen coaxed from her own body. The woman's other hand kneaded one of her full breasts, her fingers digging into soft flesh as her back arched off the bed, her hips rising to meet her touch. Her legs were spread wide, her feet planted firmly against the velvet, using the leverage to push herself deeper inside, closer to ecstasy. The sheet beneath her twisted and bunched, caught in the frantic rhythm of her movements. Her moans, low and unrestrained, filled the room, each one a pulse that seemed to vibrate through the air, drawing the audience deeper into her spell.

Yet the crowd remained still, their eyes fixed on her, their silence a stark contrast to the raw energy of her masterful performance. The woman's body was a study in contrast. Soft curves against the sharp angles of her movements, vulnerability laid bare under the weight of their gazes.

Emerson's breath caught as she watched, her feet rooted to the spot. The woman's unabashed pleasure stirred something in her, a mix of fascination and a faint, familiar ache. She had not realized she had stopped moving until Lathen leaned down, his breath warm against her ear.

"There are two empty seats if you wish to get closer," he whispered, his voice low and teasing.

Emerson gasped and turned to look at him, her eyes wide behind her mask.

Surely, he is not serious!

Lathen's expression was unreadable, but his lips curved in a faint, mysterious smile. He shrugged and gently tugged her hand, leading her across the grand arches of the open room toward another hallway. They had been down this way before, and Emerson assumed he was taking her to the Cantilever Chamber at the end. Instead, he stopped at the second door on the right and opened it for her.

Emerson peered inside, her heart still racing from the scene in the amphitheater. After what she had just witnessed, she braced herself for something astonishing. Instead, she found a simple bedroom. A four-poster bed stood at the center, its dark wood polished to a gleam, topped with a cozy blanket and fluffy pillows that invited touch. A padded bench sat at the foot of the bed, its upholstery a muted shade of burgundy. Along the wall, a small table held two chairs, their carved backs unassuming yet elegant. The room was almost mundane in its normalcy, a stark contrast to the decadence she had just seen. Emerson turned to Lathen, one brow raised in question.

"You were expecting something else, perhaps?" Lathen's voice carried a teasing lilt, his smile playful. "We can still go back and watch the performance, if you would prefer."

Emerson stiffened, standing taller as she walked into the room with her head held high. Whatever his plan was, it was obvious he was not going to hurt her. She removed her gloves, her fingers brushing against the soft fabric of the blanket as she moved to the bed.

I made a choice to run away and marry Lord Farnsworth. Lathen found out and was incredibly mad. Angrier than I have ever seen him. Yet, instead of punishing her, he brought her here, to this room. Yes, it was down here, at *Noir*, but the room could be in any house in London.

Emerson was confused. Not just because Lathen brought her here, but because a part of her felt a flicker of disappointment they were not in the Cantilever Chamber down the hall.

Is it because I wish to finish what was happening in my dream? Somehow, I know reality would be so much better. She shook her head to dispel the thought. It was foolish to imagine Lathen chaining her to some contraption, flogging her bare skin to prepare her for him, positioning her so her body was open and vulnerable, suspended from a wooden beam as he claimed her until she shattered around him, helpless to do anything but surrender to the pleasure.

No! She shook her head again, more forcefully this time.

The door closed behind her, and Lathen stepped closer. She knew this was an important moment. She could keep facing away, or she could turn and meet his gaze.

She turned.

chapter thirty-five

Lathen watched Emerson's face when she first saw the room. Her shock amused him. Now, as Emerson faced him, holding her breath, he wondered if he had made the right choice. Tonight was not going to be about punishment or pain.

Well, not too much. But I am still me.

Nor would it only be about passion. When they left this room tonight, there would be a new understanding between them. For better, or for worse. Lathen was not sure which.

Emerson licked her dry lips but said nothing. With her mask still on, she looked mysterious and sensual. He could not stop himself from lifting his hands to cup her cheeks briefly. Then he pushed her hood back to reveal her hair. It was still up in a tight twist at the top of her head. He began looking for the pins holding it in place and pulled them out. One by one. Her long dark curls began to fall past her shoulders and into the folds of the cloak. He wanted the cloak gone, so he undid the clasp that held it at her neck and let it drop to the ground in a soft rustle.

Next was the dress. It was modest and simple. Light blue, with a few buttons at her back. He turned her gently, and she did not hesitate to help him. Once unbuttoned, the dress slipped down her arms and pooled at her feet with the cloak. While her back was still facing him, Lathen went ahead and untied her stays. Soon, Emerson was standing in only her undergarments and hose. Lathen could not help but remark to himself how erotic she looked. He did not wish to keep it to himself.

"*Nyx*, I have never seen anyone so beautiful as you are now." It was simple and direct.

Emerson blushed and lowered her eyes shyly for a moment, but she did not move to cover herself. Instead, she lifted her arms to Lathen's cravat and tugged at one of the ends. He let her undress him as he had just done to her. She stepped closer to undo the long line of buttons on his lawn shirt, then pushed the shirt and his coat off his shoulders in one movement. As though she was in too great a hurry to take them off him one at a time.

Once Lathen was standing in only his breeches and boots, Emerson looked a bit unsure. Looking around for a moment, she seemed to come to a decision. She pushed Lathen toward the long bench at the foot of the bed. If Lathen did not want to go, he would have been strong enough to stop it, but he did not. He let her do as she wished and sat down where she wanted him.

Emerson bent and made to pull off Lathen's tall leather boots. It was a bit difficult, but she eventually managed before she moved on to his breeches. This she was familiar with. She opened one side and then the other and then pulled the front flap forward. Lathen's manhood was already hard and straining toward her, and she licked her lips again. Without a word, she dropped to her knees and grasped him tightly with both of her hands. Her tongue came out to give soft fluttering licks all around his wide head before she opened her mouth wide to accommodate his girth. She moved down as far as she could, until the tip of his member pushed against the back of her throat and made her eyes water, then she moved back.

Lathen reached forward and grasped Emerson's hair so he could see her clearly. She had him in her mouth. Just as he had first shown her.

Actually, she is doing more than what I taught her! Lathen marveled as he watched.

He had never come across a woman so eager to please him. He had been with too many women to count, but it never felt the way it felt with Emerson. She was naturally enthusiastic, and had a keen instinct for how to touch him in ways that made him feel like he was about to come undone.

"Yes, *Nyx*, just like that," he encouraged her and let his head fall back. But he did not want to come so quickly. He wanted to make this time together last. He tried to pull Emerson back with her shoulders, but she let out a small protest and held tightly to him, increasing her suction. Like a tiny animal mewling for something it desperately needed.

Lathen wove his fingers in Emerson's hair and pulled. Hard. She hissed and finally let go and sat back on her heels. Though she also looked up at him with frustration.

Instead of explaining to her why he stopped her, Lathen stood and bent down to pull her up. He lifted her under her arms and tossed her onto the soft bed as she shrieked in surprise. She landed with a bounce and Lathen moved to slide up on top of her. He kissed her softly once while staring into her eyes, his own expression blazing with obvious desire.

Perhaps this was not the right thing to do. Certainly, it was not going to fix their problems. It was not going to make her suddenly able to accept him. Nor would it make him want to marry her. Yet for that moment, Emerson knew they both needed this. They needed to feel the touch of one another. To have this close connection. More than just a quick dalliance in a locked room.

Lathen kissed her again. This time, she opened her mouth and let him in. Their tongues intertwined and danced. Lathen raised his hands into her hair and again pulled. But it was to position her mouth the way he wanted. She moaned and tilted her hips in response. Her hands rose to his naked back, and she scratched downward with her nails, relishing his warm skin. Lathen groaned and lifted his head.

"Now, now, do not draw blood," he chuckled.

Emerson moved her nails down to Lathen's ass and pulled him closer. The feeling of his hardened member pressing against her was tantalizing, but it was not enough. She pulled him again, digging her nails in even deeper.

Lathen's response was to lean back so he could pull her chemise down below her taut breasts. He bent forward and enveloped one in his mouth and drew on it deeply.

Emerson let out a garbled moan of desperation and she moved her hands to his head. Her fingers wove into his hair, and she barely had time to acknowledge how soft it was before he released her from his mouth with a pop and moved to do the same to her other breast. One of his hands moved to find the small button that held her lace underwear at her hips. When he found it, he pulled them down just far enough for him to slip his hand over her core. Emerson was ready for him. She was wet and dripping in need. He barely slid his finger over her before she gasped, shaking as she came apart. When he slid down further and entered her with two of his fingers, she exploded. It always amazed Emerson every time she had an orgasm, but this time she was almost embarrassed by how fast it happened.

He only needs to look at me and I am wet for him. He only needs to kiss me once, touch me once, enter me once. And I am completely undone. How am I to live without this? To marry another when I know how this is with him.

Before Emerson could dwell on it further, Lathen pulled her upright and swept her undergarments from her completely. Until she was standing there in nothing but her hose with their tied ribbons around her thighs, and the black mask.

Emerson's legs were wobbly, and she was still euphoric after her orgasm. She did not notice anything was different until Lathen pushed her down again. This time with her face downward. Before she realized his intent, Lathen pulled her arms outward like a star, and he attached one of her wrists to a leather cuff. Emerson lifted her head and looked over at it as though she could not place it. It had obviously been there all along, but she had been oblivious to everything except Lathen.

Apparently, the boring bed is not so ordinary after all.

Her other wrist was bound as well, and Emerson lay there, watching as Lathen did it. She was not worried or scared. Instead, a delicious clenching of her womanhood nearly overwhelmed her, and a shiver of excitement ran down her exposed back.

"I suppose you are wondering what is to come next. After all, you deliberately defied me again, *Nyx*. I sometimes think you do these things on purpose. Just to get my attention. Perhaps this is only a foolish wish on my part, but how do I make you understand I am always paying attention to you? I see everything you do."

As he spoke, Lathen was wandering around the room. Emerson heard him opening and closing something, then he moved back toward her. He began to stroke her back. Not with his hand. He had something soft and leather, trailing and swishing over her skin. When he was done speaking, he lifted it and let it fall onto the bedcover next to her body so she could see what it was.

Emerson gasped. It was a flogger. Eerily, it looked like the one she dreamt of while she was sleeping in the coach. It had an ornate silver handle, with long, black leather tresses. It was close to her face, and she could smell the tanned leather and count each strand as it fell against the others.

Lathen let her observe it for a few moments, then trailed it over her arm. She lost sight of it as it moved to her back again. She turned her head when he moved to her other arm so she could continue to watch.

Emerson felt weight shifting the bed as Lathen climbed onto it with her, but she could not see him, and once he moved the flogger again, she was blind to what he was doing. Except that she could feel each movement on her skin. She probably ought to have been scared or at least felt helpless. Instead, Emerson felt alive. Each time Lathen touched her, it was like a new mystery. A secret that he was sharing with her.

When Lathen finally raised his arm up high and brought the flogger down with force, it was shocking, and Emerson let out a yelp. Not because it hurt her, but because she was not expecting it.

It landed on her bottom. She tensed and tried to turn, but the leather cuffs at her wrists made it impossible.

"Lathen," she cried breathlessly.

Lathen let the flogger fall again. This time harder.

"What did you call me?" Lathen's voice had changed. Emerson recognized the commanding tone immediately.

"Master," she moaned instead, "please." She did not know what she was begging for.

Is it for him to stop? Or to go on? Or perhaps to release me, so I can watch?

Lathen seemed to understand she was confused.

"Please, what?" he asked darkly, "what do you want, *Nyx*?"

He lifted his arm and let it fall again. The flogger made a low whistling sound as it went through the air and fell to her backside again. It stung, but it still was not overly painful. Instead, it made her skin tingle, and she could feel the sensation spread all over. Even her toes started to curl, and her knees were messing up the bedding as they lifted and sawed up and down.

Again, and again, and again.

Lathen lifted the flogger, only to bring it down onto her back. The soft leather made thwacking noises, filling the room. Every so often, Lathen would pause to ask the same question.

"What do you want, *Nyx*?"

Her head thrashed back and forth. She had no answer to give him.

What can I say? I do not know what I want. He is sitting next to me, hitting me with a flogger, and I do not want him to stop.

Emerson knew, with every fiber of her being, that if she asked him to stop, he would. She let him continue. Because with every strike, her entire body lifted from itself. The tingling warmed her, the blood rushing to her skin, turning her liquid. If he kept going, she was going to orgasm just from the contact.

"You!" She suddenly realized what she wanted, and she screamed out loud, "I want you, Master!"

chapter thirty-six

Lathen's heart stopped for a moment before it started to thud quickly. He did not know what to expect. If Emerson asked him to stop, he would have helped her get dressed, walked her back up to Nox House, lifted her into the carriage and taken her home. That would have been the end of it, a quiet retreat into the shadows of regret, leaving the unspoken hunger between them to smolder like an unquenched fire.

But this...

Relief swept through him, swiftly replaced with a yearning desire to give himself to Emerson. As she asked. Her words hung in the air like a velvet command, unraveling his last thread of restraint.

Lathen did not have enough patience to unstrap the cuffs on Emerson's wrists, his fingers trembling with barely leashed urgency as he imagined the marks they would leave on her pale skin, a brand of his dominance etched into her flesh.

Instead, he tossed the flogger aside, grabbed her hips, and pulled her to her knees. Her chest and head were still down on the bed, but he did not care. Actually, in this position, her back arched sharply and her bottom was forced into the air, giving him access to her glistening core, her arousal dripping like dew in the candlelight. He felt compelled to taste her, to devour the essence of her surrender. He licked up from her clit to her opening, his tongue insistent, savoring the earthy sweetness of her as he dipped deep inside, plunging into her velvet heat that clenched around him greedily, her inner walls fluttering in desperate need.

Emerson moaned and did her best to push back against him, but she could not get any purchase with her arms spread wide, the cuffs holding her in exquisite submission. She had to take everything he was giving her, and he was grateful for it, the power dynamic sending a dark shiver of pleasure through him, his cock throbbing painfully against the confines of his breeches as he feasted on her, lapping at her with long, languid strokes that made her thighs quiver and her breath hitch in ragged sobs.

Lathen rolled over, spreading Emerson's legs until she was practically astride his face. He reached up and grasped her bottom, pulling her closer to his mouth, until her slick core smothered him with intoxicating heat. Emerson groaned deeply, her hips swiveling of their own accord, rubbing across his lips in a frantic grind. Faster and faster, her movements growing wilder, more desperate, chasing her release under his merciless tongue that flicked and circled her swollen nub, sucking with expert precision. Then, without warning, he lifted her and moved away, leaving Emerson wanting, her whimper echoing off the stone walls like a siren's plea.

"Please," she moaned, "Master." The words dripped from her lips like honeyed submission, a dark invocation stoking the flames of his dominance, making his blood roar.

Lathen knew exactly what she was begging for this time. He did not disappoint her. He came up behind, lifted her hips exactly how he wanted them, angling her with forceful hands that dimpled her skin, and slammed into her with a single, brutal thrust that buried him to the root in her welcoming depths.

Emerson screamed loudly at the intrusion while she pushed back to let him in even deeper, her body arching like a bowstring pulled taut, her inner muscles clenching around his thick length in a vise of silken heat. He stayed where he was for a moment, letting her adjust to having him inside her. She was so tight, he knew his large member was stretching her to her limits, making her ache with exquisite pain that would blur the line between torment and ecstasy, her juices coating him in a slick sheen easing his possession. He also felt the beginning quiver of another orgasm tightening around him, her body betraying her impending surrender with rhythmic pulses that pulled him deeper.

"Oh. My. God." Emerson murmured into the pillow, her voice muffled and broken, a prayer of overwhelmed bliss that sent a jolt straight to his mind.

Lathen shook with the effort to hold still, his muscles corded and straining, sweat beading on his brow as he fought the primal urge to ravage her without mercy. He waited until he heard her exclamation, then he let himself go, unleashing his passion. He pulled back until he was nearly out, the drag of his shaft against her sensitive walls drawing a keening whine from her throat, then pushed back in as deep as he could go. Which was all the way to the hilt because of the angle of Emerson being on her knees, with her head on the bed, her ass presented like a dark offering in the flickering light, making him think of other ways he wanted to possess her. He dug his fingers deeper into her hips at the idea, and pulled back again, then crashed back home with a force that thrust her forward.

Emerson was moaning wordlessly, forced to take everything he was giving her, her cries a symphony of raw, unfiltered passion that fueled his relentless pace. Suddenly, Lathen raised his hand and slapped her on the buttock. Once. The sharp sting bloomed across her skin like a brand, turning it a rosy pink that made his mouth water. Twice. The second impact echoed through the room, her flesh shaking enticingly under his palm, her gasp turning into a throaty moan. On the third loud crack, his hand connecting with a resounding smack that reverberated in the air, Emerson screamed as her orgasm bore down on them relentlessly, her body convulsing in waves of shattering ecstasy, her walls spasming wildly around him in a grip that nearly undid him. In the midst of her climax, as she shattered beneath him, Lathen traced a finger along the shadowed temptation of her rear. He teased the puckered entrance with a feather-light touch before pressing one digit into the tight, forbidden ring of her most intimate depths, invading her dark, velvet sanctuary with a slow, possessive glide designed to heighten her release to agonizing heights of shadowy pleasure.

Emerson was still coming when Lathen bent over her and unbuckled her wrists and let her go, his breath hot against her neck as he freed her, only to recapture her in new ways. He pulled out of her only long enough to flip her over onto her back and spread her thighs wide before he slid back inside, her body still quaking with aftershocks, her slick folds parting eagerly for him once more. She was still throbbing, and her eyes were unfocused and glazed over, lost in the haze of multiple peaks, her lips swollen and parted in silent invitation.

He was not done with her yet.

Lathen's hands, warm and deliberate, glided to Emerson's breasts, his touch igniting another spark across her skin, an energy that ran through the haze of her lingering ecstasy, rekindling the embers of her desire with a dark, intoxicating current that pulsed like a living thing beneath her flesh. Her nipples, already taut with anticipation, responded eagerly as he captured them between his fingertips, pinching with a precise intensity that sent a sharp jolt through her, making her arch closer, her spine curving in a desperate offering to his command, her body a willing supplicant to his unspoken demands. The sensation was a delicious blend of pleasure and pain, her nerves alight with the contrast, each nerve ending singing a duet of torment and bliss that made her breath hitch and her pulse race erratically.

Emerson's eyes refocused, locking onto Lathen's, and her breath caught in her throat, a gasp trapped by the weight of his gaze. His amber, commanding eyes held a hunger that mirrored her own, a primal need that burned through the shadows. Yet she had not fully descended from the peak of her last climax, her body still trembling, leaving her raw and vulnerable, every inch of her body laid bare to him.

His desire, however, was an undeniable force, a tide pulling her under, dragging her into depths she had not dared to explore until this moment, where the line between surrender and power blurred into something dangerously, deliciously undefined, a realm where she was both captive to his will and liberated by the intensity of their connection.

He drove into her with a slow, deliberate thrust, his body meeting hers with such depth that he touched the very core of her womanhood, the invasion both punishing and reverent, as if he were claiming every hidden part of her soul with each measured stroke, his member filling her with a fullness that bordered on exquisite agony.

A scream tore from her lips, raw and unfiltered, as the sensation overwhelmed her, her voice echoing in the shadowed chamber like a primal hymn to their shared descent, a sound that sank into the heavy air, thick with the scent of their mingled arousal. The sharp pinch at her nipples seemed to reverberate deep within, as if an invisible, erotic string tethered the two points of her body, each pulse of pain amplifying the pleasure coursing through her core, a molten current that threatened to unravel her completely, her senses drowning in the heady mix of his dominance and her yielding.

The sensations wove together, creating a symphony of intensity that left her shaking, her skin flushed and slick with sweat, every inch of her hypersensitive to his touch, his scent, the very air that seemed to throb with Lathen's command, a palpable force that wrapped around her like a velvet chain.

Emerson's mind spun, grappling to make sense of the whirlwind consuming her, a tempest of conflicting desires tearing at the edges of her carefully constructed resolve, each thrust and touch peeling back the layers of her propriety to reveal a rare, untamed woman beneath. Her body betrayed her attempts at control, already building toward another crescendo, the coil of pleasure tightening low in her belly with a ferocity that stole her breath, a pressure so intense it felt as if her very essence might shatter under its weight. This time, it was fiercer, higher. As if Lathen had unlocked another hidden depth within her, a secret chamber where her truest, most untamed desires lay waiting, now unleashed by his relentless mastery. His every movement a calculated stroke to draw her deeper into his world.

Her hips, once steady, faltered in their rhythm, moving erratically as her moans grew louder, more desperate, losing all coherence, spilling from her lips in broken syllables that pleaded for mercy and more all at once. The room closed in, the flickering candlelight casting long shadows dancing across the stone, mirroring the chaos within her. Her mind nearly broke with the realization that this was no mere act of passion but a claiming of her very soul.

"Lathen..." she gasped, forgetting to call him Master, a slip of rebellion born from her overwhelmed body, "...please." It was a fragile plea swallowed by a storm of sensation, her voice a confession of her surrender, unraveling any defense she had left. The word hung in the air, a delicate admission that she craved him beyond the roles they played, beyond the masks and the games. It was something real, a connection that terrified and exhilarated her in equal measure.

Everything was wild now. Untamed, raw, and edged with a sweet ache pulsing through her veins like a forbidden melody, each note a reminder of truths she could no longer deny. The pain was no longer just pain. It was a catalyst, heightening every touch, every movement, transforming each sensation into a sharp, exquisite note in the symphony of their union, a harmony resonating in her bones.

When Lathen released her nipples, a hot rush of blood flooded her breasts, the sudden warmth sending a shockwave through her, a visceral jolt that made her gasp as if surfacing from underwater, her body arching involuntarily as the sensation rippled through her like a tide. The echo of that release surged to her core, a rushing wave that pushed her over the edge once more, her body shattering into a blinding climax, every muscle tensing as pleasure consumed her, her inner walls spasming around him in a desperate, rhythmic grip that seemed to pull him deeper into her essence, a claiming as much hers as his. In that same moment, she felt Lathen's own release, a warm, answering flood that mingled with her own, sealing their connection in a shared surrender, his seed a dark, primal claim marking her as his in ways transcending the physical, binding them in a moment of unspoken intimacy that left her shaking with the weight of its significance.

chapter thirty-seven

Emerson's cheek pressed against Lathen's broad chest, the steady thrum of his heartbeat slowing beneath her ear, a rhythm that steadied her amidst the storm of sensations still coursing through her. His breaths, once ragged with exertion, now softened into a calm cadence, though the heat of his skin still radiated against hers, a lingering fire making her pulse quicken with unspoken need. Somehow, in the midst of their climax, Lathen had maneuvered them, flipping their positions so Emerson now rested atop him, her body molded to his, her curves pressed flush against the hard planes of his form. He remained inside her, his arousal only slightly softened, filling her with a delicious fullness pulsing with lingering desire, a decadent ache throbbing deep within her core, teasing her with possibilities. Despite the tender ache between her thighs, a greedy spark ignited within her, a ravenous hunger curling low in her belly, whispering of pleasures yet to be claimed.

I want more.

Testing her power, she shifted her hips subtly, a teasing roll that drew a sharp hiss from Lathen's lips, the sound a low, primal growl sending a thrill of triumph through her, her body wondering at what control she could wield over him in this fleeting moment.

"I guess I am not the only one," she murmured, her voice low and playful, a mischievous, untamed glint dancing in her eyes.

The sensation of dominance surged through her, intoxicating and bold, a heady rush that emboldened her to claim what she craved. She pushed herself upright, straddling Lathen as if riding a stallion, her thighs gripping his hips with newfound confidence, the muscles flexing with each deliberate movement. The image of herself in britches, commanding a bareback horse, flashed through her mind, and a soft giggle escaped her lips, the sound light yet laced with a sultry edge hinting at the fire simmering beneath her playful facade.

Lathen's amber eyes lifted to meet hers, a warm smile curling his lips, softening the hard edges of his features with a tenderness that made her heart stutter.

"You are alright?" His voice was a tender caress as he reached up, tucking a wayward strand of her black hair behind her ear, his fingers lingering against her flushed cheek. The touch was a delicate contrast to the raw intensity of their earlier passion, yet no less potent in its intimacy.

"Oh, yes," Emerson replied, her grin wicked as she leaned forward, deliberately shifting her hips again to tease him, the slow grind against his pelvis sending a jolt of pleasure through her, making her breath catch. "Master," she added, her tone dripping with playful defiance, knowing the word would stir him, waking a beast that craved her own submission.

Lathen's eyes fluttered shut, briefly savoring the exquisite friction, a low groan rumbling from his chest as his hands quickly found her hips, gripping them firmly to still her movements, his fingers digging into her flesh with a possessive edge that made her gasp.

"Emerson, we need to talk," he told her, his voice strained, a plea for her to focus, yet revealing how deeply she affected him.

"We can talk later, Master," she purred, her eyes gleaming with mischief. "I am not done with you yet."

Emerson had no interest in conversation. Not now, when her body still burned with insatiable want, her core aching with the memory of his possession. His grip might have pinned her hips, but her hands were free, and she intended to use them. Her long hair cascaded around her like a silken cloak, parting naturally to reveal her breasts, their pert nipples standing proud and begging for attention. Curious and emboldened, she mimicked his earlier touch, taking her nipples between her fingers and pinching them firmly. The sensation was not as sharp as his touch, but it sent a warm ripple of pleasure through her, coaxing a soft moan from her throat. More thrilling, though, was the way Lathen's eyes darkened, his pupils dilating, his gaze fixed on her hands as if hypnotized. Emerson felt both worshiped and desired.

Lathen's resolve wavered, and his hands rose to cover hers, guiding her fingers with a gentle pressure, amplifying the sensation. His touch was a silent command deepening the ache within her, her breasts tingling with the heat of his palms. Seizing the moment, Emerson lifted her thighs, sliding up his length before dropping back down, the slow, deliberate motion drawing a guttural groan from Lathen, fueling her audacity. His hands fell away from her breasts, drifting to her waist as he watched her with near reverence, making her feel like a goddess.

His goddess. His Nyx.

Emerson's movements were clumsy at first, unpracticed, and she winced once when she took him too deeply, the stretch bordering on pain, a delicious burn that made her cry out. But her enthusiasm was boundless, her body driven by an instinctive need to chase the pleasure building within her, each rise and fall a step closer to ecstasy.

One of Lathen's hands roamed to her abdomen, the other to her chest, guiding her with a gentle nudge to lean back.

"Like this," he murmured, his voice husky with desire, a low growl sending a shiver through her core, his words both instruction and seduction.

The new angle shifted him inside her, his length brushing against a sensitive spot that made her gasp, a spark of pure bliss making her eyes flutter shut. Emboldened, she gripped his thighs for leverage, lifting herself high before sinking down slowly, each descent sending sparks of ecstasy through her core, her body trembling with the intensity of the sensation.

The tip of him rubbed against something she had not known existed, a hidden trigger that sent waves of pleasure radiating through her, and when she realized the angle was the key, her eyes widened with delight, a wicked smile curving her lips. She quickened her pace, dragging herself along his length, chasing the electric sensation, her breaths coming in short, desperate pants, her body slick with sweat and desire.

Lathen watched her, seemingly captivated by her unbridled passion, his amber eyes burning with a mix of awe and ownership, as if she were both his conquest and his queen. His fingers found the bundle of nerves nestled in her curls, swollen and slick with their combined arousal, the touch sending a shock through her, making her hips buck. He traced small, deliberate circles over the sensitive bud, watching her hips swivel instinctively as she sought the perfect pressure, each stroke a masterful tease pushing her closer to the edge, her body trembling under the onslaught of sensation.

"Oh. My. God!" Emerson gasped, her voice a garbled plea as her head fell back, her spine arching until her tight nipples pointed skyward, her body an instrument of surrender and strength. Her hair fell back, spilling across his legs. Her hips jerked forward, grinding hard against his fingers, demanding more with every movement, her body a live wire of need, each touch amplifying the fire threatening to consume her.

Lathen's restraint suddenly snapped, a roar escaping his mouth as his control shattered. With a swift motion, he sat up, his hands seizing her waist as he flipped her onto her back, the sudden shift making her gasp, her breath catching at the raw power in his movements, a dark promise of what was to come. He spread her legs wide, the position exposing her completely to his gaze, her core glistening and vulnerable under his scrutiny. He drove into her with a force that stole her breath, each thrust deeper, harder, hitting that sensitive spot with unrelenting precision, the rhythm a relentless assault on her senses. Her body arched beneath him, her nails digging into his shoulders as she surrendered to the onslaught of sensation, her moans escalating into cries filling the room. His visceral moans joined her, a primal cacophony of their shared hunger. Harder and higher, each thrust pushed her closer to oblivion, her body trembling on the brink of another shattering release. Until she was screaming as she came apart once more, her climax a blinding wave destroying her, her inner walls clenching around him in a desperate, pulsing grip, her voice a raw hymn to the dark, consuming passion that bound them in this moment of exquisite surrender.

chapter thirty-eight

The room, once charged with restless tension and unspoken anticipation, now cradled a delicate intimacy, a sanctuary woven from the raw vulnerability of their shared experience. The air felt soft, almost tangible, a cocoon of entwined breaths, each exhale a testament to their closeness. Lathen and Emerson lay together, their bodies still slick with sweat, cooling slowly in the silence. Their minds, however, were far from still. Reflection twisted their thoughts, each grappling with unspoken questions.

Emerson's thoughts were a tempest, a swirling chaos of emotions she could not fully grasp. Her heart raced as she replayed the night in vivid detail, her body still humming with echoes of passion. Every moment was etched in her consciousness. The way Lathen's hands claimed her. The feeling of leather on her back. How her own body betrayed her fears and her ultimate surrender to desire. She had been so certain Lathen's talk of his 'needs' meant something harsh, something that would shatter her boundaries and leave her hollow and broken. When he spoke of pain, her mind had conjured visions of cruelty and unyielding dominance that would strip her of herself. She had braced herself for a breaking point, a moment where she would be forced to recoil, to flee from the intensity she feared would consume her.

But tonight?

I wanted it. I wanted it all.

The realization sent a shiver coursing through her, not entirely unpleasant but laced with a thrilling edge of danger, like standing on the precipice of a cliff, the wind tugging at her resolve. Her body had responded to him in ways she had not anticipated, her skin alight with every touch, every press of his body against hers. The sharp sting of his fingers on her nipples had been a jolt, a spark that ignited a fire deep within her core. His deep, deliberate thrusts had filled her so completely, each movement a revelation of pleasure that bordered on overwhelming. She had not only endured them, she craved them, leaned into them with a hunger that startled her.

Was he right about me all along? The thought was both exhilarating and unsettling, as if Lathen had peeled back a layer of her soul she did not know existed. Exposing an animalistic need.

She wondered if this fierce, uninhibited version of herself was who she truly was, or if Lathen had unlocked a hidden part of her, a secret self that thrived on the intensity of their connection. Her fingers fidgeted with the edge of the sheet, twisting the fabric nervously, though she longed to trace the contours of his skin instead, to draw slow, teasing circles across his chest and feel the heat of him beneath her touch. She wanted to voice the questions burning in her mind, to shatter the silence and demand clarity about what this night meant. For them, for her. But the words felt too heavy, too raw, caught in her throat like a secret she was not ready to confess.

Or perhaps it is his answers I am afraid to hear.

Lathen, too, was lost in his own labyrinth of thoughts, his mind a tangle of satisfaction and unexpected wonder. The night had unfolded far differently than he imagined when he first saw her in the back garden. In that moment, he envisioned something darker. There was a need to dominate, to bend her to his will, to shape her into the submissive partner he always thought he wanted. Control had been his goal, a way to assert his power and mold her into his vision of perfection.

But when the moment came, the idea of forcing Emerson, of breaking her spirit, felt wrong. Repulsive, even. Instead, their connection had been a revelation, a dance of mutual desire that defied his expectations. Letting Emerson be herself, being himself...it left him exposed. Now, as he lay beside her, his fingers tracing slow, reverent paths along the curve of her spine, he marveled at how natural it felt to simply *be* with her. Her softness, the quiet strength in the way she met his passion with her own, had unraveled him. Her body yielded to his, not out of submission but out of a shared, electric want. A rhythmic dance that pulsed between them, raw and unscripted.

She is not what I expected, he thought, his fingers pausing as realization settled deep within him, *but perhaps she is exactly what I need.* The admission was both comforting and disquieting, challenging the walls he had built around his heart, the rigid beliefs he held about control and power. Emerson gave herself to him, not as a conquest but as an equal, her enthusiasm and openness a gift he did not anticipate. It made him question everything he thought he knew about desire, about love.

The soft rustle of the sheets as Emerson shifted pulled him from his reverie. He wondered what thoughts danced behind her eyes, whether she was as stunned by the night's events as he was. He had expected resistance, perhaps even resentment, but instead, she embraced the moment, her body arching beneath his, her moans a symphony that still echoed in his mind. The memory of her, hips grinding against his, her tight nipples jutting forward as she teased herself, the slick heat of her arousal coating his manhood, stirred him even now, his body responding with a fresh wave of desire.

Lathen's hand resumed its slow journey along her back, savoring the warmth of her skin, the gentle curve of her hip beneath his touch. Without thinking, driven by an instinctive need, he reached for her hand, the one twisting nervously in the sheets, and guided it to his chest, pressing her palm against his heartbeat. He needed her touch, needed the reassurance of her presence to anchor him in this unfamiliar territory.

Through the haze of his thoughts, one question burned brighter than the rest. He knew he wanted Emerson as she was. She was fierce, honest, impetuous, and perhaps most important, unapologetically herself.

But does she feel the same? Could she accept the parts of him that were raw, unpolished, driven by needs even he was only beginning to understand?

"I am the way I am," he broke the silence, his voice carrying a rare vulnerability that surprised him. "Can you accept me for that?"

Emerson's eyes flicked to his, a mischievous spark igniting in their depths. "Only if you can keep up with me, *Master*," she teased, her voice light but laced with a challenge that sent a thrill through him.

"Emerson, please," he urged, his tone firmer now, though still soft. "I need you to hear me. This matters."

Her lips curved into a playful smile, but she shifted closer, her fingers tracing a slow, deliberate circle over his chest, her touch both teasing and calming. The gesture was a promise, a silent acknowledgment that she was listening, even if her mischief lingered. Their bodies, still entwined, spoke a language of their own. Her thighs brushed against his, the heat of her skin reigniting the embers of their earlier passion. The night had changed them both, and as they lay there, the unspoken questions between them began to take shape, demanding answers that would define what came next.

chapter thirty-nine

The sun was barely brushing the eastern windows with a faint glow as Emerson slipped back into the sitting room she shared with Hazel, her footsteps light to avoid waking her friend. The effort was pointless.

Hazel sat in front of the fire, a book open but unread on her lap, her eyes fixed on the flames. With a heavy sigh, Emerson eased the door shut and sank into the chair beside Hazel, her gaze drawn to the fire's hypnotic dance. The weight of the night pressed on her chest, urging her to speak. Not because Hazel would demand it, but because Emerson craved her friend's counsel to navigate the turmoil within her mind.

Where do I even start? she thought. *I could trace it back years, to when Lathen first stirred something in me, or leap to tonight, where everything unraveled.* The night's events felt like a knot she could not untangle alone.

"We made love once more," she began, her voice barely above a whisper. "I cannot seem to stop myself."

Hazel's eyes flicked to her, curiosity mingling with concern. "He took you to Nox House?"

"No, we went below again. To *Noir*." Emerson's cheeks warmed at the memory.

Hazel said nothing, her gaze returning to the fire, her silence heavy with unspoken thoughts.

"I wanted him," Emerson added softly, needing to clarify. "He did not force me. I chose it."

Hazel turned back, her eyes glistening with unshed tears. She opened her mouth to speak but faltered, the words caught in her throat.

"Oh, Hazel," Emerson came closer, leaning over to wrap her friend in a comforting hug. "What is wrong?"

Hazel mumbled something, her words muffled against Emerson's cloaked shoulder, lost in the fabric.

"What, darling?" Emerson pulled back, searching Hazel's tearful eyes with concern.

"I am...so very...sorry," Hazel blurted, her voice breaking between soft sobs, her hands trembling as she clutched Emerson's arms.

"Sorry for what?" Emerson asked, her brow furrowing. "I chose to be with him. He would have let me leave at any moment. I know that in my heart."

Hazel's gaze dropped, her voice barely audible. "I betrayed you, Em. I was the one who told His Grace you were planning to run away with Lord Farnsworth."

Emerson froze, the revelation hitting like a cold wave. The night had been so consuming. Lathen catching her in the garden. His anger, their passion, the way he held her after. His words about acceptance. She had not paused to question how he knew her plans. Her mind raced, piecing together Hazel's confession, but the sting of betrayal faded quickly. It did not matter. Not now. She would have been days away from a loveless marriage to Lord Farnsworth, a man she did not care for, did not even think of during her night with Lathen. Not once.

It has always been Lathen, she realized. For years, every reckless act, every flirtation, every attempt to run. They had all been to capture his attention, to provoke him into pursuing her. *Even trying to marry another was to force him to stop me.*

"Hazel," Emerson said, leaning forward to cover her friend's trembling hand with her own, "it is alright. You did the right thing."

Hazel looked at her, eyes wide and red rimmed, searching for sincerity. "Em, are you sure? I feel wretched."

Emerson squeezed her hand, her voice firm but gentle. "You saved me from a terrible mistake. I do not love Farnsworth. I never did. I never *could!* I feel for him with friendly affection, if that. But I need more. You have always said I deserve love, and you were right."

"I only wanted what is best for you, Em," Hazel's shoulders sagged in relief, a weak smile breaking through her tears. "I could not let you throw yourself away."

Emerson nodded, her heart swelling with gratitude for her friend's loyalty. Even when she did not understand she needed it most.

"I know. You are the wise one, Hazel, as always. While I am the impulsive fool. Running to Gretna Green would have been a complete disaster."

Hazel dabbed at her eyes, her smile steadier now. "What are you going to do now?" she asked, her tone pointed but soft, urging Emerson to confront the question she had been avoiding.

Emerson paused, her thoughts drifting back to Lathen. How his anger melted into tenderness, the way his hands had claimed her with a mix of ferocity and care.

"Honestly, I do not know," she admitted. "I believe there is a future for us, but I am still not sure if he sees it. When he parted, he told me I need to take him as he is, but he understands if I cannot."

Hazel frowned, leaning closer. "What does that even mean, Em? Take him as he is? That is so vague it is maddening."

Emerson gave a small, rueful laugh. "If I could answer that, Hazel, everything would be simpler. Lathen is...complicated. One moment he is fire, all anger and need, and the next he is holding me like I am the only one who matters."

"Do you love him?" Hazel reached for Emerson's hand, squeezing it tightly.

Emerson's breath caught, the question cutting through her haze. "I do," she whispered slowly, the words feeling like a confession. "But it scares me. I want him so much. I want this version of us, even the parts I do not understand."

They fell silent, hands clasped, lost in the moment.

"How do you feel about...what he does?" Hazel asked cautiously, her eyes searching Emerson's face. "The things he needs and where he takes you. Does it frighten you still?"

"It did, at first." Emerson blushed, her gaze dropping to their joined hands. "I thought his needs would break me. But I cannot explain it, Hazel. It is like the ache and the pleasure were one, and I wanted them both. They make me feel whole. He makes me feel whole."

Hazel's eyes widened, but she nodded, her expression softening. "Then you need to talk to him,

Em. If you love him, you owe it to yourself to understand what he is asking of you. And what you are willing to give."

A soft knock at the door startled them, their heads jerking toward the sound. It was far too early for visitors. Emerson rose, her heart pounding as she crossed the room and opened the door to find Lathen's aunt standing there in her nightclothes, a tightly tied robe cinched around her.

"Lady de Clare?" Emerson said, her voice tinged with shock.

"Hello, my dear," Lady de Clare replied, her tone polite but firm. "I am sorry to bother you at this hour, but I must speak with you. Would you come to my sitting room?" It was phrased as a question, but Emerson recognized the command. Even if it was given graciously.

Emerson nodded, casting a glance back at Hazel's surprised face before stepping into the hall, closing the door behind her.

chapter forty

Emerson followed Lady de Clare down the grand staircase, her chest tight with a mix of apprehension and curiosity. They walked into a cozy private sitting room. The space was a warm haven, adorned with rose colored chairs, a plush settee, and lush green plants basking in the soft light streaming through the south facing windows. The fire crackled in the hearth, its gentle pops and hisses filling the silence as they settled across from one another. Emerson's fingers twisted nervously in her lap, her mind still reeling from the night's events, unable to fully wonder why she was there. She waited, her breath shallow, for Lady de Clare to speak, unsure of what this conversation would unearth.

"You may call me Aunt Lillian," Lady de Clare started warmly, her voice cutting through the quiet with a gentle authority. "For the conversation we are about to have, it feels right. I want to discuss what happened tonight."

Emerson's cheeks flushed, a wave of heat rising as her thoughts spiraled. *What does she know? About* Noir, *the flogger, the way I surrendered to Lathen?*

Her throat tightened, but she forced herself to focus. There was more about tonight than her moments with Lathen. That must be what Lillian was referring to.

"Aunt Lillian," she finally began, her voice trembling, "I guess you heard about my attempt to elope with Lord Farnsworth. I assure you, I will not be trying that again. It was impulsive and thoughtless. I thought running away would free me, let me start anew, away from His Grace."

Lillian's brow arched in genuine surprise, her lips twitching with a hint of amusement. "Elope? No, my dear, I had not heard that tale." She leaned back, her eyes twinkling with curiosity. "But let us set that aside for now. I am more concerned about your late return to de Clare House with Lathen. And how he has been acting this season. Completely out of character, I might add, and it always seems to revolve around you."

"Oh," Emerson whispered, mortified, her hands clenching in her lap. The realization that their connection had been so visible, so exposed to others, sent a jolt of embarrassment through her. "I did not realize...I thought we were discreet."

Lillian leaned forward, patting Emerson's hand with a knowing smile. "Do not fret, darling. It was not you who made it so obvious. I have known Lathen his entire life, and he is predictable as the tides. Always composed, always in control. But these past months? He is different. Smiling at odd moments, stammering when your name comes up, watching you when he thinks no one notices. He turns away when you look, but his eyes linger, Emerson. He cares for you in a way I have never seen before. I do not mean just from him. I mean I have never seen someone care so much about someone else. And remember, I have seen a lot. It is one of those things that comes with age."

Emerson's breath caught, her heart quickening at the words. "His Grace? Truly?" she asked, her voice barely above a whisper, as if saying it louder might break the fragile truth.

"Oh, yes," Lillian chuckled, her eyes gleaming with amusement. "Lathen has always been guarded, shaped by my father's iron hand. He was molded to be cold and controlled, detached from an early age. My father ensured it. Nannies, tutors...no attachments were allowed. Mrs. Jaymeson, bless her, was dismissed for daring to show him affection, and she was not the only one. Lathen learned to keep everyone at arm's length, to shield himself from loss."

Emerson frowned, a memory surfacing. "Mrs. Jaymeson once told me she was sent away for being too kind to him," she said softly, her heart aching for the boy Lathen had been.

"My father was relentless," Lillian nodded, her expression tinged with sadness. "He tried first with my brother, but he escaped and Lathen became his new project. The other children, Lennox and Leighton, were left to us, thankfully. But it was not until school, with your brother and Lord Warwicke, that Lathen began to open up, to find a semblance of connection. Those friendships gave him a glimpse of joy, something my father could not take away."

"What about Lennox and Leighton?" Emerson asked, her voice curious. "He is so protective of them, so brotherly."

"It took time," Lillian admitted, her gaze softening. "He was afraid to care too deeply, especially after Lincoln."

"Lincoln?" Emerson's voice was soft, the name unfamiliar yet heavy with significance. "Who is he?"

Lillian's expression shifted, a veil of grief settling over her features. "Lincoln *was* Lathen's younger brother. They were only a year apart. Lathen adored him. Everyone did. He was a bright, loveable child, with a laugh that could melt even my father's stern heart, in his own way. But Lathen was caught neglecting his studies to play with him, and my father would not tolerate it. He sent my brother and his wife to another estate, taking Lincoln with them. Not long after, Lincoln caught a fever and passed away. Lathen was so young, but I have always believed he blamed himself, thinking his love caused it."

Emerson's heart clenched, the pieces of Lathen's guarded nature falling into place like shards of a broken mirror. Every time his eyes shuttered suddenly made sense.

"That is why he holds back," she murmured, her voice trembling with realization. Her words were more for herself than Lillian. "Why he says he cannot change, that I must take him as he is. He is afraid his love destroys."

"Exactly," Lillian sighed. "He is terrified to love. Afraid it will break him. Or someone he cares for. But with you, Emerson, he is different. You have cracked that shell, just as Leighton did with her stubborn charm. He is letting himself feel, and I think it scares him more than anything. But I see it. He is falling for you."

Emerson's mind raced, leaping from one revelation to the next. It explained everything. Lathen's need for control, his fear of marriage, of children, his insistence that she find someone else.

"Aunt Lillian, do you think he could love me? Truly love me, despite his fears?"

Lillian's eyes softened again, a knowing warmth in her gaze. "I think he already does, dear, but he is wrestling with it. He does not know how to love without fear. You are showing him it is possible, but he needs to believe it too. Do you not feel his love?"

Emerson blushed, her thoughts once again drifting to earlier that night. The way Lathen's hands bound her wrists, the sharp sting of the flogger against her skin, the heat of his body as he claimed her with deliberate, consuming thrusts.

Is that love? she wondered. But then she thought about after. When he held her. There was a moment when his eyes told her what his words could not.

"I do," she admitted, her voice barely audible. "I feel his love. I just wonder if I can be what he needs."

Lillian's expression turned fierce, her voice hard. "Emerson, you are enough as you are. The question is, can you trust him to meet you halfway? To love you without trying to control you completely? He is trying, I can see that, but he needs you to show him."

"I want to," Emerson's voice cracked. "But I am scared too. Of what it means to love someone like him, with all his complexities. His needs..."

Lillian tilted her head, her gaze probing. "His needs? You mean the way he loves, the way he expresses it? Tell me, dear, what exactly frightens you?"

Emerson's cheeks burned, realizing she almost said too much.

"I suppose I am scared I cannot love him the way he needs," she answered diplomatically.

Lillian nodded, her smile both understanding and encouraging. "Then you are already halfway there, my dear. Love is hard. Simply understanding that, knowing you must try, and not give up, is enough. And you must stop running from him, dear. Stop making him chase you. Instead, meet him halfway."

Emerson swallowed, her heart pounding. Lillian did not know how appropriate her words were. Yet they gave her hope.

Stop running away. Go to him.

Even now, with Lillian right there, Emerson desperately wanted to find Lathen. Her fingers itched to touch him, but she knew she had to wait for this meeting to end.

"You will know, your *heart* will know when it is right. I believe in Lathen, and in you," Lillian added, her voice steady. Then she paused, considering her next words. "You have both been shaped by fathers who failed you, who left you to navigate love and trust alone. I understand that. My own father ignored me, focused only on my brother and Lathen. Yours was absent in his own way, was he not?"

Emerson nodded, her throat tight, a sharp pang in her chest at Lillian's sudden change of subject.

"He was," she finally admitted with a confused frown. "I learned to rely on myself. Trusting Lathen feels like stepping off a cliff."

"Yet you are not alone in that leap, my dear. Lathen is taking it with you, even if he does not know how to land yet."

Rising, Lillian crossed to a wooden box over the mantle, lifting the lid and a hidden tray to reveal a stack of letters tied with a faded blue ribbon. She sifted through them with care, her fingers lingering on one, the paper aged and crackling as she turned it in her hands, as if weighing its significance.

"I am not sure if this is right," she hesitated, "but it might answer some of your questions, or stir up things you have buried to protect yourself. Either way, I pray it is for the best."

She handed the letter to Emerson, who took it with trembling fingers, as if it might catch fire in her hands. Her eyes fell to the scrawled address. Lady de Clare, with her father's name and Havenfield as the return. Her breath hitched, tears welling unbidden as the weight of her father's words loomed before her.

"Yes, dear," Lillian said softly, her voice filled with compassion. "It is from your father."

chapter forty-one

My dear Lady de Clare,

I sincerely hope this letter finds you well. I know it has been many years since we last spoke, but I heard you lost your brother recently, and I wished to send my deep regrets. He was a good friend to me for many years and brought many joyful moments during our shared youth. I well remember the last time we all met, when you were coming out in London. My own darling Imogen was delighted by your charm and once said you were the prettiest debutante she had ever seen. I am afraid I was always too filled with watching my beloved to notice, but I know she was usually right about such things.

As you probably heard, I lost my son a year ago. Your nephew, the new Duke of Windemere, was the one who brought him back to us, and I will be forever grateful to him. But that is not all I have to thank His Grace for. I am immensely glad he was such a good friend to my son. Kit was a gregarious boy, and your nephew always brought a bit of seriousness he sorely needed. He was always sure to remind my son of his responsibilities.

Never was that more apparent than when he came to Havenfield, two springs past, with my son. His Grace met my daughter, Emerson, on this trip, for the first time. To say he was appalled at her condition was an understatement. He lectured Kit and me on how we had both failed her. And he was quite right.

You see, I realized I had never even looked at my daughter since her birth. I had seen her, but never really looked at her. That day was the worst I ever experienced. My beloved, my Imogen, lost her life shortly after Emerson's birth. I held her in my arms, begging her not to leave me. But of course, it was her time to return to the Lord, and I could not stop it.

My Imogen, oh, how she loved music, and how she poured that love into the child she carried. In the months before Emerson's birth, she would sit at her piano, her fingers dancing over the keys, composing lullabies for our unborn child. She would laugh, her eyes alight, saying each note was a promise of awaiting love. I can still hear those songs in my mind, though they pain me now.

After Imogen's death, I stood before that piano, consumed by grief, and nearly smashed it to pieces, unable to bear its silent reminder of her joy. Instead, I locked it away, the room she once loved most a tomb.

When they put Emerson into my arms the next day, her red face was pinched, and she was screaming louder than any babe I ever heard. Then she suddenly stopped and opened her eyes to stare at me. They were Imogen's eyes staring up at me. Eyes like the lavender that grew in our eastern fields. I say grew because I had them all torn out after she died because they too reminded me of her.

I am not proud to say I was too broken to see them coming out of another's face. Even from my own child. I gave her back to the nurse and walked away. I crawled into a bottle and to be honest, I have been deep inside my cups for nearly twelve years.

Recently, however, it has caught up with me. The doctors tell me that I am soon to leave this world. My only consolation is I will soon be with my beloved Imogen. At least that is my hope. Perhaps that was always my hope, and it has taken this long to get my wish.

This will of course leave Emerson all alone in the world. We do not have any close family, as both Imogen and I were only children, and our parents have long since also left us. There are a couple of second and third cousins in the Americas I considered but dismissed, as they live in a place I could never imagine Emerson residing. A marshy land filled with fever, called Louisiana. She is an English rose, nay English lavender, and she belongs here. Her children belong here. At Havenfield. Perhaps to bring some life back into this place.

I have given a lot of thought to where she should go after I am gone. She deserves so much more than the indifference she has always received from me. I understand my weaknesses and heartbreak are no excuses for not being a proper father to her, and it is far too late for me to show concern. But alas, I feel my impending mortality has sobered me enough to really think of Emerson's future.

To that end, I reached out to your brother last year and received his help with securing a special remainder for Emerson. She will now be the Earl of Haven in her own right, with all the benefits which come with that. I also had my lawyers come last week and I updated my will. I am leaving everything to Emerson. I know this will bring her many suitors when she comes of age, and not all of them will have her best interests in their own hearts. So, I have also made His Grace, your nephew, her guardian. There will be many who will question why I have done this. After all, though I was once close with your family, especially your brother, we all know I lost touch long ago. And as far as your nephew is concerned, he has only come to Havenfield twice and only met Emerson once, I believe.

However, as I explained earlier, His Grace was the first person to show any concern for Emerson's future. Kit, my son, of course loved his sister deeply, but he also allowed her to run wild and found her unladylike ways to be amusing. He never thought to have anyone around who might teach her how to become a lady, or who could show her even the smallest facsimile of a mother's love. It was His Grace who really saw her and saw the need for such. He was the one who brought Mrs. Jaymeson into her life. I have taken the time to notice Emerson has blossomed in the last year since. Even after losing Kit, she has managed to survive because of having someone to show her love and hold her through it all. I can never express just how grateful I am to His Grace for that.

As for me, I still struggle to look at my daughter, because as she grows, her every look and mannerism is so much like my darling Imogen it breaks my soul. It is not fair to her in any way, I know this. But it is the truth. Besides, I feel it is for the best she will not miss me when I am gone. I will be the merest echo in her heart she may never hear. But if she does, the sound will hopefully not affect her over much.

She will move on, grow, and will have Mrs. Jaymeson to help her. I have made provisions for that dear woman to stay with Emerson until her dying day, or until she wishes to retire. It is my hope Mrs. Jaymeson will safeguard Emerson's happiness and growth into a woman, while His Grace ensures she is brought out into society properly and marries someone he approves of. Thus, Emerson will have a future worth something.

There is not much I can give her besides a title, money, and a home. But I am hoping I finally made the right decisions for her. Fatherly decisions.

I hope you can understand all I am saying, and you do not disapprove of me and my failures as a father too much. I also hope you will help your nephew with all I am asking of him. I know he is still a young man himself, and he has many new responsibilities that come with being a duke.

Perhaps, if it is not too much to ask, and honestly, I know it likely is, can you please watch out for her as well. Please see that she finds a husband worthy of her and makes her happy. Hopefully, one that is stronger than her father ever was. She is a good child and deserves all of this and more.

I thank you for your consideration and look forward to your reply, and I hope all is well with you and your family at this difficult time.

Yours in Friendship,
Christopher Haven
Earl of Haven

chapter forty-two

Emerson sat for some time, long after the sun finished rising, each ray a soft reminder of the world moving forward despite her inner turmoil, before she finally returned to her own rooms. She had long since read her father's letter, its creased parchment now resting on the small, ornate table beside her, the ink smudged in places her tears had fallen. Her heart was heavy with the weight of revelations she had not been prepared to face. Now, alone in her own dressing room, she sat before her mirror, the cool glass reflecting a version of herself she barely recognized. Her dark hair was disheveled after her night with Lathen, strands clinging to her damp cheeks, and her lavender eyes still shimmered with tears, their depths clouded with a sorrow she had not fully acknowledged until this moment.

She had started to cry as she was getting undressed and into her nightclothes, the soft silk of her gown whispering against her skin like a lover's caress, even though she had not realized the tears were falling until she caught sight of herself in the mirror's unforgiving surface. The reflection showed a woman caught in a storm of emotion, her face pale yet flushed with the rawness of grief and discovery, her kiss-swollen lips trembling as she traced the contours of her own features. She now understood her face echoed her mother's in a way that must have haunted her father daily, a mirror to a loss he could never escape.

Occasionally, he would be so drunk he would acknowledge her, his slurred words tumbling out in rare moments of vulnerability, telling her of her mother. He would say her laugh was a melody that could brighten the darkest days, her gentle touch a soothing balm for his restless spirit. Mostly it was talk of her eyes.

But that was the extent of their interactions, fleeting glimpses of connection drowned in the ocher of his vice, moments too brief to bridge the chasm between them. Mostly, she learned to avoid him as well, seeking solace beyond the confines of the manor, wandering the sprawling property where the air was crisp with the scent of apple blossoms and the earth was alive with the hum of life. A sanctuary where she could escape the weight of his absence.

She spent her days among the crofters, her hands stained with the juice of apples destined for the cider mill, her mind occupied with their laughter and labor, their simple joys a stark contrast to the shadowed halls where her father drowned his sorrows with that same cider.

She never would have supposed he had sobered up enough to make decisions regarding her future. She thought his mind was too clouded by drink to care, the assumption a bitter shield against the pain of his neglect. To be honest, she had been so preoccupied during that time, helping the crofters with planting, she barely remembered seeing her father in the weeks before his death. She certainly never realized how ill he was, how the sickness had crept into his body. Or that his final days were spent in a clarity that now reshaped her understanding of him.

Yet, here was proof he not only was thinking of her at the end of his life, he did what he thought was right for her. Ironically, she spent years being angry at him for making Lathen her guardian. In fact, she had thought it was only because Lathen's father was one of the few people her own father could remember from before he began to drink.

It was not like that, was it? He tried. Yes, he was who he was, and I cannot forget his weakness. However, he tried, and perhaps I can forgive.

She thought of his explanation about how Lathen brought Mrs. Jaymeson into her life. Lathen always seemed concerned for her. He was a strength, a presence, someone who changed her life for the better. Apparently, his concern and strength were enough to penetrate her father's haze of drink.

All this time. Lathen cared. And my father cared. He just could not show it. Lathen is not good at showing it with his words either. Instead, he shows it in his actions. Perhaps actions are better than words.

Emerson's mind found purchase and her thoughts winnowed their way to one distinct reflection she could not ignore.

Lathen cares, and so do I!

chapter forty-three

Even as Emerson's realization hit her, Lathen's words from earlier kept repeating in her head on a loop.

'I am the way I am. Can you accept me for that?'

After everything, it stuck with her the most. He did not want her to answer right away. He had brought a finger to her mouth, asking for her silence. She complied. Instead, she watched as he stood, their time that night coming to an end. She saw his body move like the animal he was, all sinew and muscle, as he dressed quickly in the candlelight. Then he helped her dress in silence and brought her home. They came in the front door, Giles seemingly unconcerned about how Emerson had managed to leave.

Now, after speaking to Hazel and Lillian, and reading her father's letter, she realized she could accept him. Exactly the way he was. After all, she spent the last seven years trying to be something she was not. Not her femininity. She felt like she had grown into her womanhood. But the need to be proper and ladylike all the time, especially before the *ton*, had strained her. To not be exuberant or free to do as she wished. All of it stifled her. So, asking him to change for her seemed wrong.

I can accept him. His sexual needs. His domineering nature. The Master. I want him exactly how he is.

Emerson trudged to her bed and lay down with her eyes closed. In the quiet of early morning, the chaos in her mind finally settled, and she knew what she had to do. Well, not what she *had* to do. What she *wanted* to do.

She got up again quietly. Slipped her nightdress off, pulled on a soft silk robe, and tiptoed quietly down the stairs, then down the hall to Lathen's chambers. She did not bother to knock for fear of others in the household hearing.

Inside, the heavy drapes were shut, and it was dark except for a single candle still burning on a small table and a fire that had burned to near embers. They cast a warm, moody flicker across the room and revealed Lathen was still awake as well.

He was sitting in a large high backed chair in front of the low fire, wearing only his unbuttoned white lawn shirt, leaving his chest bare, and breeches that were halfway undone and hanging low on his hips. His boots were removed and lay in a pile, and Emerson thought briefly even his bare feet were sensual and manly.

Lathen was holding a snifter of brown spirits, raised halfway to his lips, pausing as she entered the room. In his other hand was a fragrant cigar with smoke that was rising in a haze and made him look mysterious. Obviously, just as she was, he was being kept up by his own thoughts.

Lathen's brow rose as she came closer, and Emerson saw the day-old growth of his beard. It made the hollows of his cheeks and chin darken, and he looked almost piratical. Still, they both kept the silence.

Emerson watched his face as she reached down for the drink in his hands and took it from him. She took a large swallow. And almost lost all her poise when the whiskey inside scorched a path down her throat, straight to her stomach. She had been expecting brandy! In response, she noted Lathen's look, which she interpreted as respect. It emboldened her to take another drink before she turned to put the nearly empty glass on the table next to Lathen's chair.

Emerson untied her robe and pulled it back from her shoulders and let it fall to the floor. She heard Lathen's sharp intake of breath and had to smother an answering smile. The knowledge her nakedness affected him gave her the confidence she needed to continue.

Still not speaking, she came forward and crawled up onto his lap. All the while, they kept eye contact. Her moody lavender irises holding his intense amber gaze hostage. She felt a powerful surge of energy coursing through her body. Despite their earlier lovemaking, her core blossomed, making her almost desperate to feel his touch. He did not disappoint her.

As soon as she settled, Lathen put out his cigar. His arms snaked up, pulling her to him, and his mouth caught hers in a rough kiss, matching her own need. She could taste the earthy tobacco and spiced whiskey as his tongue swooped in and captured hers in a dance she was now familiar with.

Even though she knew the movements, there was a different feeling to this kiss. For the first time, she belonged in his arms. It felt right. As though all the questions of whether she should be there or not were answered.

Still, there were no words. They had spoken them all in the last months. This was about finishing what they started. It could be their beginning, if they wanted it to be.

Lathen took a moment to lean back, pulling his shirt off completely. Emerson's hands explored his chest, letting them drift lower. Then lower. Without hesitation, Emerson slipped open the last buttons on his breeches and as his hard manhood sprang free, she grasped it tightly and stroked him, root to tip, the way he liked.

"Fuck!" Lathen hissed between his teeth, the tendons in his neck jumping with restraint. His hands went to her head and tilted her face so he could kiss her deeper.

Lathen's hips moved slowly while she continued to caress him, tighter, bringing him to the brink. He growled suddenly and pulled Emerson's hands to the small of her back. A whimper escaped her, but her eyes gleamed with acceptance and desire.

She was so beautiful. Her lips red and soft from his kisses, parted slightly, begging him silently. Her perfect, petite breasts, heaving from her excitement, pushed forward from the position of her restrained arms, taunting him. Lathen lowered his head. First encircling the tip of one nipple with his tongue. Then blowing on it and watching while it hardened to a tight point. Before moving to the other and giving it the same treatment. He took his time, driving Emerson wild. She soon writhed on his lap, trying to pull her arms from his grip, but he kept her hands still. Scooping his free hand under her bottom, he rose to his feet, pressing her to him.

He strode quickly to his bed and laid her down on the soft mattress. He let go of her, stepping back so he could enjoy the sight of her on his bed before he slipped out of his breeches and climbed up to join her. He began kissing a path down to her abdomen and over to one of her hipbones, where he nipped at the hollows beneath. His hands slid to her knees where he grasped them roughly to push them apart and up high. He could see her beautiful entrance. It was nestled in her dark curls like a delicate secret only he could discover. The wetness on her upper thighs proved she was already burning for him, but he wanted her dripping and begging before he took her. He hoped to spare her as much pain as he could because his plan for her was going to be hard and fast.

His head dropped again and, much like when he kissed her, his tongue entered her deeply. He was ravenous, eating at her like a starved man. Sucking her nether lips and using his tongue to go around her budlike clit as it swelled and flowered for him.

Emerson grabbed his hair tightly in her fists, but he barely noticed. He had to use his own hands to hold her hips in place because she was lifting them almost violently to get even closer to him. Just as she was quivering, tightening, ready to explode, he stopped.

The memory of him not letting her come once before must have still been fresh. A fierce expression made her eyes gleam as she pulled back on his hair, exclaiming through clenched teeth, "You had better not halt!"

"Shh, *Nyx*, I promise," he whispered and grinned devilishly. No other woman would dare try that with him, but his night goddess dared such and more. She tugged one more time, making him wince, before she let him go. He climbed back up to look her in the eye. His look was its own question. The same as before.

Is this her answer? Can she accept me?

Emerson's response was to reach up and pull him down to kiss her again. She could taste her essence on his lips. It was a heady combination with whisky and tobacco. She was eager with desire and struggled to hold still when she felt him settle between her wet thighs. She spread them as wide as she could to accommodate his hips. His manhood lay heavily against her lower belly, making it clench with heated anticipation.

Lathen stopped kissing her and held her with a look. He braced himself on his elbows and his hands were at her scalp with his fingers woven into her black silken hair.

Without warning, he pulled his hips back and entered her deeply, in one swift motion. Emerson gasped as she felt him buried deep, stretching her with an almost unbearable fullness. It was painful, but it was the answer to the emptiness she had been feeling since he left her earlier.

Lathen stayed still, as though he was waiting for her to get used to him. Her hips began to make small circles. Testing. Then she tilted them to bring him deeper. With a groan, Lathen gathered her close, burying his face in her neck, and started to move.

It was a miracle. Emerson felt him push her thighs up and enter her even deeper, trying to sheath his whole length. For a moment she worried she might not be able to take all of him, but that fear was quickly quelled when she dug her heels into his ass and felt him grinding against that magic part of her that brought an explosion of color to her vision. Each time he withdrew, a breath of sadness escaped her, only to be dispelled with a moan when he slammed back home. Relentless, circling, panting. Emerson's nails dragged down Lathen's back, pulling him even closer.

Still inside her, Lathen rolled over, pulling her with him. He sat up, edging back until he was settled, sitting up against the headboard. He lifted her knees until they were spread wide, with her feet flat on the bed. It was an intimate position. Their faces were even, and they looked into one another's eyes, shared the same desperate breaths. Lathen leaned forward and kissed her roughly, but he left their pace up to her. Emerson wrapped her arms around Lathen's shoulders, and with her eyes still holding his, she slowly moved against him, tilting her hips and grinding her pelvis against his. Deciding what felt best to her.

Lathen looked like he was hypnotized. He moved his own hands to her hips, but it was to feel her motion, not to control her, his thumbs drawing small circles on her skin. Emerson felt something building in her. A zenith getting higher and higher.

Just as she was about to explode, Lathen sat up higher, grabbed her nape and pulled her onto him. He kissed her hard, swallowing the scream she could no longer contain. She came undone.

When the spasms hit, the force made Emerson lose her rhythm and she nearly fell from Lathen's lap. But he grabbed her ankles, spreading them apart for leverage. Then he grasped her hips and drew her even closer.

Once. Twice. He pulled her tight and lifted into her until he poured his seed inside. The sensation of being connected so completely was overwhelming and Emerson realized she wanted him to be inside her forever.

chapter forty-four

Lathen leaned back against the headboard, its familiar contour pressing into his spine as he drew a steadying breath. Emerson was still astride him, her feet braced on the rumpled sheets, knees bent high, her body a warm, living tether to his. Where they still joined, their connection pulsed in the quiet of the room. The candlelight flickered, casting her in a soft glow, her skin a canvas of shadow and light, her curves etched in silhouette.

He reached for her ankles again, guiding them forward with a gentle pull, wrapping her thighs around his waist. His hands settled at the small of her back, fingers tracing the delicate arc of her spine, holding her close as if she were the only truth that mattered. He bent to kiss her, lips brushing hers with a tenderness carrying the weight of everything still unspoken. Slowly, he moved against her again, each motion deliberate. They had made love several times that night, each encounter more fervent, more consuming, as if time could be persuaded to pause. Sleep, rest, food. None of it mattered. Only her. Only this. Only now.

This was his precipice, not the fleeting surge of release, but the raw, searing closeness binding them. The conviction. Emerson had chosen him, here, tonight, in this space of vulnerability. He did not drag her down to *Noir*.

She came to me.

Tonight, he asked if she could take him as he was. Flaws and all, unpolished and ardent, and she had not turned away. She chose him. Her acceptance was a revelation, a salvation that reshaped the contours of his soul. It was more than desire. It was a promise of something he never dared to want until now.

He kissed her again, deeper, his lips lingering as he tasted the warmth of her breath, the faint tremor of her pulse. The kiss was a confession, a plea, a vow sealed in the heat of their closeness. His hands tightened on her hips, fingers pressing into her skin as if to memorize her. Leaning back, his chest rose and fell, his breath shuddering with the weight of what he felt.

Words burned within him, forged in the fire of their shared moments, undeniable now as they rose to his lips. He met her eyes, their depths catching the candlelight, reflecting a truth he could no longer contain. His voice was low, steady, but laced with a raw intensity that stilled them both.

"Emerson, will you marry me?"

chapter forty-five

Perhaps I heard him wrong.

Emerson's heart lurched, a wild, stuttering beat that stole her breath. She had crossed the threshold of Lathen's room with a single certainty. Tonight, they would become lovers, their bodies entwined in a passion she had long craved. She was accepting him exactly as he was, convinced that having him, even fleetingly, was worth any cost. Marriage, though, was still a distant dream, too impossible to fathom.

"Your Grace, surely you do not mean it!" Her voice broke, a soft sob slipping past her lips, honest and unguarded. Tears pricked her eyes, not from sorrow but from the overwhelming weight of his words, heavy with promise.

Lathen's gaze softened, his eyes catching the flicker of the candles, their depths warm and unwavering. A tender smile curved his lips. It was gentle, uncomplicated, a glimpse of a man who was baring his soul.

"I told you, *Nyx*," he murmured, his voice a low caress, "when we are alone, in this house, call me Lathen."

With that, he drew her closer, his hands firm yet reverent on her hips, pulling her tight against him. He was deep, the angle pressing him against the core of her, and a sharp ache bloomed where their bodies met. It was a delicious pain, one that sent shivers racing through her, teetering her on the edge of ecstasy. Astonishingly, it stirred her anew, her body already trembling with the promise of another release.

"Well?" he pressed, his voice rough with desire as he moved beneath her, thrusting upward with a slow, deliberate rhythm. Each motion fractured her further, her senses splintering under the intensity. His question, his body, his everything. Her hands gripped his shoulders, nails making half-moons on his skin as she fought to keep herself in this moment. With him.

"Yes!" The word tore from her, a cry that mingled with a gasp as her body arched, unraveling in a wave of pleasure. "Yes, Lathen, I will marry you!" Her voice was a fervent plea, a surrender to the truth she had not dared name until now. She wanted him. Not just tonight, but forever.

Lathen's growl was primal, a sound of triumph that rumbled through his chest as he surged into her, his release crashing with hers. Their bodies trembled together, again, locked in shared ecstasy. A vow.

The colors in the room faded, the world narrowing to them alone. New words would come. Real vows would be spoken before others. Yet, at this moment, they were irrevocably bound.

chapter forty-six

Lennox trudged down the stairs. His head was pounding, and the world was spinning. It took everything he had not to rush to one of the potted plants on the second floor landing.

An odd night, certainly, he thought while he rubbed circles on his temples.

He had spent last night doing a favor for his brother. *'I need you to see Lord Farnsworth is occupied for the whole of the evening,'* Lathen told him yesterday morning.

Lennox had questions regarding the reason why, but his brother had looked at him so intently he kept them to himself. It was rare for Lathen to ask him for favors, and it felt good to help his brother. Especially since Lathen had been upset with him ever since the incident with Lady Haven leaving town.

He and Warwicke had done exactly as Lathen asked. They found Farnsworth at White's, playing cards, and they joined him. When he left, they followed and 'helped' him along to a tavern down by the docks. The poor sod was not used to having many friends, so he was not sure how to say no. Even though, to his credit, he tried to excuse himself when he realized where they were going, his cheeks flushing with embarrassment. After they also helped Farnsworth get quite drunk, dropping a few silver crowns into a doxy's hands was all it took to ensure he was kept in a room above for several hours.

It worked. Lord Farnsworth would likely be waking up quite happy, all things considered. *Though perhaps with his own aching head and a few things crawling in places on his body that ought not to be!* The thought made Lennox chuckle, then wince, as he turned into the breakfast room.

He stopped short when he saw the only other person in the room was Hazel. They had not spoken since the other night. When he caught her leaving his brother's rooms. In the bright light of the orangery, he felt a little bad about how he handled that situation. After all, he had no right to make judgments on her behavior. He was neither her brother nor her lover, and he was certainly no choir boy himself.

"Miss Atwood," he nodded politely to her. She lifted her head from the book she was reading to stare at him. Not for the first time, he was struck by how astonishingly blue her eyes were. Especially as the morning sun hit her perfect face. Today, they narrowed in irritation before she lowered them back to her book.

"My lord," she acknowledged him. Barely.

Yes, she is mad. He thought to himself.

It was an unusual occurrence for him. Most unmarried ladies of the *ton* went out of their way to catch his attention. After all, being an earl with property, he was considered a catch. Even if he was not exactly looking to be caught yet. The idea that Hazel was annoyed enough to show him was a novel experience. It made him think of making amends to her in some way.

Perhaps if I find some kind of trinket, she will forgive me. He grinned at the thought. After all, it worked with his mistresses.

He pulled a chair out and sat across the table from her. A footman came over and placed a plate in front of him and poured his tea while he waited. During all of this, Lennox watched Hazel while she studiously ignored him.

"A good book?" he asked her with the most charming smile he could muster. The one that normally had ladies melting in his arms.

"Yes, quite so," Hazel responded pertly, still without even glancing at him. He frowned to himself. He was about to think of something he could say that would get her to pay attention to him, when his aunt and sister walked into the room.

Hazel looked up immediately, placed a bookmark, and smiled. Lennox saw genuine cheerfulness light up her face and he immediately felt better. Even if it was not meant for him, it gave him a warm feeling in his chest.

"Lady de Clare. Leighton. Good morning," she said merrily.

"Good morning." They replied together.

The footman rushed to them as well. A conversation began about the play they had all gone to the other night. Lennox listened casually, but he was mostly watching the animation on Hazel's face. He had never noticed the small crinkles at the corners of her eyes when she was truly happy. She was so wholesome. Bright and clean. Very unlike the women he usually spent time with. Perhaps that was why finding out she had been in his brother's room was such a shock.

No, that is not it. Because it was not a shock that I felt. I was angry. Truly furious.

Lennox was roused from his thoughts when he realized everyone at the table had fallen silent. They were all looking at something behind him. He turned in his chair, and he too was stunned into silence.

His brother was standing at the entrance to the breakfast room. With him was Lady Haven. Amazingly, Lathen had a wide grin on his face, and his arm was protectively around Emerson's waist, keeping her close. All the while, Emerson blushed with a shy smile, her hands wringing, causing the enormous emerald ring on her finger to flash in the light streaming through the glass orangery. Lennox immediately recognized it as the de Clare Duchess ring. The one his mother wore before she died.

"It is about damn time," his Aunt Lillian was the first to break the silence. Obviously, she was not surprised by what they were all seeing.

Leighton was the next to realize what it all must mean. She shrieked, making him wince again, threw her napkin on the table, and jumped up to run to the couple.

"Oh, my goodness!" she exclaimed. "I simply cannot believe this. This is wonderful!" She wrapped her arms around her brother tightly, then around the smaller woman. "Now I get to have a true sister. Instead of just smelly brothers!"

"All right, kitten," Lathen said gruffly to her. Though still with an indulgent smile. "Lady Haven has only just agreed to marry me, so let us not break her."

Lennox had to admit he was dumbfounded, and he swung back toward Hazel. He worried she might be hurt that Lathen had played with her affections and was now marrying her best friend. But Hazel surprised him more. Tears sparkled in her eyes, but they were clearly happy ones as she was beaming, her smile generous. He frowned, confusion marring his face.

"Brother?" Lathen prodded him and Lennox turned back to the couple. Lathen's brow was high with a question. Without another thought, Lennox stood, walked to Lathen with a hand outstretched to shake with him in congratulations, and clapped his back with a quick hug. It was a little awkward as they did not usually embrace one another, but it felt right, nonetheless.

"I am very happy for you both. I am especially glad that he is marrying someone who can keep him on his toes."

Emerson blushed even more at his words. It was the truth, though. Lennox realized he was delighted. Though it was a surprise, he had to admit it made a lot of sense. Lathen had always felt a huge sense of responsibility for Emerson. Especially after his friend, Kit, died. And this season, he showed strong feelings toward her, even if Lennox did not always understand why. It was good to know he would be married to someone he obviously cared for. And he loved Emerson just as he did Leighton. She would make a wonderful addition to their family.

"When will you be married, and where?" Leighton asked eagerly.

Lennox knew she was likely imagining what flowers would adorn the church. Or whatever else girls her age thought of when the idea of matrimony was in the air. And a duke getting married was going to be a grand affair. Perhaps the wedding of the season. Members of the *ton* would be clamoring for an invitation.

"Oh, well..." Emerson trailed off as if she did not have an answer.

"All right, kitten," Lathen pulled Emerson close again, as if he sensed her discomfort. He stared down at her like he could not fathom staying away from her for even a day, let alone the weeks it would take for banns to be read. Plus, the time to arrange for a service at St. James's Church, which was really the only acceptable place for someone of their status to be married. Not to mention they would have to invite the royal family and have a celebratory ball afterward. Even Lennox understood what a hassle it would all be.

"Perhaps it might be better to just get a special license. Then Lady Haven and I could be married as soon as this weekend," Lathen suggested and looked to Emerson to see what her thoughts might be. Usually, he would be making such decisions on his own, but he obviously wanted her to be happy.

However, their aunt was not having it and huffed loudly. Her chair screeched as she stood abruptly.

"Absolutely not!" she exclaimed in a tone that brooked no arguments. Even mighty generals would have stood taller and listened as she continued, "There are certain expectations and commitments our family has. De Clares have always been close to the Royal Family, and it would not be acceptable to have a ducal marriage without them attending. Now, I know you are eager to start your married life, but the banns must be read, and we must have a wedding fit for a duke."

When she was finished, Aunt Lillian sat down primly and resumed making her tea. She did not bother to look to see how anyone was taking her proclamation as she was certain the matter was settled.

For his part, Lathen raised a brow, but decided not to argue. Lennox realized their aunt was probably right. His brother would simply have to make do and wait for at least a month before he could make Emerson his duchess.

If it was anyone else, I would feel sorry for him. But the wait will probably do Lathen some good, Lennox grinned at the thought and slapped his brother on the back once more.

chapter forty-seven

Emerson's watcher sat in the shadowed embrace of a wingback chair, before a roaring fire at White's. The premier gentleman's club, with its polished mahogany and heavy drapes, was a stage for the *ton's* elite, where decorum was a currency he wielded expertly. To be seen here, among the clink of crystal and the low hum of privileged voices, was to claim a place in their world. No one could glimpse the storm raging beneath his tailored coat, the fury that clawed at his ribs, threatening to spill over. They must never see him falter.

Never see my beast I keep chained!

He was finding it nearly impossible tonight. The Times lay open on his lap, its inked words a fresh wound, bleeding into his thoughts. He seized the brandy decanter, pouring a generous measure, and took a gulp, the liquid fire searing his throat, sharp and bitter. It did nothing to dull the rage coiling in his gut. Instead, it got tighter, threatening to strangle him. His eyes flicked down again, drawn to the announcement as if it were north and he was a compass needle. He whispered the words, voice low and venomous, each syllable dripping with loathing.

"It is announced, for the purpose of marriage, between His Grace, the Duke of Windemere, Lathen de Clare, to Lady Emerson Haven, the Earl of Haven, daughter of Lord Haven of Havenfield, at St. James's Church, on Saturday, noon, in four sennights' time."

His grip tightened on the crystal tumbler, knuckles whitening. He imagined hurling it into the fire, the glass shattering in a cascade of glittering shards, the brandy igniting in a fleeting, glorious blaze. How satisfying it would be to watch it burn, to see something break as he was breaking. Instead, he crushed the newspaper in his fists, the paper crumpling with a pathetic rustle, and tossed it into the flames. It flared briefly, curling into ash, the blackened fragments drifting up the chimney like ghosts of his plans. It did little to quell the inferno in his chest.

It had always been men like the de Clares, Havens, and Warwickes. Those arrogant, entitled bastards who trampled his life under their polished boots. Their laughter had mocked him, their easy camaraderie a wall he could never breach. He was no darling of the *ton*. Just a shadow on the fringes, watching their drunken revels and whispered trysts.

Men like them always had everything. The titles, the wealth, beautiful women throwing themselves at their feet. While I have always scraped for scraps of their notice.

It was like that when he met Marien. He could still see the night, vivid as a fresh wound, when he first glimpsed her. She had been slipping through the iron gates at Oxford, her dark hair a cascade of midnight, her eyes glinting with secrets under the moonlight. Marien was different. She was bold, untamed, her flirty confidence a siren's call.

I wanted her, needed her. To prove I was a man, not just a castoff!

When he approached and offered his company, Marien laughed, and declared she belonged to Lord Haven. The rejection still burned, a red haze clouding his vision, but he was a planner, always calculating. He spent nearly a year weaving a scheme to win her, waiting for the moment Haven's interest waned.

It almost worked. Marien, sensing Haven's growing distance, had turned to him, her flirtations a calculated game to spark jealousy. She came to his rooms, her smile a promise she never fulfilled, stopping short of giving herself to him. She teased him, dangled her beauty like a prize, then snatched it away.

Haven, for his part, never had a chance to regret any of his decisions. He tried dismissing Marien with a bag of coins as if she were a common whore.

The self-righteous, imbecilic fool!

Marien's rage had erupted, and in a moment of chaos, she pushed him. He had watched, hidden in the shadows, as Haven tumbled down the stairs, landing in a grotesque heap, his neck twisted unnaturally.

The *ton*, of course, swallowed the lie that Lord Christopher Haven died in a riding accident, a tidy tale to shield their delicate sensibilities. Then Windemere and Warwicke had spirited Marien out of England, and he did not see her for more than seven years.

Not until she returned, older but still intriguing, seeking a new protector. He took her in, but not out of desire. Her charms had faded, a husk of what they once were, but she was still useful. A pawn in his new game. His tastes had changed in her absence, honed by years of resentment. She was only a tool now, a means to exact revenge for every slight, every moment he was made to feel less.

Lady Emerson Haven was his obsession now. His everything. Ever since her smile pierced his armor. That smile promised him everything. Her heart, her body, her place in their world. Marrying her would give him wealth, status, and the sweetest victory. She was Haven's little sister, and he would be stealing something precious from de Clare. He had planned meticulously, weaving his web with care, but now it was unraveling. De Clare had claimed her, as men like him always claimed everything.

It is always the fucking de Clares of the world, taking what should be mine!

His blood roared, a medieval tide of rage and despair. He had been too patient, too careful. The fire crackled, its light casting grotesque shadows on the walls, mirroring the twisted shapes in his mind.

I cannot lose her, not now!

She was meant to be his.

A new plan took root, dark and urgent, blooming in the corners of his soul. The time for patience was gone. He would take what was his, by force if necessary. Her smile was a pledge, and he would carve it from her if he must. He imagined her fear, her resistance, and then, inevitably, her surrender.

Resolved, Emerson's watcher rose from the chair, his movements sharp and predatory, a wolf shedding its disguise. He drained the last of his brandy, the burn fueling his determination, and tossed the glass onto the table with a clink that echoed in the quiet reflection of White's.

It will have to do, for now...

chapter forty-eight

"What happened next?"

Emerson and Hazel were walking along Bond Street arm in arm. Alice, their maid, and a footman were behind them, but far enough back so they could talk privately.

It was the first time they had the chance since Emerson and Lathen had announced their engagement. Hazel was, of course, happy for her friend. She also wanted all the details!

Emerson was whispering about their encounter the other night. It was an amazing story, having gone from running off to Gretna Green with one man, to being engaged to another hours later. More importantly, she made love to him again, numerous times. Hazel blushed as she listened.

Especially when Emerson described *Noir*. Hazel was astonished. She thought she knew a lot about sex because of all her reading.

Well, as much as an unmarried woman could know.

Yet this was all more than she had even assumed. It made her wish she had her own lover, or at least the ability to see *Noir* for herself. But it seemed unlikely. And her marriage prospects had been less than stellar so far, so she did not see a lover in her future.

*Speaking of...*Hazel elbowed her friend because she saw Mr. Brown walking toward them. *I suppose I still have him, at least.*

Now that Emerson would soon be married and on her honeymoon, perhaps it was time for her to seriously consider if she could be Mrs. Hazel Brown. The idea made her wistful.

"Mr. Brown, how lovely to see you," she forced herself to greet him brightly.

"Good afternoon, M-miss Atwood, L-lady Haven," he took off his top hat and nodded.

Emerson gave an answering nod of acknowledgement and turned to Hazel with a raised brow. Then she walked a bit further, investigating the window of a hat shop. She did not need a new bonnet but did want to give her friend a bit of privacy.

"I heard His G-grace and L-lady Haven are n-now engaged," Mr. Brown smiled shyly at Hazel and ducked his head.

"Yes, is that not wonderful? We are very much looking forward to it. There is obviously a lot to be done, but it is a good match for them both."

"Of c-course, I am g-glad for them," he agreed, before he leaned closer toward Hazel, "Perhaps it w-would b-be possible to escort you to the w-wedding. If you are n-not already spoken for, that is."

"Oh!" Hazel's eyes widened in surprise. She was not expecting him to ask, and her mind raced with indecision.

It would seem I need to make a choice about Mr. Brown right now.

As her logical mind bounced quickly between the advantages and disadvantages of saying yes or no to him, she missed seeing anything out of the ordinary around them. She was not prepared when she heard a shout come from behind her.

She turned, astonished to witness the de Clare footman who was following them crumple to the ground in a heap. She was barely able to process what she was seeing before a scream came from Emerson as she was grabbed by a rough-looking man and pulled quickly toward a waiting carriage. She was thrown in so roughly her dress caught on the latch and, even from where she was standing, Hazel heard the rending of the material as the door was closed.

It happened so quickly, Hazel and Mr. Brown barely had any time to chase them before the horses were whipped and the carriage was tearing away.

Alice had dropped all her parcels to help the footman, and she was just rising to also give chase. Hazel grabbed the other woman by the arm.

"Do you know who they are?" Hazel asked anxiously.

"No, miss," Alice responded quickly, wringing her hands, "I have no idea. What shall we do?"

Hazel's mind raced with near mathematical precision while the three of them ran back to where a small crowd was forming around the young footman who was just beginning to rise. He held a handkerchief to his bleeding forehead.

"Oh, dear," Hazel exclaimed, "are you alright, Peter?"

"Yes, miss, but where is Lady Haven?"

"She has been taken by two ruffians. In what looked like a hired hack."

Even during this discussion, she was still coming up with a plan.

"Is there any way you can manage to rush back to de Clare House? We must let His Grace know what has happened as soon as possible."

"Of course, miss. But what about you? I cannot leave you alone. You should come back with me." Peter looked worried. Hazel could not tell if he was more concerned about losing both ladies he had been charged with or having to be the one to explain what happened to the duke.

Either way, Hazel was running low on time, and she was not willing to argue.

"No, you rush back, as fast as possible." Then she looked at Alice, "The two of us will take the carriage and try to follow them. They could not have gone far in this crush."

Without waiting to see Peter's reaction, Hazel lifted her skirts and ran toward the de Clare carriage that was waiting for them two blocks away. Someone grabbed her arm, halting her, and she turned to glare at the interruption.

"Wait, M-m-miss Atwood," Mr. Brown let go of her and put his hands up to calm her. "I w-will come as w-well. You should n-not g-g-go alone." His tone, despite his stutter, was firm, surprising her. Hazel did not have time to argue, but she figured having him along could not hurt, so she nodded quickly and continued to run.

She ignored the shocked looks of the well-dressed people on Bond Street, who were unused to seeing a young woman running. She soon reached the carriage with Mr. Brown and Alice and explained to the driver what had happened.

Luckily, the hack racing off with Emerson had caused such commotion the driver noticed it when it passed. Mr. Brown helped the two women jump into the carriage, and they barely got the door closed before the driver was snapping the reins to give chase.

From inside the carriage, Hazel could hear the driver shouting at people along the way, asking if anyone had seen the hack go by. Fortunately, they were pointed in the right direction, and Hazel felt she had done the right thing by attempting to follow Emerson. Especially when it was obvious they were going the opposite direction of St. James's Square.

Hazel glanced at Mr. Brown. He had been silent the whole time, but he looked determined and upset. She was grateful he was helping her, and she and Alice were not alone.

"I simply do not understand who could ever do such a thing."

"Nor do I. B-but p-perhaps we should get the authorities. What will we d-do if we m-manage to catch them up?"

Hazel had to bite her tongue. Emerson was her best friend, and she had nothing but certainty that she would do the same for her. She was saved from having to respond to him when the driver slowed and shouted down to them.

"Miss, I believe I see them several blocks up ahead. They have turned toward Bloomsbury."

Hazel put her head out of the window and yelled back up to him. It was difficult as they were going quite fast over the cobbles and turning to avoid slower traffic, so she had to hold tightly.

"Please keep back so they do not identify you, and we can follow them to their destination."

Hazel's mind was still racing. She realized Mr. Brown was correct. She had no idea what they were going to do once they found out where the men who had taken her friend were going. They only had the driver to help them, and from what she had seen, there were at least three brawny men taking part in this kidnapping.

As she looked across to Mr. Brown, it was obvious to her that he was going to be of little help. The gentleman was nervous on the best of days, and though he was obviously willing to help her, he was not going to be able to stop three large ruffians.

They were still in town, albeit in an area that Hazel did not recognize, when the carriage slowed and came to a stop. The driver jumped down after a few moments and opened the door so he could talk with them quietly.

"Miss, the hack pulled to a townhouse on the next block. I saw them bring someone inside who was covered in a cape. But, based on the size and how hard they were fighting, I believe it was Lady Haven."

Hazel leaned out so she could follow where he was pointing.

"Was it still just the three of them?"

"No, Miss. There was one other as well."

"Do you know where we are?"

"Just off Bedford Square."

"Is it safe here? I am afraid I do not know London well."

"Safe enough, but we should go to His Grace and tell him where they have taken Lady Haven."

Hazel leaned forward and made to leave the carriage. The driver, unsure of what to do, jumped back and helped her down.

"Very well, you go back, with all haste, and I will wait here."

Mr. Brown, Alice, and the driver all shouted at her in disagreement, but Hazel simply lifted her hand to stop them.

"You must rush, please," she said to the driver in a tone that brooked no more arguments. "I would like you to stay as well, if you do not mind, sir," she gestured to Mr. Brown. "We will do our best to look as though we are simply out for a stroll."

Mr. Brown had a short moment of indecision before he came out of the carriage and joined her. Hazel reached out and grabbed his arm.

"It will be alright, but we cannot abandon Lady Haven, and I can promise you the de Clare family and I would be most appreciative of you for having helped in this difficult time."

Mr. Brown seemed resigned. He blushed as Hazel put her elbow through his, but he did not argue with her again. They stood close together and walked forward, keeping to the sidewalk on the opposite side of the street from the house the driver had pointed out. It looked like any other well-kept home around the square. Not as fashionable or large as de Clare House, but still respectable.

Their carriage pulled off quickly and was already turning around the corner and back toward St. James. Hazel did her best to look confident for Mr. Brown's sake. Truthfully, she was also scared.

What if the ruffians were to come out before anyone from the de Clare House could come back? What if someone recognized her walking past, and came after them?

Nonetheless, she did her best. They walked past the house, and Hazel noted that the hack was driverless and waiting. She was assured it was the right one, seeing the strip of light muslin from Emerson's dress still hanging off the latch, blowing in the breeze. Her breath caught as they continued around the corner. There, a large tree made it possible for them to stand and keep watch without anyone from the house seeing them. The next minutes passed excruciatingly slowly as they stared at the house.

After a quarter of an hour passed, Hazel began to worry about what might be happening to her friend inside. Another plan began to form in her head. She assumed the carriage would be just getting to de Clare House. It would take them at least another ten minutes to come back with help, probably longer.

I cannot wait so long. I must go inside and see if I can find where they are keeping Em. Maybe I can sneak in, and we can sneak out together.

"Listen, Mr. Brown," she turned to her companion, "I do not expect you to help me further, but I need to go inside and see if I can help Lady Haven escape. Can you wait here for His Grace and let them know where I have gone?"

Mr. Brown's eyes widened in shock, and his face went red as he opened his mouth several times to answer her but was unable to get his words out.

"N-n-n-o. You c-c-c-cannot g-go alone," he finally said to her as he stamped his foot in frustration. With that, he started walking toward the house.

"Wait," Hazel whispered, "let us go around to the back and find a servant's entrance. We might be able to get in without anyone noticing."

Mr. Brown nodded, and they moved through an alleyway behind the block they were on. They were in luck. They found a servant's entrance, and when they checked, discovered it was unlocked.

chapter forty-nine

Rough hands pulled Emerson up a narrow stairwell, the splintered wood snagging the hem of her skirts. A brutal shove sent her sprawling onto a lumpy mattress, the musty stench of mildew and damp feathers choking her senses. The door slammed shut, the lock's metallic click echoing through what felt like an empty tomb. The two men who had snatched her from the street, along with a third who joined them as soon as they had thrown her into the hack, had not uttered a word. The ride was jolting and silent. They had bound her wrists behind her with coarse twine that bit into her skin, gagged her with a foul-smelling cloth that reeked of rot and stale sweat, and thrown a rough flour sack over her head, plunging her into suffocating, filtered darkness.

Where am I? God, where have they taken me? The uncertainty gnawed at her, her mind spinning at the possibilities. None of which were good.

The journey was brief. Surely, they were still in the city. Unfortunately, the place they brought her did not sound or feel familiar, with unfamiliar decay filling her senses.

She had tried screaming through the gag as one of her captors yanked her from the carriage, her muffled cries swallowed by the sack. The man shook her so violently her ears rang, his coarse dockside growl slicing through the air. "Keep quiet, ya hussy, or I'll addle ya brain!" The threat lingered.

When he threw her on the sagging bed, Emerson had shrunk away, her body tensing for the next violation. *What do they want? What will they do?*

The man's cruel laugh, sharp and mocking, cut through her fear as he retreated, leaving her alone in the oppressive silence. Her breaths came in shallow, panicked bursts through her nose, each inhale tainted by the gag's rancid stench. It clawed at her throat, making her chest tighten as if the air itself refused to help.

I cannot breathe! She twisted her wrists, desperate to free herself, but the twine dug deeper, carving raw furrows into her skin. Her fingers, numb and icy, tingled with painful futility. *Stay calm. You have to stay calm.*

Taking as deep a breath as the gag allowed, she forced herself to take stock of her surroundings.

All right. I am in a house. On the second floor. In a room, sitting on a featherbed which has seen better days. That much she could tell from a sliver of space beneath the sack.

Beyond the locked door, low voices murmured, their words indistinct but heavy with intent. Her pulse quickened as the door squeaked open, boots clicking across the bare floor with deliberate menace. Emerson froze, every muscle coiled, waiting for the unknown to strike.

"Hmmm," a dark laugh rang out, then a man lowered his voice. "I am not sure if I should be mad at Silas for delivering you this way, or grateful."

A prickle of fear shot down Emerson's spine. She believed she recognized the voice, yet somehow it was different from anyone she knew. Like a melody played in a minor key, distorted by his whisper and malice.

The man prowled the room, his movements deliberate. Drawers scraped open and shut, their contents rattling as he rummaged through them. The bed dipped as he sat beside her. Emerson flinched, trying to lean away, but his hand clamped onto her shoulder, nails digging into the tender flesh above her collarbone. Pain flared, sharp and burning, drawing a muffled whimper from her.

"Hold still!" the man hissed, the command clear and threatening.

He released her shoulder, his fingers trailing briefly, possessively, before tugging at the ropes binding her wrists. The twine loosened, and she felt the cold kiss of a knife slip beneath it. Emerson obeyed, but only because she wanted to have her hands free to be able to fight.

The blade sliced through the bonds, nicking her skin, a sharp sting she barely registered in her desperation. She yanked her wrists forward, fumbling to rip the sack from her head, but her hands betrayed her, heavy and unresponsive, the blood sluggish in her veins. As she shook them, sensation returned in a brutal rush, a thousand needles stabbing her flesh, each prick a scream trapped in her chest. A low moan of pain escaped her, muffled by the gag and flour sack.

"Oh, yes, my darling," the ominous whisper came to her ear, dripping with grotesque tenderness, "I love to hear you like that!"

The words were a violation, intimate and obscene, twisting her fear into something darker. Her skin crawled, her stomach churning as she finally clawed at the sack, fingers trembling with pain and desperation. Several hairpins caught, tearing at her scalp, but she yanked harder, ripping out strands of hair in her frenzy to see.

The sack dropped from her shaking hands, and the room came into focus. Dingy, shadowed, a single lamp casting jagged patterns on the walls. She turned and her gaze locked onto the man beside her, turning her blood to ice.

No! It cannot be!

chapter fifty

Lathen lounged on the deep leather couch in his study, the rich aroma of aged scotch mingling with the earthy smoke from cigars. Across from him, Lord Greyson Warwicke sprawled with the ease of a lifelong friend, his eyes warm, with a touch of mischief from the liquor.

"I have tae admit, auld man, I dinnae sae this coming. Even though I did hope for such. Lady Haven is a lovely, charming lass. And of course, it is nice tae know Kit's sister will be well taken care of." Greyson leaned forward, a teasing grin spreading across his face as he puffed his cigar. "But ye? Settlin' down? The great Duke of Windemere, tamed by a lass with a temperament as wild as a kelpie in a loch? I thought ye'd sooner wrestle a Highland coo than admit ye're in love!"

Lathen chuckled, a low, genuine sound that felt rare even to him. He took a slow sip of his scotch, the burn sliding down his throat a familiar friend.

He is not wrong. It was a shock even to him.

For years, he had told his friend his heart was an unbreakable fortress. Yet Emerson had breached those walls, slipping into his soul so deeply he had not recognized it until she was everything to him.

"You forget, Grey, I have tackled worse than bulls. Remember Abington? You with that innkeeper's daughter, and me dragging you out the window before her father came at us with a pitchfork?"

Greyson threw his head back, his booming laugh filling the study. "Och, dinnae remind me! My pride still smarts from that tumble. And ye, playin' the hero, only tae trip over yer own boots. We were a right pair of eejits." He leaned in, his voice dropping to a mock whisper. "But seriously, Lathen, Emerson's got ye smilin' like a lad with his first lass. I am happy for ye."

Lathen nodded, a soft warmth spreading through him as he thought of Emerson. Greyson was one of the few who knew him truly. Not just the duke, but the Master of *Noir*, the man who wove shadows to tame a chaotic world. Losing Kit, their best friend, in their reckless youth had shattered him, further forging his need for control. A need that *Noir* fed but never fulfilled. But Emerson, she had finally made him whole.

She challenges me, drives me to distraction, and yet makes me feel alive.

"She does at that," Lathen smiled even wider, "Even when she is calling me a pompous arse to my face."

Greyson snorted, nearly choking on his scotch. "Aye. Ye deserved it, mind, all that broodin' duke nonsense. Emerson is yer cure." He leaned closer, eyes glinting. "Just promise me, at the weddin', dinnae let her pick the music. I cannae handle ye dancin' a jig in a kilt. If ye even own one."

"No kilts," Lathen grinned, "I swear. We de Clares have gone too far from our Scottish roots for that."

"Ha, more's the pity, ye English."

"Well, here is to my future bride," he raised his glass. "Hopefully, she can put up with me." They clinked glasses, the sound bright, a toast sealed with the camaraderie of brothers forged in fire.

Greyson opened his mouth for another quip when a commotion erupted in the main hall. Shouts, scuffling feet, a door slamming shut. Lathen's stomach tightened, a flicker of unease cutting through him. He set his cigar and glass down, his movements deliberate, and he strode to the door.

Flinging it open, he saw his brother rushing toward him, gripping a young footman by the arm. Lathen recognized Peter Jenkins, a loyal servant, now battered, blood smeared across his temple, trickling onto his livery.

"Lathen, it is Lady Haven!" Lennox's voice was sharp, his face pale with urgency.

Emerson's name hit Lathen like a blade, his blood turning to ice. He straightened, a cold mask of calm snapping into place, though his heart pounded with dread.

"Come inside." He ushered them in, shutting the door with a firm click that echoed his resolve. Turning sharply, he fixed his gaze on Peter. "Tell me."

"Your G-grace..." Peter stammered, his eyes wide, the blood stark against his ashen face.

Lathen waved away the formality, impatience clawing at him. He needed answers, now.

"Tell me!" The words came out like a whip, his composure fraying.

Peter swallowed, trembling. "The Lady Haven and Miss Atwood were walking on Bond Street, when someone attacked me and then two others stole away with Lady Haven."

"Who were they?" Lathen's mind raced, images of Emerson, frightened and vulnerable, flashing like lightning.

If someone has harmed her, I will tear them apart.

"Honestly, Your Grace, I know not," Peter's voice wavered. "But Miss Atwood sent me back to tell you what happened, and..." He hesitated, fear flickering in his eyes, as if the next words might unleash hell.

"Keep going," Lathen commanded, his tone low and lethal.

"Well, even though I tried to tell her it was not a good idea," Peter rushed on, "Miss Atwood decided to take the carriage, to follow after the men who took Lady Haven."

Lathen's breath caught, his chest tightening. *Hazel, you brilliant, wonderful girl.*

"What?" Lennox shouted, making Peter flinch.

Lathen glanced at Lennox, noticing his face was etched with the same worry crawling in Lathen's gut.

"I swear my lords, I did try to stop her, but she insisted, and was gone before I could do anything. I figured it was right for me to come tell you as soon as I could."

Warwicke stepped in, his earlier mirth gone, replaced by a steady calm as he questioned Peter further. Descriptions, directions, any detail they could grasp onto. But the footman's account was sparse, his knowledge limited by the chaos of the attack and his own injury.

Lathen thanked him curtly, sending him to the kitchens to have his wound tended, but his thoughts were a whirlwind.

Emerson, where are you?

The room fell silent, the air thick with tension. Lathen moved to his desk, his hands steady despite the anguish tearing at him. He unlocked a bottom drawer, shoving aside a small box holding three pairs of torn lace underwear, relics of passion now overshadowed by terror. Beneath it lay another box. Lathen pulled it out, set it on the desk, and lifted the lid. Two pistols gleamed inside, cold and lethal. He loaded them with practiced precision, carefully pouring powder and ramming the lead ball down each barrel, the click of the flintlock a grim sound he barely heard over his own pounding heart. One went into his coat pocket, its weight a promise of retribution.

"Lathen, we dinnae even know where tae look. This could be a blunder fer all we ken." Greyson's voice was strained, his attempt at reason falling flat against Lathen's determination.

I will knock down every door in London if I must. I will find her. The thought was a blade, sharp and unyielding. Reason had no place here, only the primal need to protect his woman. He handed the second pistol to Lennox, their eyes locked in silent understanding.

"Come," Lathen said, his voice firm, striding toward the door, his steps masking the storm within.

"Lathen!" Greyson called again, reaching for his arm. "We mun wait until we ken more!"

Lathen jerked away, his jaw tight, anguish twisting his features. "Wait? When Emerson is out there, scared and alone? With God knows what happening!" The thought of Emerson's fear, her pain, was a vise around his heart, each second an eternity of torment.

The front door burst open as they reached the entry hall, admitting a gust of cool air and two figures. His carriage driver, Mac, breathless and disheveled, and Alice, the lady's maid meant to accompany Emerson and Hazel, rushed inside. Their use of the main entrance screamed urgency.

"Your Grace," the driver bowed hastily, gasping. "I bring news. Miss Atwood had me follow a hired hack that stole away with Lady Haven. They went to a house to the north, in Bloomsbury. She told me to come get you right away!"

Relief clashed with fresh dread in Lathen's chest. *Bloomsbury. A lead, finally.* He surged toward the waiting carriage, his brother and Greyson close behind.

As they climbed in, Lennox paused, his face tight with worry. "Where is Miss Atwood?"

"I am sorry, my lord, but she stayed behind to watch the house," the driver replied, scrambling up to his perch. "I did try to get her to come back here, but she insisted."

Lennox looked distressed, his jaw clenched and his eyes furious, but said nothing as he climbed in. Lathen's hand brushed the pistol in his pocket, its weight a grim comfort.

If someone has hurt her, I will kill them. No mercy will be given. The carriage lurched forward, the horses driven to a frenzy, the ride a brutal jolt over cobbled streets. Angry shouts from pedestrians pierced the air, but inside, silence reigned, heavy with Lathen's dread. Each bump fueled his anguish, his mind conjuring Emerson, terrified, crying out for him. *Hold on, my Nyx. I am coming.*

chapter fifty-one

Hazel pressed her back against the rough brick near the servant's entrance, her heart pounding like a drum in her chest. The early evening air hung heavy with a damp chill, clinging to her pelisse, seeping through to her skin. Mr. Brown stood beside her, his breath coming in short, uneven bursts. He glanced at the door they had just opened, as if still doubtful of the wisdom of entering. Hazel's fingers tightened around the small penknife hidden in her pocket, though she prayed she would not need it.

"Sh-should we really d-do this, Miss Atwood?" Mr. Brown whispered, his voice catching on the words. His eyes, wide and earnest, searched her face for reassurance.

Hazel nodded firmly, though doubt flickered in her mind.

What if we are caught? she wondered, the idea sending a shiver down her spine that had nothing to

292

do with the cold. But Emerson needed them, and Hazel could not abandon her.

"We have no choice," she murmured, slipping through the door first.

The interior hit her like a wave of neglect. The kitchen, which should have been the bustling heart of any respectable home, was a chaotic ruin. Counters overflowed with stacks of grimy plates, crusted with remnants of meals long forgotten. The air was thick with the stench of unclean pots piled in the sink, their surfaces slick with grease and dotted with flies that buzzed lazily. Worse was the underlying odor of molding food, sharp and sour, emanating from open cupboards where loaves of bread had sprouted fuzzy green patches and fruits rotted in forgotten bowls.

Pots hung askew on hooks, some dented as if thrown in frustration, and the floor was sticky underfoot, littered with crumbs and spills no one had bothered to sweep away. It was as if the servants had simply given up, letting decay creep in unchecked. Hazel's stomach churned at the sight, wondering who could live in such filth.

Mr. Brown followed her in, wrinkling his nose. "This p-place is ab-bominable," he whispered, stepping carefully to avoid a puddle of what looked like spilled milk gone sour.

They moved forward cautiously, weaving through the disarray. Hazel's shoes stuck slightly to the floor with each step, the adhesive residue pulling at her soles like reluctant hands. She scanned the room for any sign of movement, her ears straining for voices or footsteps.

Empty.

The kitchen led to a narrow hallway, its walls papered in faded patterns now peeling at the edges, revealing plaster cracked and yellowed with age. Dust motes danced in the faint light filtering from a distant window, and the air grew heavier, carrying hints of stale smoke from a hearth that had not been cleaned in weeks.

Or months.

As they rounded a corner into what seemed like a pantry, a hulking man suddenly loomed in their path. He was built like the dockworkers Hazel had seen unloading crates at the Thames. His broad shoulders strained against a threadbare shirt, arms thick with muscle and scarred from years of hard labor. His face was weathered, etched with lines from sun and salt, and his hair hung in greasy strands over a forehead furrowed in suspicion. When he spoke, his voice was a gravelly rumble, laced with a rough, clipped accent.

"Wot do we 'ave 'ere?" he growled, his eyes narrowing as he blocked their way completely. His breath carried the tang of cheap ale and weak snuff, and he cracked his knuckles with deliberate menace.

Hazel gasped, her pulse spiking as fear clawed at her throat. Instinct took over and she spun on her heel, grabbing Mr. Brown's hand so they could flee back the way they had come. But she collided hard with another chest, solid and unyielding, like slamming into a wall of flesh and bone. Strong hands clamped down on her arms, fingers digging in with bruising force. She struggled, twisting wildly, but the grip only tightened, threatening to grind her bones to dust. Hot, nasty breath washed over her face, reeking of onions and spoiled meat, making her eyes water.

"Got ourselves a lively one, eh?" the man holding her chuckled, his voice smoother than the dockworker's but no less threatening. He was taller, leaner, with a sharp jaw and eyes that gleamed with cruel amusement. Scars marred his cheeks, old knife wounds perhaps, and his clothes were finer than the other man's. He wore a vest over a shirt that might once have been white but now bore stains and slight tears.

He called out over her shoulder, his voice booming with authority. "Oi, Jack! Tommy! Get in 'ere!"

From the adjoining room, grumbling voices responded. "What does Silas want now?" one grouched, the words muffled but laced with irritation. Footsteps thudded closer, and two more men emerged, rough-looking sorts with unshaven faces and clothes patched in multiple places. They eyed the scene with interest.

Meanwhile, the hulking dockworker had lunged at Mr. Brown, who was standing frozen, his words refusing to leave his mouth. With a swift motion, he wrapped a massive arm around his neck, yanking him backward in a chokehold. Mr. Brown gasped, his hands clawing futilely at the arm constricting his throat. His face reddened, veins bulging as he struggled for air.

"Leave him be!" Hazel shouted, her voice cracking with desperation. She thrashed against the hold of the man they called Silas, her shoes scraping the floor, but it was useless. Mr. Brown's eyes met hers, wide with terror, and a surge of protectiveness welled up in her.

Silas laughed, a cruel, barking sound that echoed off the walls like shattering glass. "Shut it, ya little minx," he snarled, his fingers tightening on her arms until tears sprang to her eyes. He yanked her away from the scene, dragging her toward a side door while the three men closed in on Mr. Brown. "You lot. Find out who this blighter is. And make it quick. The lord'll want to know if we've got more pests sniffin' around."

The first man nodded, his arm still locked around Mr. Brown's neck, though he eased the pressure just enough to keep him conscious. Jack and Tommy grabbed Mr. Brown's arms, pinning him further as they hauled him toward another room. Hazel's last glimpse of Mr. Brown was his pleading eyes, his mouth opening in a silent cry before the door swung shut behind them.

Silas propelled her into a small servant's room off the hallway, the space cramped and forgotten. It was little more than a closet with a narrow cot shoved against one wall, its mattress sagging and stained with what looked like old spills. A rickety table held a few dusty bottles and a cracked mirror that reflected the room's gloom back at them. The walls were bare except for hooks where clothes and aprons might once have hung, now empty save for cobwebs draping like torn lace. Silas kicked the door shut behind him, the latch clicking with finality.

He released her arms but positioned himself between her and the exit, his frame filling the doorway like a barricade. Hazel backed away until her legs hit the cot, her breath coming in ragged gasps. She glanced around wildly for an escape. There was none.

Silas loomed closer, his eyes raking over her with undisguised hunger. "The lord said we weren't to touch the dark-haired lady," he said, his voice dropping to a low, menacing purr. "But 'e never said nothin' about you, did 'e? Pretty thing like yerself, sneakin' in where ya don't belong. One would think ya were asking fer it."

He snickered as she cowered, pressing herself against the wall, her hands trembling at her sides. The penknife in her pocket felt heavy, but with him so close, she feared reaching for it. His shadow fell over her, blocking out the weak light from the tiny window high on the wall, and she could see the yellowed teeth in his grin, the veins in his neck pulsing with excitement as revulsion twisted in Hazel's gut.

Silas took another step, pressing his body to hers as his hand grabbed her chin, forcing her to look up at him. "Don't worry, luv. I'll make it quick...or maybe not. A doxy with bosoms like yers deserves some time after all."

Rage boiled over, smothering Hazel's fear. In a flash, she drove her knee upward with all her strength, connecting squarely with his groin. Silas howled, doubled over, his face contorted in agony. She did not hesitate, pulling the penknife out, gripping it in her fist, and wielding it in a wide arc until it hit his neck.

Blood sprayed as it sliced through his skin. Hazel's heart pounded, adrenaline surging as the crimson jet splattered her trembling hand, warm and slick. She gripped the knife tighter, its handle digging into her palm, her breath ragged, and pulled it out. His gurgling gasp clawed at her ears, raw and desperate, as she saw his hands scrabble at the wound, fingers slipping in the gushing red. Her stomach churned, a chaotic swirl of fear and relief, as she watched the man who attacked her stagger, his life spilling onto the ground in a dark, relentless pool.

Hazel stood there, chest heaving, the room spinning from what she had done. She took several deep breaths, desperately trying not to look down as Silas made one last reach for her, before his hand dropped, stilling. Several moments passed before she wiped her penknife on her skirts, slipping it back in her pocket with a trembling hand. Then she forced herself to move, stepping over Silas's motionless form toward the door. Freedom, and perhaps rescue for Emerson and Mr. Brown, lay just beyond.

chapter fifty-two

Lord Virgil Farnsworth stood beside the bed, a mere shadow of the refined gentleman Emerson had known and nearly wed just days prior. His once impeccable hair, normally tamed with Macassar oil, now hung in disheveled strands, tumbling over his bloodshot eyes. Those green eyes, once warm and friendly, now glinted with a feverish intensity, sending a chill through her. His tailored coat, usually pressed to perfection, was creased and sagged off his shoulders. The cravat, which he always tied with meticulous care, dangled around his neck, its ends loose as if he had tugged at it in frustration, then forgotten it. Even his spectacles, normally polished to a gleam, were smudged with fingerprints and perched crookedly on his nose, one lens catching the dim light in a way that made him appear unhinged.

"My dear Lady Haven," he said, his voice dripping with mockery as he swept into a deep, exaggerated bow. The gesture was not the courtly deference she remembered but a cruel parody, his lips curling into a sneer. Emerson's heart pounded as she tore her gaze from him to take in her surroundings. The room, though clearly once a place of grandeur, had succumbed to time's decay. Heavy velvet curtains, their rich burgundy faded to a sickly rose, hung limply at the windows, their edges frayed and moth eaten. The floorboards beneath her feet were warped, groaning under the slightest shift of Farnsworth's weight, and a musty odor clung to the air, thick with dust and abandonment. The sparse furnishings, a sagging bed with a threadbare coverlet and a rickety table barely supporting a chipped porcelain washbasin, only deepened the room's desolation. Yet, the walls told a different story. They were adorned with hundreds of small, tarnished frames, each encasing a butterfly, their delicate wings pinned in eternal stillness, their vibrant colors undulled by time. The sight sent a shudder down Emerson's spine, each tiny corpse a silent testament to an obsession she was only beginning to comprehend.

"My lord," she said, forcing her voice to remain steady as she met his gaze, "what on earth is going on? A lout injured one of the de Clare footmen, and two other ruffians stole me away in broad daylight. Off Bond Street, no less!" Her words carried the indignation of a woman accustomed to respect, but beneath them lay a tremor of fear she could not fully mask.

Farnsworth's laugh was a jagged sound, devoid of warmth. "Oh, yes, I know. Those men have been trying to get to you for weeks, but the duke is usually more protective of his *possessions*." The last word was spat with venom, his lips twisting as he stepped closer. His boots scuffed against the warped floor, the sound grating in the oppressive silence. He reached out, his fingers brushing toward her face, and when Emerson flinched, he seized her chin with a grip that made her wince, his nails digging into her skin.

"This face," he rasped, his voice hoarse as though scraped raw by emotion, "it bound you to me three years ago, when you gifted me your first smile." His words hung in the air, heavy with a delusion that made Emerson's breath catch. She stared at him, her mind reeling.

Three years? She had met him only this spring, their relationship mostly one of polite encounters and carefully measured exchanges. Yet his eyes burned with a conviction that chilled her to the core.

"Every step you have taken since then, I have been there," he continued, his voice dropping to a fervent whisper. "I have nearly bankrupted myself, sacrificing everything to ensure your safety. You have been my own butterfly, my precious creation, waiting to emerge from your cocoon. And now, like all butterflies, you are ready to be caught and preserved." From his pocket, he produced a small, gleaming pin, its sharp point catching the flickering light of a single candle on the table. From his waistband, he drew a dagger, its blade dull but menacing in his trembling hand.

Emerson's temper flared, fueled by fear. "How dare you, sir!" she shouted, her voice echoing off the walls. "You must know that His Grace and I are to be married. I sent you a letter explaining everything!" Her words were a desperate attempt to anchor him to reason, to remind him of the world beyond this decaying room.

Farnsworth's face contorted, and in a flash, he backhanded her across the cheek. The force sent her sprawling to the floor, her gasp swallowed by the sharp sting of pain. The taste of copper filled her mouth as she touched her cheek, her fingers trembling. She stared up at him, tears welling in her wide eyes. No one had ever struck her like this, not the village boys she had brawled with as a child, not even Lathen in his sternest moments of discipline. Farnsworth's rage was different, a twisted, consuming fury that seemed to feed on her fear.

"Shut up, you bitch!" he roared, leaning down until his face was inches from hers, his spittle flecking her skin. "How dare I? You promised yourself to me, and you think a *letter* makes everything alright?" His voice cracked, veering between rage and despair, as if he were unraveling before her.

Emerson scrambled backward, her hands and backside scraping against the rough floorboards, but Farnsworth was faster. He seized her shoulders, his fingers biting into her flesh, and yanked her to her feet. He shook her with such force that her teeth rattled, her vision blurring.

"Please, my lord," she cried, her voice breaking, "you are hurting me."

His lips twisted into a maniacal smile, and he laughed again, a sound that sent chills racing down her spine. "Oh, my dearest Lady Haven, you have not seen anything yet." He raised his hand and struck her again, the blow snapping her head to the side. Pain exploded across her face once more, and she cried out, dazed, as blood trickled from her lip. His expression lit with a sick satisfaction, his eyes gleaming as if her suffering were a prize he had won.

"Please, stop," she whimpered, her voice barely audible, her body trembling with a terror she had never known.

"Oh, I will stop," he said, his tone icy and deliberate, "but only after I get what I am due." The words sent gooseflesh prickling across her arms, her skin crawling under his gaze.

"What do you mean, my lord?" she asked, forcing the words out despite her fear. She needed to keep him talking, to buy time, to find some crack in his madness.

Perhaps if I can calm him, he will see reason, she thought, though her hope felt fragile in the face of his delirium.

"Well, my dear," Farnsworth's eyes narrowed, his smile turning predatory, "you promised me a bride. While I cannot force you to marry me, I will still have my wedding night. Then we shall see if the duke will want such soiled goods as will be returned to him." His words were a blade, cutting through her mind, and she felt her knees weaken.

A sudden commotion sounded outside the door. Thuds, curses, and guttural groans drifted toward them, shattering the tension, making it possible for Emerson to breathe again. Farnsworth whirled toward the sound, his face twisting in irritation.

"I told you bloody fools not to disturb me!" he bellowed, his voice echoing in the hollow room, bouncing off the butterflies.

The door burst open, and two of the ruffians who had kidnapped Emerson stumbled in, dragging a bloodied Mr. Brown between them. His face was a mess of cuts and bruises, his head lolling to one side as if his neck could no longer support it. Emerson's heart lurched.

"Mr. Brown!" she screamed, lunging toward him, but Farnsworth's hand shot out, seizing her hair and yanking her back against his chest. Pain seared her scalp, and she gasped as the cold edge of his dagger pricked her chest, drawing a thin line of blood. He then released her hair, and took the pin he still held, tracing it down her cheek, its sharp point grazing her skin in a grotesque mimicry of affection.

"This is your fault," he snarled, his breath hot against her ear. "You lured him here, you whoring temptress!"

The ruffians chuckled darkly, their eyes glinting with amusement as they threw Mr. Brown's body in the corner. Then they retreated, slamming the door behind them.

Farnsworth's grip tightened, his dagger still pressed against her. "I will take what you have so freely given others, my butterfly," he whispered, his voice a chilling promise, "before I pin your wings."

Emerson's mind raced, her heart hammering as she searched for a way to escape the nightmare closing in around her. The butterflies on the walls seemed to watch, their own pinned wings a silent warning of the fate he intended for her.

Farnsworth laughed again, the knife in his hand raising high.

chapter fifty-three

Emerson's breath was ragged as she braced for the dagger to pierce her heart. The cold metal hovered inches from her skin, its glint a cruel promise of what was to come.

He is deranged, she thought, the realization sinking into her bones. A lord of the realm did not threaten a lady with such vile intent, nor did he orchestrate a kidnapping in the heart of London's bustling streets. Yet here she was, trapped in this decaying room, its faded grandeur a mockery of the life she knew. Her thoughts spiraled to Lathen, his steady presence a distant memory in the face of her terror.

Will he still want me after Farnsworth has taken me? Will I even be alive? The questions clawed at her, each one sharper than the blade in Farnsworth's hand.

"Please, Lord Farnsworth," she said, her voice trembling but firm, "you cannot mean this. I know I have hurt you, but truly, that was not my intent." She turned her neck, forcing herself to meet his gaze, searching for any flicker of the man she had once known, the one who had courted her with polished words and gentle smiles. The one who brought her small sketches and books of poetry. But the man before her was a stranger, his bloodshot eyes wild with a fury that seemed to consume him.

"Was it not?" Farnsworth's lips curled into a mocking smile, his voice dripping with contempt. "I think you enjoyed playing with me, letting de Clare win over me yet again." He leaned closer, his breath hot and sour, the scent of stale brandy mingling with the musty air of the room. The walls, lined with their macabre gallery of pinned butterflies, seemed to close in, each delicate wing a silent scream echoing her own dread.

"Of course not," Emerson protested, her words tumbling out in a desperate bid to reach him. "Indeed, I made the arrangement for us to marry in good faith. It was not until that very night we were to go to Scotland that circumstances changed. I swear to you!" Her voice cracked, her hands trembling as she clasped them together, as if the gesture could hold her fraying courage in place.

Farnsworth's sneer deepened, his face contorting with rage. "You swear?" he roared, seizing her shoulders and spinning her to face him completely. His scream reverberated in the hollow room, making her shrink back. "You lie so prettily, Lady Haven. As if I do not know that you have been cavorting with de Clare like a doxy for months! While I was there, waiting for you, always patiently waiting. So many times, I have watched you coming and going to that den of fornication, *Noir*. I even saw you open your legs for de Clare as he took you against a tree! Like a common whore!"

Emerson gasped, her breath catching in her throat as his words struck her like a physical blow.

Oh, good heavens, she thought, her mind reeling. This is what Marien meant when she said someone was watching me! The memory of that woman's cryptic warning flooded back, and with it, the sickening realization that Farnsworth's obsession had twisted him into a lunatic, an animal who had stalked her every move. Her stomach churned, not just from his accusations but from the violation of knowing he had spied on her most private moments.

"Yes, my dear, I have seen everything," he continued, his voice dropping to a poisonous whisper. "You gave de Clare what was to be mine. You no longer have your virtue to bargain with, do you? Well, circumstances will simply have to change again. Now be a good girl and remove your clothes."

"No!" Emerson cried, her voice raw with defiance. His words were similar to ones Lathen once used, but their meaning was completely different. It renewed her fight. She twisted in his grasp, her arms straining against his iron grip, but his fingers only tightened, digging into her flesh until she felt the bones beneath protest. The pain was sharp, piercing her mind, even as her heart screamed for escape, pounding so fiercely she thought it might burst.

Farnsworth shook her again, his rage a living thing that seemed to pulse through his hands. With a snarl, he threw her down, her body landing half on the sagging bed, the worn feathers spreading under her weight. Before she could scramble upright, he was upon her, his hands seizing the edges of her walking dress at her bosom. With a savage yank, he tore the fabric apart, the delicate muslin ripping to her waist and exposing the thin chemise beneath. The fine linen, already stained with a trickle of blood from the earlier nick of his dagger, clung to her skin, revealing the curves of her breasts in a way that made her feel utterly exposed. Emerson cursed the new garments she had once delighted in, their delicate craftsmanship now a betrayal that left her vulnerable.

Farnsworth froze, his eyes raking over her with a hunger that made her skin crawl. "Bloody hell," he whispered, his voice hoarse as he licked his lips, the gesture grotesque in its greed. He looked up, his gaze accusing. "These should have been mine!"

"Please, Lord Farnsworth, you must stop," Emerson pleaded, her voice trembling as she tried one last time to appeal to whatever shred of humanity remained in him. But his eyes only darkened, his expression hardening into something predatory.

"Oh, no," he said, leaning down until his face was inches from hers, the stench of brandy overwhelming. "This is going to be something you will never forget." His hand shot out, grabbing her right breast with a roughness that made her gasp in pain, his nails biting into her delicate skin. The touch was nothing like Lathen's, whose hands had always known exactly what she needed. This was evil, ugly, a violation that twisted her stomach with revulsion and fear. Tears welled in her eyes, not just from the pain but from the creeping dread that Farnsworth's words might hold truth. Lathen might turn away from her after this. She might be forever tainted in his eyes.

Memories of Lathen's touch flooded her mind unbidden, a cruel contrast to the brutality she now endured. She tried to cling to those memories, to let them pull her away from the moment, but Farnsworth's hands were relentless. He grabbed her chemise and yanked it from her body, the fabric tearing with a sound that echoed like a death knell. Her skirts followed, then her bloomers, until she lay exposed, her skin prickling in the chill air of the room. She did not bother to wipe the tears streaming down her face, letting them fall as she retreated into her mind, desperate to escape the reality of what was happening. She fixed her gaze on the butterflies, counting them, each one a fragile tether, holding her sanity together.

Farnsworth straightened, his eyes roving over her naked form with sick satisfaction. He began to shed his own clothing, tossing his coat and shirt aside with careless haste. When he placed the dagger on the rickety table, its blade clattering against the chipped washbasin, Emerson did not move. She could not. Her body felt leaden, her mind detached, as if she were watching this horror unfold from a distance.

Farnsworth, misinterpreting her stillness, smirked. "See, I knew you wanted this," he said, his voice smug as he returned to the bed, his hand stroking himself as he approached.

The sight of his body, so different from Lathen's, yet him so confident in his delusion, sparked something unexpected in Emerson. A flicker of absurdity bubbled up from the depths of her fear.

Surely, that is not a weapon worth worrying about, she thought, and the notion was so ludicrous a giggle escaped her lips. It started softly, a nervous hiccup, but then it grew, swelling into uncontrollable laughter that shook her body. She rolled to her side, clutching her stomach as tears of hysteria mingled with those of terror. *Perhaps I am going mad too.*

"What the hell?" Farnsworth froze, his hand stilling as confusion and anger flashed across his face. Her laughter seemed to drain the passion from him, his body deflating as he stared at her, baffled.

Emerson could not stop, the sound spilling out of her like a dam breaking. It enraged Farnsworth, his face reddening as he lunged forward and struck her again, his fist connecting with her cheek. "Stop! Stop it!" he screamed, his voice cracking with fury.

She raised her arms to shield her face, curling into herself as he rained blows upon her. Turning to her side, she caught a glint of gold in the fading light filtering through a crack in the tattered drapes.

It was a rough-hewn piece of amber, suspended on the wall, a butterfly trapped within its warm translucent prison. The sight stirred a fleeting memory, a whisper of something she could not quite grasp.

Is this me? Forever trapped here? The thought pierced her, but then the amber brought Lathen's eyes to her mind. Warm, golden, steady. The idea of never seeing them again hurt more than the blows raining down on her body.

Farnsworth, furious, spittle flying from his mouth, screamed again, "Cease!" Then he jumped up and grabbed the dagger from the table. Emerson's thoughts sharpened, and in a surge of clarity, she rolled to her side just as Farnsworth plunged the blade into the mattress, missing her by inches. Ignoring her nakedness, she scrambled to her feet and snatched the chipped washbasin from the table. She swung it blindly behind her, the porcelain connecting with Farnsworth's jaw in a sickening crack as it shattered. He staggered, blood spilling from his mouth, but he slashed out with the dagger, catching her arm. Pain seared through her, blood pouring down her forearm, but she pressed forward, fueled by desperation and the hope of Lathen.

She kicked at his knee, and when it buckled, she drove her forehead into his nose with a force that made him scream. Farnsworth flailed, his dagger slicing through the air, but Emerson dodged, her bare feet slipping on the warped floorboards, tiny porcelain shards cutting her feet as she darted back to the table. Farnsworth stumbled to his feet, lunging after her, his face a mask of blood and rage. She circled the table, her breath coming in sharp gasps, and when he was on the opposite side, she leaned forward with all her strength, shoving the table against him. It trapped him against the wall, the dagger knocked from his hand with a clatter on the floor.

"Of the two of us, look who is pinned!" Emerson gritted out, her muscles straining as she held the table in place. Her arms trembled, her strength waning, but she clung to her defiance. Farnsworth's eyes blazed, and he pushed back, the table creaking as he fought to free himself.

"You bitch!" he screamed, his voice filling the room, echoing off the framed butterflies.

Behind her, the door splintered open with a deafening crash. Emerson realized, heart-wrenchingly, she could do no more. Farnsworth's henchmen were too much for her to handle. In silence, she fell to the floor as darkness claimed what was left of her fragile mind.

I am sorry, Lathen. I tried.

chapter fifty-four

As the carriage barreled through London's twisting streets, a cool rain began to fall. For nearly a quarter of an hour, Lathen, Lennox, and Greyson had sat in taut silence, their bodies jostling with each sharp turn, their faces etched with grim determination as the city blurred past. When the driver yanked the reins, the horses skidded to a halt, their hooves scraping the wet cobbles. The men leapt from the carriage, their boots splashing in shallow puddles that reflected the dying light of the sky. The driver, his face haggard under a weathered cap, raised a trembling hand and pointed across the street to a house. Its normalcy, despite what might be happening inside, seemed almost grotesque. Lathen did not hesitate, charging toward the door, his fist hammering against it with a force that rattled the hinges.

The door opened, revealing a young maid, her face pale as chalk, her dark eyes wide with terror. Her apron hung limp, crumpled from nervous twisting, and her hands fidgeted as if unsure whether to flee or stand her ground. Lathen surged forward, seizing her shoulders.

"Where is she?" he growled, his voice a low, feral snarl that seemed to vibrate through the dim foyer, its walls peeling with faded wallpaper.

"Sir?" the maid squeaked, her body trembling, her gaze darting like a trapped animal's.

Greyson, with his steady presence, stepped forward, his broad shoulders casting a calming shadow. He gently nudged Lathen aside, his touch firm but measured.

"I'm verra sorry if we scared ye, lass," he said, his burr soft and soothing, like a balm to the chaos. "We're looking for a young lass taken earlier today, and we believe she is here. Can ye help us?" His eyes, warm and earnest, held hers, offering a kindness she rarely knew.

The maid blinked, astonishment flickering across her pinched features. In this house, kindness was a foreign thing. Lord Farnsworth's words cut like blades, and the housekeeper's cruelty followed suit, her hands quick with pinches or slaps. Less than an hour ago, the maid had been slapped for daring to question the sight of a woman being dragged up the back stairs and shoved into a room. And then there were the shouts and desperate cries she covered her ears to block out. The injustice burned in her chest, and she felt no loyalty to her master.

"Up to the top of the stairs, down the hall to the left," her voice was steady despite the tremor in her hands. "Third door, milord."

"Good lass," Warwicke said, patting her hand with a gentle smile before turning to follow Lathen and Lennox, who had already bolted toward the staircase, their boots pounding against the worn floor, the sound reverberating through the house like a call to battle.

Before they could reach their goal, three hulking figures blocked the narrow stairwell, their silhouettes a wall of menace. The man in the middle, a brute with a scarred face and a nose twisted from past breaks, sniggered, his lips curling to reveal yellowed teeth.

"Oi, more bleedin' rich toffs struttin' in 'ere like they own the place!" he spat, shoving his sleeves up to reveal forearms thick with muscle, veins bulging under grimy skin. His companions flanked him, their faces twisted in matching sneers. One, with a jagged scar running from ear to chin, cracked his knuckles with a sound like snapping branches, while the other, shorter but broad as a barrel, flexed his hands, his fingers calloused and bruised from countless brawls.

Lathen and Lennox exchanged a glance, their eyes glinting with unspoken agreement. Before they could move, Greyson charged past, his fists raised, his face a mask of cold fury, his earlier calm forgotten. The air exploded into chaos as he collided with the leader, his fist smashing into the man's jaw with a wet crunch. Blood and spittle sprayed, the brute staggering as his head snapped to the side. He roared, swinging a wild punch that clipped Greyson's shoulder. Greyson did not flinch, driving his fist into the man's mouth, knocking a tooth free. The yellowed shard skittered across the floor, glistening with blood, as the thug howled, clutching his face. Greyson pressed his advantage, slamming his elbow into the man's temple, sending him crumpling like a felled tree, his body thudding against the wall, dislodging flakes of peeling plaster.

Lathen tackled the scarred man, his fists pounding into the thug's ribs, each blow eliciting a sickening crack. The man grunted, his face contorting in pain, but he fought back, landing a heavy punch to Lathen's jaw that snapped his head back. Blood trickled from Lathen's lip, but he roared, seizing the man's collar and slamming his head against the banister. The wood splintered, and the thug's eyes rolled back as he slumped, blood streaming from a gash on his forehead.

Lennox, agile and precise, faced the third man, dodging a swinging fist with ease. He drove his knee into the thug's gut, the impact forcing a wheezing gasp from the man's lips. The thug doubled over, his face paling, but he lunged again, his fist grazing Lennox's cheek. Lennox twisted the man's arm behind his back, forcing him to his knees, his grip unyielding as the thug bellowed in pain.

As the fight raged, Lathen saw his chance and sprinted up the remaining stairs, leaving Lennox to circle the last standing thug. At the top, a loud crash echoed from below. Lathen leaned over the railing, his breath catching at the sight. The third ruffian lay sprawled on the ground, his skull bloodied, a heavy candlestick beside him, its base dented from impact.

Standing over him was Hazel, her small frame trembling, her face and clothing streaked with blood and grime, her eyes wild. She panted heavily, her chest heaving, the candlestick clearly her weapon of choice.

Lennox rushed to her, sweeping her into his arms and lifting her effortlessly, carrying her toward the open front door. Relief flooded through him that Hazel was safe, and he returned his focus to Emerson, racing down the hall to the third door on the left.

A man's voice, raw with rage, cut through the air. "You bitch!" Lathen's blood ran cold, his heart pounding like a war drum. He grasped the door handle, finding it locked, and threw his shoulder against the wood. The lock shattered, the door swinging open with a splintering groan, revealing a scene that burned itself into his soul.

Against the wall stood Lord Virgil Farnsworth, his naked body pinned by a broken table, its jagged edges digging into his pale, sweat slicked skin. His face was a mask of fury, his eyes wild with pain and madness, his lips split and bleeding. Before him, with her back turned, was Emerson, her body trembling with exhaustion, her screams feral as she pushed against the table with all her fading strength. She was nearly naked, blood dripping from a gash on her arm. As Lathen watched, her strength gave out, and she crumpled to the ground in a small, broken heap.

Lathen's control shattered. In a heartbeat, he was across the room, seizing Farnsworth by his unkempt, greasy hair. He yanked with such force that Farnsworth's head snapped back, his body thrown to the ground with a heavy thud. The man lay there, stunned, his eyes wide with shock, blood trickling from his mouth. Lathen straddled him, his fists a blur as they pounded Farnsworth's face. Each blow landed with a sickening crunch. A cheekbone splintering, nose collapsing, lips splitting wider. Blood sprayed across Lathen's knuckles, staining his sleeves, as Farnsworth's face became a swollen, unrecognizable mass. Lathen's vision blurred, his rage a roaring tide that drowned out everything else.

Greyson's voice cut through the red haze, sharp and commanding. "Lathen, stop!" Strong hands seized his arms, dragging him back, but Lathen thrashed, his body still burning with the need to destroy. "Enough, mon! Ye will kill him!"

It was Emerson's voice, soft and broken, that finally broke through his fury.

"Lathen," she whimpered, a sound so fragile it pierced his heart. He turned, shrugging off Greyson's hold, and his breath caught at the sight of her. She stood unsteadily, a worn coverlet wrapped tightly around her trembling form, her eyes downcast, her face streaked with tears and blood. The sight of her, so small and shattered, drove a spike of guilt through him. He strode to her, his movements gentle despite the storm within, and scooped her into his arms, cradling her close. Her body shook against his, her soft sobs muffled against his chest. Without a glance back at Farnsworth, he turned to leave, trusting Greyson to deal with the wretch.

As he reached the doorway, a garbled shout stopped him. "De Clare!" Lathen spun around. Farnsworth was on his feet, swaying, a pistol trembling in his bloodied hand. Lathen realized it was his own, and it must have fallen from his pocket. Its barrel glinted, aimed at them, Farnsworth's swollen eyes blazing with hatred. Lathen had no time to react beyond instinctively turning and curling his body to shield Emerson, bracing for the shot. But a loud crash shattered the moment, followed by the crack of the pistol. Lathen realized nothing struck him, and he quickly searched Emerson's limbs. Seeing she was also not hit, Lathen turned around again.

When he turned back, Farnsworth was gone, the window behind him a jagged maw of broken glass, shards glinting on the ground. Mr. Brown stood in his place, bloodied and trembling, his face pale but resolute. He had tackled Farnsworth, sending him crashing through the window to the street below. On his shoulder was a rapidly spreading bloom of blood. Their eyes met, and Mr. Brown nodded, a silent vow of loyalty. Lathen bowed as best he could, still holding Emerson, then turned and carried her out.

As he descended the stairs, each step heavy with the weight of his failure, Emerson's soft weeping tore at him. Each sob was a reminder that he had not protected her, a duty he had sworn to uphold. His arms tightened around her, as if he could shield her now from the horrors she had endured. He had to maneuver past the three ruffians, still unconscious on the floor at the bottom of the steps, lying in heaps. At the front door, left wide open, he stepped into the cool evening air, the carriage waiting like a promise of refuge.

Behind him, the maid's small voice called out, trembling but insistent.

"Milord, what about the other lady upstairs?"

chapter fifty-five

Lathen's body went rigid.

Another woman? The question burned in his mind, a fresh wave of dread crashing over him. Before he could press further, a sharp voice cut through the dim foyer.

"Molly, keep your tongue to yourself!" An older woman stormed in, her face pinched with malice, as she took in the chaos and crumpled bodies on the floor. Her eyes, cold and unyielding, bored into the young maid, who shrank back, her shoulders hunching as if bracing for a blow. Lathen's gaze flickered between them, noting the fear in Molly's eyes and the housekeeper's menacing stance, but he had no time for their drama. Emerson's soft sobs were a fierce reminder of the urgency. Without a word, he strode past them, his boots thudding against the worn carpet as he carried her to the waiting carriage.

Outside, the evening air was sharp, the sky bruised with the last hues of twilight. Lathen lifted Emerson gently into the carriage, her trembling form light as a broken bird in his arms. Inside, Lennox sat with Hazel, his arms wrapped protectively around her. Hazel's dress was a ruin, soaked crimson with blood that glistened wetly in the dim light, her face pale and hollow, her eyes staring blankly as if lost in some distant horror. Lathen's instinct was to ask if she was alright, but Lennox's gaze met his, a subtle shake of his head silencing the question.

Yet despite her own evident distress, Hazel slid from Lennox's lap and reached for Emerson, enveloping her in a tight, steadying embrace. Their shared grief hung heavy in the confined space, a silent bond forged in suffering. Lathen locked eyes with Hazel, and for the first time, he truly saw her. Not just as Emerson's friend, but as a woman who loved her as fiercely as he did. A wordless understanding passed between them, a vow to protect Emerson at all costs. He nodded, his throat tight, before closing the carriage door and turning back to the house, his mind now consumed with the possibility of another captive.

"Show me," he demanded, his voice a low growl that left no room for defiance as he faced Molly. The maid's eyes darted to the housekeeper, who shook her head sharply, her lips pressed into a thin, disapproving line. Molly swallowed hard, her resolve hardening, and nodded once. Lifting her skirts, she scurried up the stairs, her small frame moving with surprising speed. Instead of heading toward the room where Emerson had been held, she veered right, leading Lathen down a narrow hallway to another locked door.

"I am sorry, milord, but I do not have a key," Molly said, her voice quivering as she stepped back, her hands twisting in her apron.

Lathen did not say a word. Determined, he brushed past her, his shoulder slamming into the door with a force that splintered the wood, tearing the lock free again. He rushed in, his breath catching at the sight before him.

A woman lay on a sagging bed, her body a map of brutality. Her wrists and ankles were bound with coarse rope, the knots cutting into her swollen, bruised skin, leaving raw, oozing welts. Her face was barely recognizable, swollen to a grotesque mask, one eye sealed shut, the other a slit amidst purpled flesh. Long, brown, matted hair clung to her cheeks, streaked with dried blood, obscuring her features. Her thin dressing gown, torn and barely clinging to her frame, revealed more bruises. Dark, mottled patches bloomed across her arms, chest, and thighs, some fresh, others faded to sickly yellows and greens. The sight twisted Lathen's stomach, rage and pity warring within him.

"Your Grace?" The woman's voice was a hoarse, trembling whisper, barely audible, but it struck Lathen like a thunderbolt.

Marien. The woman he had been searching for, for weeks, the one whose actions had long cast a shadow over his life with Emerson. Despite her unforgivable deeds, the sight of her, broken and battered, ignited a fresh surge of anger. No woman, not even Marien, deserved this. The realization that Emerson had narrowly escaped the same fate fueled his fury, his hands flexing as he crossed the room.

Without hesitation, he knelt beside her, his fingers working quickly to untie the ropes. Molly rushed over to help him. The knots were tight, the fibers biting into her flesh, and each tug drew a faint whimper from her lips. Her skin was clammy, her body trembling as they freed her wrists, the ropes leaving deep, bloody grooves.

Gently, he slipped the thin blanket from the bed, wrapping it around her to cover her frail body, its coarse fabric a poor shield against her vulnerability. He lifted her carefully, her body light and brittle, her head lolling against his shoulder as he carried her from the room.

As he descended the stairs, Greyson appeared, his shoulder supporting Mr. Brown, whose face and chest were a bloodied mess, one arm hanging limply, his breaths ragged. The young maid, Molly, rushed ahead of them, reaching the front door and holding it open, her eyes still wide with fear but determined. Lathen paused as he passed her, realizing the danger she faced for aiding them. The housekeeper's glare burned into her, promising retribution.

"My household finds itself in want of capable and diligent help," Lathen's voice was firm but kind. "If you would like to come with us."

Molly's eyes snapped up, hope flickering in their dark depths. They darted to the housekeeper, whose face twisted with rage, but the girl's determination held. "Truly, milord?" she asked, her voice barely above a whisper.

"Yes, come along," he said, nodding toward the carriage.

Without a glance at the housekeeper's furious shouts, Molly scurried after them, her small frame nearly lost in the shadow of the men. The carriage awaited, its door still open, a cramped haven for the battered group. Inside, Lennox held Hazel, her eyes still vacant but softening as she clung to him. Emerson sat beside her, wrapped in her coverlet, her shivering unabated. Greyson helped Mr. Brown inside, the younger man wincing with each movement, his face a patchwork of bruises and cuts. Marien, still in Lathen's arms, was placed gently beside Emerson, her blanket slipping to reveal the extent of her injuries. Molly squeezed in last, her hands clasped tightly in her lap, her eyes darting nervously.

Lathen climbed in, pulling Emerson onto his lap both to make room and to feel her close, her quivering body a painful reminder of his failure to protect her. Her shivers vibrated through him, each one a silent accusation. He wrapped his arms tighter, as if he could shield her from the terrors still lingering in her mind. The carriage lurched forward, the wheels grinding against the cobblestones as they headed toward de Clare House.

The journey was silent save for the soft whimpers from Emerson and Marien, their pain a shared thread weaving through the cramped space.

Lathen's heart hardened with each cry. No matter what, he would do everything in his power to keep Emerson safe, to rebuild the trust shattered in that house of horrors. The weight of her in his arms, the warmth of her against his chest, was a promise he would never break again.

chapter fifty-six

The bruises on Emerson's skin had softened to faint shadows, their once angry purples and blues now mere whispers of the violence she had endured. The wounds, too, were mostly healed. Only the deep laceration on her arm, a jagged scar that snaked from elbow to wrist, still gnawed at her, its itching a constant reminder of that night. She scratched at it absently, wincing as the healing skin tugged beneath her fingers.

Standing before the tall, gilt framed mirror in her dressing room, she watched as Mrs. Jaymeson deftly pinned her hair, weaving delicate lavender roses into her black curls. The flowers' soft petals brushed her scalp, their soft purple hues mirroring the Baroque pearl she wore around her throat. The pale purple silk of her gown, which clung to her frame, caught the light in a way that made her eyes glow. The gown, with its intricate lace bodice and flowing skirts, was a vision of elegance, crafted by

Madame Delphine for tonight's intimate gathering, a prelude to the grand wedding in four days. The past weeks had been a whirlwind of preparations, but Emerson had poured her heart into readying herself for her life with Lathen, her final wedding dress fitting looming in three days like a beacon of hope.

Lathen, for his part, had been relentless in tying up the loose ends of their shared ordeal. He had spent weeks ensuring the shadows of the past were banished, his influence wielded like a blade to sever any threat to their future. Marien, the woman whose betrayal had once haunted Emerson, was now an ocean away, exiled to a comfortable but isolated home in India, never to return. Emerson's heart twinged with pity for the horrors Marien had endured, her body battered and broken in that wretched house, but her crimes were unforgivable. Exile was a mercy she scarcely deserved, yet it was a clean break, a way to keep the past from tainting their new beginning.

Lord Virgil Farnsworth, too, had been dealt with, his fate a grim testament to Lathen's wrath. The man's face, once haughty and cruel, had been reduced to a swollen, bloodied pulp under Lathen's fists, his bones shattered from the fall through the window after Mr. Brown's desperate shove. His recovery would be slow, his body marked forever by a limp that would hobble his steps, a fitting punishment for his sins.

Instead of Newgate's dank cells, Lathen's influence had secured his banishment to a penal colony in Australia, a place reserved for the worst offenders. Farnsworth would sail as soon as he could stand, his name erased from London's gossip, sparing Emerson of the scandal that would have followed a public trial. It was a calculated mercy, one that ensured he could never harm anyone again.

Emerson drew a deep breath, her reflection steady in the mirror. The weight of her past, her brother's death, the terror of that night, had lifted, replaced by a quiet certainty. Lathen had been her protector all along, his love a shield she had not fully understood until now. She traced the edge of her gown's sleeve, the silk cool against her fingertips, and felt a surge of gratitude for the safety she now knew.

"My lovely girl, my poppet," Mrs. Jaymeson cried, her voice thick with emotion as she tucked the final curl into place, a lavender rose nestling against Emerson's temple. The governess's eyes shimmered with unshed tears, her hands trembling as she adjusted a pin.

Emerson hid a smile, warmth blooming in her chest.

If she is this emotional for a small gathering of friends, what will she be like on the wedding day?

She squeezed Mrs. Jaymeson's hand, her touch gentle but firm, a silent thank you for the woman who had been a mother to her in all but name. With Mrs. Jaymeson's guidance, Emerson felt ready. Not just for tonight, but for the life ahead, perhaps even motherhood someday.

The door to the sitting room she shared with Hazel burst open, and her friend swept in, a vision in a dark blue gown that hugged her curves and made her eyes sparkle like sapphires. The dress, tailored to perfection, shimmered as Hazel moved, its rich hue a striking contrast to her pale skin and blonde hair. Emerson's heart lifted at the sight, a flicker of pride for her friend's resilience. Hazel had endured her own horrors that night, yet here she was, radiant and strong.

Emerson turned toward her, a playful smirk tugging at her lips. "Good heavens, Hazel, you look like you stepped out of a painting! That gown is practically unfair to every other lady in the room."

"Oh, Em, you are too kind," Hazel twirled, the fabric catching the light with a soft shimmer, and laughed, "but do not think you are stealing all the compliments tonight. Besides, Lathen is out there, practically wearing a hole in the floor waiting for you to grace him with your presence."

Emerson's eyes glinted with mischief. "Is he now? Poor man, pining away. Though I believe he is not the only one smitten. I saw Mr. Brown hovering by the drawing room, looking quite eager for a certain sapphire vision."

Hazel's cheeks bloomed pink, her laugh nervous, before she swatted the air and deliberately changed the subject.

"Oh, posh, stop it! Let us talk about something better. Like that dessert table. It is calling our names, do you not think?"

Even Mrs. Jaymeson laughed at that, but Emerson could not help but think of Mr. Brown, the man who had saved Lathen's life with his selfless act. Guilt pricked her for her past judgments of him, now replaced by deep respect.

He deserves my apologies, she thought, and perhaps Hazel's admiration.

Mr. Brown was still recovering from his injuries, especially from a pistol shot he took for Lathen. He was staying with them at de Clare House, his place secured for as long as he needed. He would join tonight's dinner, a small, intimate gathering of those they most trusted. Lennox, Greyson, Hazel, Leighton, Aunt Lillian, and Mrs. Jaymeson. Each was a pillar for the new life she was building.

Emerson preferred it this way, a quiet celebration of love and survival, far from the spectacle of the grand wedding to come, where half the *ton* and the Royal family would fill the cathedral with their pomp and scrutiny.

She sighed, shaking off the tingle of apprehension at the thought of that looming event. The weight of expectation, the eyes of the elite, and the whispers of her past. It all paled against the truth that steadied her.

It is worth it, she told herself, her heart swelling with certainty, *to be married to the man I love.*

Her reflection smiled back, the lavender roses in her hair a promise of the joy awaiting her, the pearl a token of Lathen's adoration. Both told of a future built on love and hard-won peace, a future where the echoes of her past served not to haunt her but to remind her of how far she had come, and how bright the path ahead could be. It would be a journey filled with the promise of laughter, love, and the quiet joy of a life reclaimed.

tangled truths

The fog draped London's streets like a shroud, swallowing the clatter of hooves and the creak of carriage wheels in its damp embrace. Inside the swaying carriage, a woman clutched her dark cloak tighter, the heavy velvet failing to ward off the chill of the late spring drizzle seeping through the cracks. Her gloved hands trembled as she adjusted her hood, pulling it low to shadow her face. Her heart pounded, a frantic rhythm that echoed the urgency of her mission.

She had to confront Lord Virgil Farnsworth, to pry the truth from his lips, no matter the cost. The answers he held could unravel everything, and she would not be deterred. Not by the risk of discovery, nor by the dread that coiled in her chest.

Ahead, gas lamps pierced the mist, their feeble glow casting halos around the squat infirmary. Its stone facade loomed, grim and unyielding, the windows dark save for a few flickering lights hinting at the suffering within. The carriage slowed as it approached an iron gate, and a watchman shuffled forward, his tarred coat slick with rain. He raised a small lamp, its weak beam cutting through the fog to illuminate the carriage window. The woman's gloved hand slipped a purse into his, the leather bulging with coins that clinked softly.

"For your troubles," she murmured, her voice low, barely audible over the patter of rain. The watchman weighed the purse, his fingers tightening greedily before he grunted and stepped aside, waving the carriage through with a lazy flick of his hand.

The driver guided the horses around to the rear, where a small, unmarked door waited, its paint chipped and peeling, meant for scullery maids and discreet deliveries. The footman, his face half hidden by his collar, helped her down, her expensive boots sinking into the muddy gravel. The door opened silently, revealing another guard, his eyes glinting with suspicion under a low brimmed cap. She tossed him a heavier purse, its contents jangling loudly as he fumbled and nearly dropped it. He recovered, pocketing it with a smirk.

"Do you know who I need?" she asked, her tone haughty, betraying none of the fear gnawing at her.

"'Course I do," he muttered, lifting a lamp with a cracked glass cover. "Yer man was clear."

She followed him down a long corridor, the walls damp and streaked with grime, the air heavy with the moans of unseen patients echoing like ghosts through the stone. The guard's lamp cast jittery shadows, illuminating a damp stone stairwell that led them downward, into what must be a basement. At last, he stopped before a heavy iron door, its surface rusted, a large ring of keys jangling in his hand as he fumbled for the right one.

"Ye've only got ten minutes, ye hear?" he told her, his voice gruff as he wrestled with the lock.

The woman drew herself up, indignation flashing in her brown eyes. "I will need more than that!"

"Well, that be all ye've got 'fore the next guard comes 'round," he snapped, his tone brooking no argument. "And 'e ain't one for bribes, ye hear?"

She sighed, her resolve wavering but unbroken. "Very well, open it up then!"

The lock clicked, and the door screeched open, its hinges protesting. Darkness swallowed the room beyond, a void that seemed to pulse with despair. The guard thrust the lamp into her hands, its flame flickering as if reluctant to illuminate what lay within. He retreated, leaning against the weeping stone wall, his silhouette a grim sentinel. The woman squared her shoulders, gripping the lamp tightly, and stepped into the close, oppressive room.

The weak light revealed Lord Virgil Farnsworth on a narrow cot, his body a broken relic of the man he had been. His leg, encased in crude wooden splints, was propped awkwardly, the bandages stained with faint blood. His face was mottled and twisted, the skin a thousand shades of yellow and green, stretched taut over sunken cheekbones. His nose was no longer straight, but sitting at several clumsy angles, and his lips were cracked and bloodless.

The fall had shattered more than his limbs. It had stripped him of any semblance of the lord she knew, leaving a hollow shell. Chains rattled as he shifted, the iron links binding his wrists to the cot, marking him a prisoner even here. He stirred at her approach, his bloodshot eyes widening with recognition, but he said nothing, his silence heavy with acknowledgement.

"Lord Farnsworth," she said, her voice soft but edged with purpose, "it is terrible to see what has become of you. I hear you are soon to set sail on a frigate bound for Australia's penal colony. They say the mines there are brutal. I certainly hope they spare you such labor."

Farnsworth's lips curled into a sneer, and he spat, the spittle landing on the cot's threadbare linens, his chains clinking with the effort.

"Are you here to gloat?" His voice was hoarse, raw with pain and bitterness.

"Oh no," she murmured, stepping closer, the lamp casting harsh shadows across his battered face. "I come for truth."

He tilted his head, his eyes narrowing as if probing her motives. Then, a twisted grin spread across his lips, revealing missing teeth. "Truth? A slippery thing, is it not? But I shall indulge you." His voice dropped to a conspiratorial whisper, weaving a tale of betrayal that dripped with venom. He spoke of Lady Haven, painting her as a siren who had ensnared him with false promises of affection, only to betray him when he claimed what she dangled before him.

"She tricked me," he told her, his emphatic voice cracking with feigned hurt, his eyes glinting with malice. "She cast me as the villain when I was merely a pawn in her games. All to trap de Clare into marriage."

The woman's grip on the lamp tightened, her knuckles whitening beneath her gloves. "What of the other woman?" she asked, her voice steady despite the storm in her chest. "The one they say you...kept?"

"A simple misunderstanding," Farnsworth replied smoothly, waving a chained hand in dismissal, the gesture weak but calculated. "A dalliance gone awry. Neither she nor Lady Haven were truly harmed. Besides, Lady Haven frequents places no virtuous woman would dare. A club, hidden beneath the grand homes of the *ton. Noir*, they call it. It is a den of vice where masks conceal more than faces. She revels there, sharing her favors, while de Clare remains blind to her depravity."

Her breath caught, the name *Noir* slicing through her thoughts. Whispers of such a place had reached her ears before. Tales of shadowed rooms where the elite shed their morals like cloaks. If Lady Haven was entangled in such a scandal, it would ruin her, shattering the facade of virtue she wore so convincingly. His Grace deserved better than a woman steeped in such debauchery, a liar who played the innocent while reveling in sin.

Farnsworth's gaze sharpened, reading the flicker of doubt in her eyes. "You see it now, do you not?" he whispered, low and insidious. "She is unfit for him. A liar, a conniver, a whore. You could free him. Expose her for what she is." His grin widened, a grotesque parody of charm.

The woman met his eyes, her purpose hardening like steel in a forge. The lamp's flame wavered, casting fleeting shadows across the room, but her persistence burned steadily.

"And you, Lord Farnsworth? What do you gain from this?"

"Me?" He chuckled, a dry, hollow sound that echoed off the stone walls. "As you said, I sail for Australia any day now. What have I to lose? But you...?" His voice trailed as his eyes gleamed with amusement. "You have everything to gain."

She stood silent, the possibility of his words settling over her. The lamp trembled in her hands, its light flickering as the guard's footsteps echoed in the corridor, signaling her time was up. She turned, her cloak swirling, and stepped toward the door, her mind a storm of doubt and determination.

"Best of luck to you," Farnsworth snickered. "As you have seen, Lady Haven is a formidable opponent!"

The iron door slammed shut, and the guard locked it. Farnsworth's grim laughter followed her as she rushed away.

emerson and lathen's story will
continue in:

master at night

coming 2026

p.s. to my amazing readers. Writing the *at Night Series* has been an incredible journey, and I have been overjoyed to hear about how *Awaken at Night* has resonated with so many of you. Your reviews, recommendations, and passion for Emerson and Lathen's story has made this series a success, and I can't thank you enough for spreading the word and your support.

If you've enjoyed *Pursued at Night*, I'd be immensely grateful if you could take a few moments to leave a review on the platform where you found it. Reviews are vital for indie authors, helping new readers find the *At Night Series* and allowing me to continue crafting stories for you.

Love, Harlow

special acknowledgements:

To S&M. Always my first readers! I am so grateful for your incredible love, support, and insightful feedback. And now, whenever I write, I hear a little voice (with a lovely laugh) asking, "But where is his hand now?" and "Did she land like Spiderman?"

To G. Thank you for your endless patience and willingness to wander with me through the weeds, even when my paths might lead us toward a cliff. Your steadfast openness to my detours makes the journey extraordinary. I look forward to endless adventures together! And I will even say shrimp are better than cucumbers...(even if they're not)

Once again, to my Alpha, Beta, and ARC readers, and my amazing street team. I am always overjoyed to hear your thoughts. I literally could not do this without you!

www.ingramcontent.com/pod-product-compliance
Lightning Source LLC
Chambersburg PA
CBHW030245120726
47903CB00005B/1624